Gilded CAGE

KJ CHARLES

Gilded Cage

Published by KJC Books
Copyright © 2019 by KJ Charles

Edited by Veronica Vega
Cover art by Vic Grey
Cover design by Lexiconic Design
Print layout by eB Format

ISBN: 978-1-912688-13-5

This is a work of fiction. Names, characters, places, and incidents are either the product of the author's imagination or are used fictitiously. Any resemblance to actual persons living or dead, business establishments, events, or locales is entirely coincidental.

All rights reserved. Aside from brief quotations for media coverage and reviews, no part of this book may be reproduced or distributed in any form without the author's permission.

kjcharleswriter.com

I'll sing you three-O
Green grow the rushes-O
What is your three-O?
Three, three, the rivals
Two, two, the lily-white boys
Clothèd all in green-O
One is one and all alone
And evermore shall be so

Green Grow The Rushes-O, British folk song

Once again for May Peterson, who cleared the way

Reader's advisory: This book contains discussion of a character's miscarriage.

CHAPTER ONE

November 1895

It was two o'clock in the morning, and the house should have been silent.

It *had* been silent. He'd let himself in, sliding through the door and closing it to keep out the hoots and rustles of other, noisier night-time predators. The house stood half a mile from the nearest human habitation. There had been no sign of life on the riverbank as he'd approached; he'd seen no lights from outside, and saw none now beyond his own dark lantern. There should be no noise except for the creak of old wood settling in a cold November night, and Mr. Montmorency's snores, and the eventual clicks and cracks when Templeton Lane opened the door of the safe-room and stole the Samsonoff necklace.

All the same he stood frozen now, his pulse thudding in his ears, because he'd bloody heard something.

He wasn't even sure what. Perhaps a sound made in sleep. Perhaps some creature behind the wainscoting, or a cat at work. Perhaps the inadvertent murmur of a policeman waiting in the safe-room to arrest the notorious jewel thieves the Lilywhite Boys. They'd doubtless be irritated when it turned out there was only one present, but not nearly as irritated as Templeton was, because Jerry ought to be here. He had sharp ears to go with his clever fingers and iced nerves;

he was just the man one wanted while breaking into a house at two in the morning.

But Jerry wasn't here, so Templeton stood, still and silent as a fox caught by moonlight, straining for sound, and enraged at himself for this fuss at what was probably the housekeeper's dog farting.

He gave it time anyway. That caution was how he and Jerry had earned their name: the Lilywhite Boys, never so much as arrested. They'd been very neatly trapped indeed this summer, but even then they'd got away with their freedom, and enough jewellery to sink a ship.

And then given it all back because of Jerry's new boy friend. The thought was an irritation, a stone in Templeton's shoe. His once-ruthless partner was hopelessly in love and softening like old leather under the emollience of Alec Pyne, duke's son, whose big eyes and soft voice were turning Jerry into some sort of respectable citizen. He'd actually insisted they return thirty-four thousand pounds' worth of perfectly good stolen jewels to their previous owner merely because he was Alec's brother. Bastard.

It wasn't that Templeton had any personal objection to Jerry's choice of bed-warmer. That wasn't his affair. But Jerry's new aversion to risk, the time and energy and focus that were going to his lover rather than his work—those *were* Templeton's affair, and he resented them with a smouldering savagery that might possibly have clouded his judgement a little.

For example, this wasn't a one-man job. The house was big, the security well-considered, the jewel dealer wary. Most of all, the jewels he was after were opals and everyone knew that opals made the Lilywhite Boys' fingers itch. Diamonds were easier to fence, emeralds more valuable, but opals sang to Templeton and he couldn't resist their song.

A matched set of black opals, Jerry had said scathingly. *Really. Was there also an advertisement placed in the paper for the attention of Templeton Lane? For Christ's sake, if the Met aren't waiting for you, the Lazarus firm will be.*

He'd ignored that as he'd ignored their fence Stan Kamarzyn's more measured words of concern, and his own doubts. He was sick of Jerry's caution, sick of wondering if the Lazarus firm were on his tail, sick of the way his life seemed to be slipping from his control. Sick to death of Jerry, who'd not just forgiven Alec's treachery in helping Susan Lazarus but worked, actually *worked*, with the woman as if she were his *friend*—

His breath was too fast. He pushed down the anger that had been a clenched fist in his chest since the events of the summer, and set himself to wait again, this time paying attention.

There was no sound, he concluded after a while. Probably there never had been.

Templeton moved forward. He was a big man, but he knew how to be light on his feet, and his dark lantern was set to the narrowest possible beam. He padded silently through the hall and up the stairs, keeping to the sides to avoid creaks, and stopped at the top to look around. The house was laid out in a rectangular shape around a full-height central atrium that went all the way to the roof. He could see every door on the first floor. No lights shone through any cracks. There was no movement.

The first door in front of him was Mr. Montmorency's, Templeton knew from the plans he'd studied. The dealer had had a safe-room installed in a windowless corner of his bedroom, which he locked when he retired at night. Templeton had come prepared with skeleton keys, pliers, and tiny oil-dropper to let himself in silently. But the bedroom door was open.

He had to look twice to be sure that the dark crack wasn't a misleading shadow. It wasn't. The always-locked door was without question ajar.

He ought to have left then. He ought to have slipped away as he'd come, silent and stealthy, to have made his way to the riverbank unnoticed, crossed the Thames and vanished into the night. He ought to have gone, but…

…a necklace of eight black opals of the most vibrant colour and superb clarity, each between fifteen and twenty-two carats, cut to matched ovals at a medium cabochon and set in gold, surrounding the forty-carat fire opal known as the Great Nebula…

Doors weren't left open for the convenience of jewel thieves. Anything out of the ordinary during a job should be treated as a warning, not a gift. But the Samsonoff necklace was so close to being his, and the opals were singing.

Templeton slipped his cosh from his pocket, just in case, and pushed the door wider. The hinges barely whispered.

He could smell the wrongness at once. The room reeked of it. And he should have run then, that very moment, but he beamed his dark lantern onto what lay on the floor—a huddled form, white hair matted dark and glistening, head surrounded by a wet, gleaming puddle—and up to the door of the safe-room which gaped wide and black.

Templeton stood and stared for too long, and then he stepped forward. He knelt by the body, shone his lantern onto the face, touched the skin, saw that the eyes glared in death. He rose to his feet again. Opals to his left, escape to his right.

He really should have run.

Two days later, Templeton Lane headed eastward along the Hackney Road, under the cover of night and the shadow of the gasworks. His hat was pulled down over his brow, and he wore a thin coat despite the icy drizzle. The hue and cry was up for a large man; he couldn't afford to emphasise his bulk. He couldn't afford to be noticed at all.

He kept to the walls, twisting politely out of the way of anyone who passed, and made no eye contact. A policeman in a rainproof cape stood on one corner. Templeton walked past, looking neither at him nor away, just as an innocent man would. His shoulders were hunched, but so were everyone else's, and the constable was doubtless too busy being wet and miserable to look out for suspected murderers. He told himself that, but his muscles didn't slacken until he was a hundred yards away.

Every breath hurting, every heartbeat a thud of panic, he walked down ill-lit streets into smoke-black damp-dark Bethnal Green and the little row of shops on Florida Street.

It was past ten at night and the bulls-eye windows of Kamarzyn Repairs were dark. Templeton didn't look around because he didn't have to: he'd been aware of everything on the street from the first step he took onto it. He unlocked the door and slipped in, relocked it from the inside, and made his way to the back of the shop and the door behind a curtain.

Light spilled through the cracks. Templeton manoeuvred himself behind the curtain to ensure none would be visible through the shop windows, opened the door, and went into the kitchen, ducking to avoid the painfully low ceiling.

"Evening," he said.

It was warm in here, and cosy too. The patent stove glowed, the gaslight was bright, the bottle of gin open. It was all entirely welcoming except for the expressions of the two people who sat at the table.

Stan Kamarzyn had been tinkering with the mechanism of a watch, his usual habit when worried, though his hands stilled as Templeton entered. He had a mop of curly black hair, and very black eyes behind wire-rimmed spectacles; he wore a waistcoat and shirtsleeves, which were rolled up displaying sinewy forearms, despite the cold. His face was smudged and his fingers stained. He looked like an honest artisan, in fact, which went to show you couldn't trust appearances, because he'd been the Lilywhite Boys' fence for five years.

He also looked appalled at Templeton's bedraggled appearance, which was fair enough. It had been a shitty few days.

Next to Stan, Jerry Crozier didn't look appalled, or sympathetic, or anything but pissed off. His mouth was set, his eyes cold, and his eyebrows slanted in a way that usually heralded violence.

"The fuck, Templeton," he said. It wasn't much of a greeting, under the circumstances.

"Good evening to you too." Templeton grabbed a tumbler and a chair, sat with a thump in the latter, and filled the former with gin. "Nice to feel welcome."

"My days," Stan said. "Where've you been?"

"I walked from Mortlake. The long way round."

"Nice weather for it," Jerry said. "Again: what the *fuck*?"

"Oh, it's all an amusing misunderstanding. We'll laugh about this one day."

Jerry's hand flexed. Stan said, "For pity's sake. This ain't funny."

Templeton knocked back a mouthful of gin, oily and juniper-scented. "Not very, no. What do you want, an apology?"

He was being a prick and he knew it, but fear and fury were stifling him. What sort of welcome was this from his best friends after the last two days and the shit he was in?

"It wouldn't be misplaced." Jerry had on his gentleman's voice, the officer's drawl that he'd had to learn in the Army because he was nothing more than a jumped-up grammar-school boy. "Considering the stupidity of your actions from start to—I'd say finish but I don't suppose we're anywhere near finished. What the devil happened?"

Templeton topped up his glass, slowly. "I'm surprised I need to say anything, if you know so much already."

"Temp!" Stan slapped his hand on the table, making the watch-pieces jump and roll. "There's a hue and cry for murder, you and that cursed necklace are all over the papers, and this is no time for you two to be at each other's throats *again*. Answer the fucking question!"

Jerry's brows shot up, as well they might. Stan rarely raised his voice. Templeton had seen him upset on a handful of occasions, angry almost never. He looked angry now.

"I'm surprised you call the necklace accursed, Stanislav," he said, playing for time. "I thought you didn't have truck with superstition of that sort."

Stan made a strangled noise. Jerry said, "Let me rephrase the question. Did you kill the old man, you stupid cunt?"

Templeton found his mouth open. "What? No, of course I didn't."

"It's hardly 'of course'," Jerry snapped. "You've been in a hell of a mood for months. I've seen you deal with obstacles, and I've seen you with opals. So—"

"You've never seen me club an old man to death." Templeton's lips felt stiff. He was dimly aware of a new anger rising up, a bright spear of insult. "For God's sake. He was about seventy, and half my size and you think I felt the need to smash his skull in?"

"I don't know what you did. You tell me."

"I *did* tell you. I didn't kill him."

"So the housekeeper lied?"

"How should I know? I haven't had time to read the newspapers. I went in around two, the house was still, his bedroom door was open. I walked in and found his body on the floor."

"On the floor," Jerry repeated.

"With his head smashed like an eggshell in a pool of blood." Templeton remembered the feel of the soft, papery skin, still warm. He rubbed his fingertips on his coat.

"So who killed him?"

"How the devil should I know?"

"Did you hear or see anything?" Stan asked.

"I'd heard a noise some minutes previously. It might have been the murderer at work, or an owl. I didn't hear anything else and I didn't see anyone at all. I found him as I said, in his bedroom, with the door to the safe-room open."

"Did you look for the killer?" Stan asked.

Templeton glared at him. "Am I an enquiry agent? I saw the fellow was dead, concluded nothing more could be done for him, and went to see about the necklace."

There was a short silence, then Stan said, "You serious?"

"What?"

"You stepped over a corpse to steal jewels?"

There was no point trying to convey the nightmarish quality of the room: the stink of death, the silence thudding in his ears, the opals' song. "I was there for jewels," he said shortly. "Don't tell me you wouldn't have done the same."

Stan's expression told him exactly that, but Stan got his hands dirty at one remove. Jerry, a practical man, said, "Can't help the dead. That said, my first thought might have been to search for the murderer."

"Because you're so law-abiding these days?"

"Because I'd prefer not to have my skull caved in from behind by some desperate character trying to escape."

"There was nobody there but the corpse. Nobody in the safe-room. Nobody at all."

"So he'd killed the old man, taken the necklace, and gone?"

"No."

"No, he hadn't gone?"

"No, he hadn't taken the necklace," Templeton said. "It was still there, on the shelf, along with everything else."

"Someone killed Montmorency, opened the safe-room, and didn't rob the place? What was the point of that?"

"No, hold on." Stan flapped a hand. "The Samsonoff *was* stolen. It's in all the papers. If this killer didn't take it, who did?"

Jerry pinched the bridge of his nose. "Oh God."

"Of course I did," Templeton snapped. "As you just said, what was the point otherwise?"

"So you clambered over a corpse, took the necklace from the conveniently open safe-room, and then what?"

"The housekeeper arrived. Or, at least, an elderly woman in her nightgown." He'd emerged from the safe-room, opals in one hand and he could almost have sworn they were glowing, dark lantern in the other, as the woman had pushed open the door. He remembered the blaze of light to his dark-adapted eyes, the soundless stretch of her mouth into an O that made her lined face look like that of a child. "She screamed. I took that as my cue to exit and ran like hell, down the stairs and out." He grimaced at the memory of the desperate chase. "The house was up faster than you would believe. Lights everywhere, people shouting, and one of them had a gun. I made it over the wall and down to the river with a mob on my heels and bullets flying—thank God he was a poor shot—to discover my sodding boat had come unmoored and was gone." He saw Jerry's brows rise. "It really wasn't my night. I had to swim, with the Samsonoff in my pocket, and bloody cold it was too."

"And what about the valet?"

"What valet?"

Jerry looked oddly at him. "Montmorency's valet."

"Never saw him."

"Did you go in the valet's room?"

"Of course not. Why would I?"

"Because he might have come in and seen you?"

"Well, he didn't," Templeton said. "I didn't encounter a soul until the woman arrived, after which I was preoccupied. What about the valet?"

Jerry ignored that. "So the old man was killed just before you got there, and the alarm was raised soon after. But nobody found another intruder. Nobody saw anyone who wasn't meant to be there, except a very large man standing over the body with a necklace in his hand."

"What do you want me to do about that? I wasn't looking for murderers."

"Yeah, well, the police are," Stan said. "They want the big man who clubbed Montmorency to death, cut his valet's throat, and stole the Samsonoff."

"*What?*"

"Valet. Throat. Weltering in pool of blood in the next room." Jerry raised his eyebrows expectantly.

"But— That wasn't me," Templeton said blankly.

"Do you realise how bad this sounds?" Stan demanded. "Someone killed two men and opened the safe-room just before you got there, but he didn't steal anything, and nobody saw him?"

"And you just happened to turn up at the very moment a murderer had done all the work for you," Jerry said. "It makes perfect sense."

Templeton looked from one to the other. "Are you calling me a liar?"

"I'm calling your story nonsense. Why would someone murder a jewel dealer and open his safe-room, but not take anything?"

"Presumably I interrupted him."

"Then *presumably* he'd have been in the damned room along with the jewels and the corpse and you," Jerry snapped. "Except that you told us there was nobody there."

"So he did it before I got there, had an attack of conscience, and went off to drown himself in remorse. I don't sodding know."

"If you think a jury's going to accept that, you're mad," Stan said. "You need to run, Temp. You need to run far, fast, and right now."

"The papers haven't named you yet but it's a matter of days if not hours," Jerry added. "Get out of the country or you'll swing. Stan, what have you got in the way of an identity?"

"Are you trying to get rid of me?" Templeton demanded.

"To save your life, you stupid fuck." Jerry's brows were twitching with tension. "Two men dead, a witness who can identify you, and

Gilded Cage

you, with your stupid bloody obsession with opals and the fucking Samsonoff in your pocket, have nothing to offer but this? Christ. If you are arrested, *you will hang*."

Templeton's jaw felt oddly awkward. "I didn't kill him."

Jerry's breath hissed. "It doesn't matter. Can you not grasp that? It makes no difference at all, because you were burgling the place, you were seen, and your story isn't worth the breath it took to tell it. Come out with that in court and the judge will laugh his black cap off. We need to get you out of the country before your name and face are pasted up on every street. And, indeed, before Stan and I are taken down with you. Stan!"

"William Hertford character. Bank details and pocketbook." Stan put a brown-paper bundle on the table. "The earliest boat train leaves from Cannon Street at twenty past seven tomorrow morning. Though if you ask me you should go up to Harwich, avoid the London stations and southern ports. They're more likely to be watched."

"You can't just bundle me off to the Continent," Templeton said. "I didn't kill him. I'm not going to be blamed for someone else's crime."

"Yeah, but you are," Stan said. "That's already happening."

"This isn't a debate," Jerry added. "We don't have time to play the fool. Stan needs to get our affairs cleaned up fast, and I have to make sure none of this touches Alec."

Templeton snorted. He didn't mean to: it was a reflex, a stupid habit he'd got into at mention of Alec because it annoyed Jerry. He wouldn't have done it if he'd been thinking. But he wasn't, and he did, and cold anger lit Jerry's eyes. "Yes, Alec, the Duke of Ilvar's brother, with his own murder scandal only just died down. If anyone links the Lilywhite Boys to the Ilvar affair, Christ alone knows what might happen. And if you think I'm risking him for your sake— Fuck you, Temp. Fuck you, and fuck this horseshit you expect us to swallow."

"Jerry," Stan said. "Stop it."

"No." Jerry's fingers were flexing. "You've been an arsehole for months; you went off on this job in a stupid reckless mood. You will not bring us all down because your self-esteem has been dented."

"My self-esteem?" Templeton said. "What the devil is that meant to mean?"

"It means," Jerry said icily, "that you sulk like a schoolboy at the very mention of Alec, as though you resent every iota of time I give to him rather than you, and it is frankly embarrassing."

"You can't be serious. What I resent isn't your boy friend, it's your work ethic. You've done fuck all in three months, because every damn job is *too risky* now. You've lost your nerve."

"I'll show you my nerve," Jerry snarled. He shoved his chair back with a clatter. Templeton matched the action. "And if your idea of nerve is smashing an old man's skull—"

"I didn't kill him, damn you!"

Stan clutched his hair. "Oh my days. Shut up, sit down, and stop it. This is not the time!"

"It's precisely the time," Templeton said. "If Jerry's priority now, with all of us at hazard, is bloody Alec—"

"Alec didn't kill anyone," Jerry said. "You are a danger to all of us, and every minute you stand here, the danger grows. I am not going to be prosecuted as an accessory to murder because you won't piss off, or see Stan in the dock, still less Alec, and by Christ if you make it necessary for me to deliver you to the Met, don't think I won't!"

"You think I did it," Templeton said. "That I murdered that man, two men, for opals. Don't you?"

"I'd find it easier not to if you'd come up with a marginally less ridiculous story. Or if I hadn't seen you drop a man out of a window in a fit of pique, or if you hadn't been in an increasing rage for three months, or if you were being remotely reasonable now. As it is…" He gave a slight shrug. It carried all the insult of a foul-mouthed tirade.

"I believe you, Temp," Stan said. "I'll believe whatever you like as long as you clear off, because Jerry's not wrong. Come on, be reasonable."

"I did not kill him," Templeton said, enunciating every word. "Either of them. Not the old man, not the valet."

"Fine. I don't care."

"I do. And I will not allow my name to be smeared like this."

"For Christ's sake." Jerry actually laughed. "Your *name*?"

Templeton straightened to his full height, and inevitably cracked his skull on a ceiling beam. "I used to have one, and I still retain some regard for it. You might not understand that."

"Nope," Stan said. "Common as muck. What I do understand is seven years for receiving stolen goods and who knows what for accessory to murder. There's fifty quid in there. Write me when you've got an address and I'll send you more, now will you please fuck off?"

He shoved the paper bundle further across the table. Templeton took it. "This is a devil of a way to end five years' friendship."

"At least I didn't do it with a razor," Jerry said. "Give it ten minutes after we leave, and use the front door. *We* are going out the back."

CHAPTER TWO

Susan Lazarus glared at the remnants of the kipper on her plate as though the fish had done her an injury for which being gutted, smoked, and eaten was insufficient penance. The kipper looked back with a single blank-white eye.

It wasn't the kipper's fault. It was the newspaper slapped next to her breakfast that had curdled any milk of human kindness she might have possessed.

The *Illustrated London News* had gone to town. That was only to be expected. It had illustrations of the house at Mortlake—which here looked like some sort of Gothic mansion in the depths of an Italian forest—the accursed Samsonoff necklace itself, and, largest of all, the Bloody Scene. In the picture Mr. Montmorency lay dead and a brutish ogre stood astride the corpse with the necklace clutched in one hand and a cosh in the other. The housekeeper stared in horror from the doorway.

Susan wondered who'd drawn it. Surely not Alec Pyne. He worked for the *Illustrated*, but she couldn't imagine he'd touch this subject. Alec's ill-judged love affair with Jerry Crozier seemed to be progressing with an unexpected lack of disaster, but Crozier was partner-in-crime to the man who called himself Templeton Lane. The man in the illustration, who was a murderer.

It didn't matter who'd drawn the pictures. She did, however, want to slap whoever had written the words. She read the text again, carefully, taking in every detail.

Mortlake Opal Murder: a Man is Named

The tragic demise of Mr. Joshua Montmorency which appalled the nation six days ago remains a matter of horror and bewilderment. The Police wish to speak to the following individual: Templeton Lane, also known as William Hertford or Maurice White. Lane is around 6 foot 5 inches tall and broad-shouldered, with thick brown hair of a deep hue, blue eyes, and a substantial moustache. Detective Inspector Wilby begs that anyone with knowledge of his whereabouts will not confront this man, who is considered a danger to the public, but rather contact the Police at once.

A reward of £100 is offered for any individual who lays information leading to the conviction of Mr. Montmorency's murderer.

There was a supplementary piece to update any reader who'd somehow missed the story. Clearly the *Illustrated* intended to milk the tragedy for all it was worth.

Mr. Joshua Montmorency, an elderly bachelor of solitary habits, resided in Sorley House, an isolated building some distance from Mortlake town on the south bank of the Thames. A dealer in precious stones, Mr. Montmorency kept his jewel holdings in a safe-room which he had caused to be constructed in a corner of his bedroom. The door to this was reinforced, and secured by the most up-to-date locks. Moreover, three servants slept on the premises, all doors were locked and bolted nightly, and all casements were shuttered.

Mr. Montmorency's nephew and sole living relative, Mr. Harrison Stroud, was living with his uncle, having come to England from India three months ago. Mr. Cecil Brayton, Mr. Montmorency's solicitor and friend of many years' standing, was also a guest on the night of the tragedy.

The three gentlemen dined together on the fatal evening. Mr. Montmorency invited his guests to admire his recent acquisition, the Samsonoff black opal necklace, a gem of exquisite beauty, immeasurable value, and ominous reputation. (At the

Inquest, Mr. Stroud recalled his uncle explaining that the necklace was said to labour under a curse, and repeating with great amusement, "If even a tenth of the so-called cursed gems that passed through my hands had any effect, I should have been in my grave twenty years ago!" The Jury was deeply struck by the melancholic irony.)

The gentlemen retired to bed by eleven o'clock, and the doors were locked and bolted as usual.

The housekeeper Mrs. Hendrick woke in the small hours of Tuesday morning, concerned she had heard an unusual noise. She crept along the corridor to her master's door, hoping to see for herself that all was well.

The bedroom door stood ajar, against all habit. Fearing Mr. Montmorency was unwell, Mrs. Hendrick peered within. What a sight met her eyes! Her master lay on the floor, the white hair that should have protected him from insult splashed with his own gore, and over him stood a hulking form, clutching in one hand a club stained with guilty blood, and in the other a glittering gem.

"I looked into the monster's face," Mrs. Hendrick told the jury, "and I saw the crime writ on it like the very mark of Cain."

The housekeeper cried for help as the brute pushed her out of the way and fled. Mr. Stroud and Mr. Brayton, disturbed by the cries, quickly emerged from their rooms and Mr. Stroud, having taken the precaution to arm himself with a revolver, joined several men of the household in pursuit of the murderer. They followed the villain to the bank of the Thames, only to discover that their quarry had plunged into the great river. It is not known if the murderer's efforts to cross were successful or if he met his deserved fate in the freezing waters; there have been various reports of sightings across the country in the days since, but none have been confirmed.

Returning to the house, the pursuers made a horrid discovery. Mr. Montmorency's valet, Francis Peevy, slept in an adjoining room to his master. His absence from the chase had been noted, for he of all men should have heard the commotion. Any blame that Mr. Brayton might have thought to cast on an idle servant was most sadly stifled on finding Peevy dead on the floor of his own room, his throat cut.

The safe-room was examined and it was discovered that only one piece was missing from the glittering ranks of treasure: the Samsonoff necklace.

The opal displayed on this necklace as centrepiece to eight perfectly matched lesser stones is known as the Great Nebula. It has been said that to desire the Great Nebula brings madness, but to possess it, death. The tragedy of Mr. Montmorency's demise at the hands of a criminal who would stop at nothing to obtain the jewel will only confirm the worst fears of those who believe in the Samsonoff curse.

Susan closed the newspaper, shaking the pages to tidy them. She folded it in equal halves with precision, folded it again, smoothed out an invisible wrinkle, threw it at the wall as hard as she could, and said, "Balls." Nobody replied, not even the kipper.

She wanted to talk to someone. She hated it when that happened.

There were her guvnors, of course. Her boarding house on Beauchamp Street was halfway between Nathaniel's lodgings in Baldwin's Gardens, and Robin Hood Yard where Justin lived. She could go north to find Nathaniel or south to seek Justin, and it scarcely mattered which because both of them would tell her the same thing. They agreed on very little on a day-to-day basis, but they'd agree that Templeton Lane deserved to hang if he wasn't already dead. He was a thief, a villain, a coward, and a killer. The only difference would be that Nathaniel would call it justice, whereas Justin would revel in vengeance.

She didn't want to talk to the guvnors right now.

She readied herself for the day, wondering who, if anyone, she did want to see. Susan was a woman to whom people brought problems rather than the reverse; she wasn't in the habit of pouring out her soul, and particularly not on a subject as stupid as this. After all, what was there to say? *A villain will receive his just deserts. He had plenty of warnings and every chance in life but has come to a bad end.* What could anyone reply except *Serve him right?* None of her family would wish James Vane, under whatever ridiculous alias, any good; none of them would waste compassion on someone who didn't deserve it. Susan wasn't wasting any compassion on him either. To hell with James-Vane-Templeton-Lane-whoever.

Only, she wanted someone to help her unpick why this all felt so…she wasn't even sure how it felt. Miserable. Peculiar. Stupid.

She was thirty-four, a professional woman, an enquiry agent. She knew plenty of criminals and a few of them had hanged thanks to her. What difference did it make that she'd known this one seventeen years ago, when his path hadn't seemed to head so steeply downwards?

Cara would have let her talk it out and asked good questions, but Cara was dead. Susan missed her brutally all the time, but especially now. Cara would have understood *why* she needed to talk about this and helped her unpick it. It would be nice if someone did.

Alec might. Cara's little brother, now Jerry Crozier's lover, Alec was thoughtful, sensitive, and far too kind for his own good. He understood unpleasant, complicated layers of feelings because he was a decent man in love with a criminal. And Crozier would have surely talked to him about the business, so maybe Susan could learn something useful while she was wallowing in sentiment.

She would talk to Alec. *After* she'd finished the report on her current case, and the invoice that would go with it, and delivered them both to the client. Those things were important, unlike James bloody Vane.

Susan didn't make it to Mincing Lane until five that evening, by which time she was in a thoroughly bad mood. Alec's landlady gave her the usual disapproving look when she announced she was going up, but as a duke's brother he was a law unto himself in the building, a fact he didn't exploit nearly as much as he could have.

Alec answered the door to her knock after a few moments, with a questioning expression that dissolved at once into a smile so warm that Susan found herself smiling back. He was an attractive man in a gentle

Gilded Cage

sort of way: soft-spoken, open-hearted to a fault, with a vulnerable air that had used to make Cara fret because it had seemed inevitable such a lamb would attract predators. She would have been relieved by Jerry Crozier. There was no need to worry about dogs now that Alec had leashed a wolf.

"Hello, Alec. Can I come in?"

"How lovely to see you." Alec stepped back. His room was lit with both gas and oil lamps, and a pen lay on the large desk together with a lot of papers.

"You aren't trying to draw in this light, are you?"

"Just sketching," Alec said apologetically. "I have rather a tight deadline before Christmas. Would you like tea? I just put the kettle on the fire."

It was pleasantly warm in here after the relentless dark cold drizzle outside. Susan seated herself. "Thanks."

"Bad day?"

"Grim." She caught his look of concern. "Not for me, for the client. I'd like to deliver good news more often, you know. Discover the missing person or the valuables safe and sound and return them to a loving family. It must be nice to hand people pictures that make them happy."

"I'm sure it would be," Alec said, with a comically rueful look at his desk. "My last revision letter was three pages. So you were giving bad news today?"

"Mmm. I was hired by a woman to find her long-lost daughter. Got into trouble, family threw her out, fled to London."

"That's not usually a story that ends well."

"And it didn't this time. She ended up working for a man called Kammy Grizzard."

"The fence?"

"You oughtn't know who he is," Susan said severely. "And an honest person would say 'receiver of stolen goods' and don't you forget it. Yes, the fence, but he's got a sideline in selling flesh as well. He buys debts, trains up girls, puts them in the way of wealthy gentleman friends—or ladies—and sells what they steal."

"I know," Alec said surprisingly. "He did it to a friend of mine, a few years ago. She's well out of his clutches now."

"Glad to hear it. So Kammy takes the profit, his tools take the risks. But when this one got caught in the act and had the police called on her, she decided to squeal. To lay information against him."

Alec winced. "What happened?"

"She was ready to testify what Kammy was doing and that he had forced her into the life. But she was held in Holloway, and before the trial another inmate threw vitriol in her face."

"My God!"

"She took the hint and withdrew her allegations. That annoyed the judge, and she got six years for theft. Needless to say her mother had known none of this when she decided to find out what had become of her daughter. I tracked her down and went to see her—it wasn't pretty—and reported to the mother today, and...ugh."

"Was the mother very distraught?" Alec said sympathetically.

Susan rolled her eyes. "You really are far too kind for this world. Of course she wasn't; she was disgusted. She'd wanted to hear her daughter had repented through hardship and was waiting to beg her mother's forgiveness, not that she was sitting in gaol with a ruined face. Not *real* consequences. I told her, if you didn't want your daughter living a desperate life, you shouldn't have driven her to desperation. That didn't go down well."

"I expect not," Alec said. "Goodness, Susan."

"Well, it was true. But she took umbrage and said she wasn't going to pay me, and the whole thing was a blasted nuisance."

"Did she pay in the end?"

"Obviously. So it wasn't a pleasant day, but never mind. How are you?"

Alec accepted the change of subject. "Oh, very good. My brother has settled that lawsuit, the baby has got over colic, and we're expecting my sister to announce her engagement soon."

"Congratulations," Susan said. "I asked how you are, though."

"Work's going awfully well."

"Alec. Do I need to have Crozier's legs broken?"

"No, no, no, good God! Don't be silly. Jerry is marvellous. I know you don't believe a word I say on this subject, but—"

"All right, all right," Susan said grumpily. "Why the long face then?"

Alec spooned tea into the pot as the kettle began to whistle. "He's not terribly happy at the moment. Not with me, but in general, and I'm quite sure you know why."

"What does he know about this Mortlake business?"

Alec shot her a look. "Why? That is, is this a professional question?"

"Crozier's rubbing off on you," Susan observed. "You used not to be suspicious."

"I used not to realise I needed to be. And?"

"It's not professional. I'd like to know, that's all."

Alec filled the teapot before he answered. "Again, why? Because if you're here to discuss Jerry's business, that seems to me more than a casual chat."

He'd used to be significantly easier to push around as well. Susan added a grudging tally mark to her very short list of Crozier's worthwhile qualities. "I'm not professionally involved; I don't need to be. If Templeton Lane is still alive the police will pick him up soon enough, and he'll hang."

"That seems to be everyone's conclusion."

"What does Crozier have to say about it?"

Alec took a moment getting out a couple of chipped cups, scarcely the sort of thing for Lord Alexander Pyne-ffoulkes, brother to the Duke of Ilvar, then poured the tea. Finally he said, "Is this for you?"

"The tea?"

That earned her a look. "The information."

"I told you—"

"You're not professionally involved. Is this for you, personally?"

"I'm not asking for information, just opinions. I... Damn. You know I used to know him, when he was James Vane?"

"Well, I'd grasped you'd met," Alec said. "You tried to shoot him, yes?"

"We were childhood friends."

Alec's mouth dropped open. "You were *what*? How did that happen? I thought you were a spiritualist's assistant! How—but—why didn't you tell me? You arrested him!"

"I *was* a spiritualist's assistant. My guvnor took me off the streets to work for him when I was eight or so. I was probably twelve when he met Nathaniel and turned reputable, and he had to find something to do with me. He sent me to school, but I was a foul-mouthed professional cheat with a lot of tricks. Got myself kicked out after three days the first time. The next one took eight. I told him if he made me go to boarding school I'd burn it to the ground, and he believed me, as well he might."

"I see," Alec said faintly.

"But Nathaniel had a friend, lady called Miss Rawling who was all about educating girls. She'd retired from being a headmistress herself, so she taught me privately. Lessons, deportment, speech, and manners. I dug my heels in about that, until she sat me down and explained that I'd be a far better kiter if I could pass for a wealthy flat, so she was actually teaching me my trade." Susan grinned at the memory. "Brilliant woman. By the time I was fifteen I was more or less civilised, and then her nephew came to stay. I say nephew, he was a second cousin of some sort, but he called her Aunt. Her mother had been a Vane, of the Cirencester family, and they'd asked her for help with him because young James was a troublemaker. He'd been expelled from school, not for the first time, and they wanted her to take him in hand. We hit it off at once."

"Really?"

"Well, he asked if I could pick pockets, so I kicked him in the shins. When he stopped swearing he explained that he wanted me to teach him, and after that we were inseparable."

"I may need a moment to picture this," Alec said. "Good Lord."

"I was a scrawny, skinny scrapper, and James was about five foot ten. I taught him to pick pockets and jimmy locks—you needn't say anything—and he taught me boxing. We used to sit on the roof and smoke and talk." And that was quite far enough down Memory Lane for anyone's good. "The point is, he was my friend once. That's long gone, but even so…"

"You don't want to think he's a murderer."

"No, I don't." Susan turned the cup, pressing her hands to its sides. She felt chilled and weary. "I know he's a thief, a villain, and a selfish swine. I despise everything he's done with his life. I did try to shoot him, and I didn't miss on purpose. And he has an unhealthy fascination with opals. But I didn't imagine he—not the boy I knew, not even the man he's become—would smash an old man's skull and cut another's throat for the sake of jewels."

"No," Alec said. "Jerry feels much the same."

Susan found herself reluctant to ask the necessary question. That was ridiculous, since she knew very well it was what she'd come for. "Does Crozier believe James is guilty?"

"I'm honestly not sure what he thinks. I don't know if he knows himself. He's mostly swearing."

"Aren't we all."

"What else is there to do?" Alec made a face. "Templeton—James Vane, I mean, but I think of him as Templeton—denies it, if that helps."

Susan sat up. "He's alive? Are you sure? Has Crozier seen him?"

"A couple of days after the murders. Apparently Templeton gave him a story that a child couldn't swallow. Jerry was spitting feathers about it. He's... I don't know quite how to put it. Disappointed."

Susan wasn't concerned with Crozier's feelings, although it was interesting to discover the man had a moral threshold, albeit one set staggeringly low. She was more concerned by the jumble of her own: outrage at the crime, resentful anger that James had let everyone down yet again, and an irritating relief he hadn't drowned in the cold, dark Thames. That was a vestige of the past that she needed to forget as soon as possible. "Disappointed because James is a murderer?"

"Because Jerry thinks he lied. He was insistent he didn't do it."

"And Crozier didn't believe him?"

Alec stared into his cup. "The thing is, they haven't been getting on very well. Jerry's been lying low for my sake, and Templeton resented that. Jerry refused to touch the Mortlake job because he said it was an invitation to walk into a trap. They had an almighty row and Templeton stormed off to do it himself in a dreadful temper."

"That sounds like James."

"I think Jerry feels guilty he didn't go with him, that perhaps he could have stopped it going bad. But he didn't. Templeton did the job and reappeared a couple of days later, with a story that didn't make any sense and—well, that. With this story."

He'd caught the stumble neatly enough that many people would have missed it. Susan gave him a look. "James reappeared with a story *and* something, did he? Would that be an opal necklace?"

"Susan..."

She sighed. "Fine. What was the story?"

"I don't know. Jerry didn't go into detail."

"Right." Susan finished her tea and put the cup down. "Damnation. Damn."

"Were you planning to do something?" Alec asked tentatively.

Gilded Cage

"There's nothing to be done. If he can't convince his partner in crime that he's not guilty, he won't stand a chance with a jury. I hope he's long gone, if only for old times' sake. But that's down to him."

"That's what Jerry said. He looked fairly miserable about it too."

"I am not miserable. I wanted to know if there was anything worth regretting in James Vane's imminent bad end, and now I've found out there isn't. That's worth knowing."

"Mph. I suppose." Alec twisted the cup in his hands.

Susan narrowed her eyes. "What is it?"

"Nothing. I don't know. It's just… The thing is, I don't much like Templeton. We didn't get off on the right foot, and he hasn't welcomed me as Jerry's—you know, and to be honest I find him quite intimidating. I wouldn't have said he'd beat an old man to death for opals, but people do awful things all the time. He might very well have done it."

"As established," Susan said thinly.

"Yes. The part I don't believe is him lying to Jerry." He was staring into his tea again. "It's probably silly of me. Jerry always says that betrayal is the one inevitable in his profession. But I've seen how they work together, that *us against the world* attitude. How much they need one another, even if they'd both rather die than voice it. The truth is, if he did it, I think he'd have told Jerry. *I lost my temper* or *I didn't realise his age before I struck* or even just, *I killed him, what of it?* Perhaps I'm wrong."

"You always think the best of people. I've warned you about that."

"But I *don't* think the best of him. I can quite believe he's a murderer. I just don't think he'd tell that particular lie."

"Did you tell Crozier this?"

"He wasn't in a listening mood," Alec said. "And of course I've barely seen him. He's keeping out of sight because of the police looking

25

for Templeton. So is Stan Kamarzyn. It's…" Alec waved his hands, apparently trying to convey the repercussions of a manhunt for homicide in mime. "Inconvenient."

"I dare say." Susan rose. "Well. Thanks for the tea."

"Just a minute. Are you all right?"

"Of course I am."

"If you say so. But you came over here to talk about James Vane, so if you want to do that, there's more tea in the pot."

Susan gave it more consideration than she should have. There was no point dragging up the dead past, or harking back to seventeen years ago, when the world was young and bright and explosively full of excitement and potential. She'd started in life with nothing, briefly believed she could have everything, and learned the hard way to cherish what she had and shrug her shoulders at the rest. James Vane and his bad end fell firmly into the 'shrug' category. He'd chosen his path, she'd chosen hers.

She'd come here to talk to someone who wouldn't be actively glad James Vane was going to hang. Perhaps she'd harboured a lingering hope that there might be some question as to his guilt; well, if the only person expressing doubt was Alec with his misplaced confidence in humanity, that was no question at all.

"Nothing to talk about," she said. "I'd better be going. Keep well. Tell Crozier that if he lands you in trouble I'll break his neck before the hangman has a chance to."

Alec smiled as though she'd expressed some sort of goodwill. "Thanks, Susan. I'll see you soon."

She made her way back through what had turned from a drizzle to a relentless downpour, trudging through the mud and slime as great drops of rain carried the filth out of the air and onto the streets, the buildings, and her. Bloody November, bloody England, bloody James.

Alec lived some way east of Leather Lane, and Susan was thoroughly wet by the time she'd reached Farringdon. She thought about ducking into Robin Hood Yard on her way home instead of returning to her cold and solitary rooms. There would be fires there, warmth and comfort. Justin would be there with Mark, who had established the enquiry agency in the first place and to whom Susan really ought to report about that client. Nathaniel might well be with them; certainly Emma, who'd been with Justin as long as Susan had and was now housekeeper. This was her family, chosen by love rather than bound by birth, and infinitely stronger for it.

They all loathed James Vane. They'd all have read the papers and would want to discuss it, or even worse, would carefully *not* say anything in case they upset her. She couldn't summon the strength.

She stopped for a hot meal at a Lyons instead, and ate it in an atmosphere that resembled the greenhouses at Kew thanks to the battle of overenthusiastic heating with the November chill. Steam boiled off the customers' wet coats like anger made visible. Susan stayed until her unpleasantly cold and damp clothing became unpleasantly hot and damp, then headed out into the dark where she immediately got cold again.

Her boarding house was on the corner of Beauchamp Street and the nameless alley that ran south to Greville Street. Susan glared down into the alley as she passed, swinging her lead-weighted cosh in a pointed fashion, and caught the eye of an urchin who was hanging around with no good intent. She hissed at him as one would a cat. He gave a yelp of alarm followed by a shrill whistle, and fled.

Probably a look-out for a job. Susan cast a quick glance around but the nearest gaslamp was out and the driving rain made it impossible to see more than a few yards in any direction. Any bastard committing crimes on a night like this would get his deserts in the form of pneumonia. She hunched her shoulders, shook the rain off her coat, and let herself in, squelching up the narrow flights of stairs to her second-floor room without any enthusiasm at all.

Her room was significantly colder than she'd expected. She hung up her coat and hat, and lit the gas, shivering. The fire was laid, so she lit that too, eased her wet boots off, then padded over in slippered feet to draw the curtains.

If she lived at Robin Hood Yard, she'd come home to lit fires every winter night, and Emma's cooking instead of meals out at coffee shops, and company. She'd also have to find a new job, because there might be people who could both work for and live with their family but Susan wasn't among them. It didn't do to put all your eggs in one basket, to rely on other people day in, day out. She'd taught herself not to cling to Justin after he remade her life around her for the second time, and then she'd taught herself not to cling to anyone at all when it turned out that people were far more weak and self-centred and unreliable than one could imagine.

"Oh, stop whining," she said aloud. She had a fire and a good book; what more did a woman need? Drink, of course. She poured herself a generous whisky, added a shovel of coals to the fire, picked up her book, and sat down with a sigh.

She read a paragraph. Then she skipped ahead three pages, and then she sat very still, eyes on the book without seeing a word.

She was reading *Diana Tempest*, with its "heir to a fortune discovered to be illegitimate" plot, a situation that had played out considerably differently when she and Justin had encountered it. The book, a cheap edition, had been splayed face down on the table, the way she'd left it. But it was now on the wrong page, at the start of the chapter that she'd got half way through.

So either she had put it down carelessly enough to turn pages but not carelessly enough to crease them, or someone else had picked it up and put it down at the wrong place. The housemaid? But she couldn't read more than her name, and habitually dusted around things rather than picking them up.

Susan took a very long, shallow breath through her nose, but couldn't detect anything over the smell of the coal fire, her wet coat, and the sharp scent of whisky. She rose as silently as possible, remembering the boy in the alley and the unusual cold of the room. She was surely too high up for casual robbery. That meant, if someone had broken in, it was personal.

She couldn't see anything missing at first glance, and her desk looked as she'd left it. Her bedroom door was closed. Best to check there first, then.

Her gun was safely stored in a bedroom drawer, a decision that had seemed sensible up until this moment. She picked up the poker in her left hand, looped the cosh's leather string over her right wrist, stepped quietly to the bedroom door, and kicked it open.

The door slammed back and bounced off the dresser without impediment. She stood and listened, hearing not a sound, not a breath. She could see no disturbance, no sign that anyone had invaded her privacy. This might just be a book she'd put down at the wrong page.

She took a step forward into the room, and another, and *then* she heard it, *then* she turned, but it was too late. A huge hand came over her mouth, muffling her involuntary cry. Susan thrust her elbow into her assailant's torso, then jerked her forearm up. She meant to put the poker into his chin and right through his skull, but he'd moved already as though he'd predicted the attack. His other arm—too strong, too large—wrapped around her, pinioning her upper arms as he said something she didn't listen to. She stamped savagely on his foot, cursing that she'd put on slippers, shook the cosh down into her palm as she did it, and tried her best to swing it at his balls with the little purchase she had. He grunted, but his grip didn't relax, and he was just too damn strong. She thrashed her head, trying to bite his hand—

"Sukey!" her attacker rasped, and the breath hissed out of her against his skin, for all the world as though she were the one who'd taken a blow where it hurt.

"Sukey," he said again. "Susan. It's me. Templeton. I won't hurt you, damn it. Just don't scream." His hand lifted slightly from her mouth.

"I never scream," Susan said through her teeth. "Let me *go*."

"I won't hurt you. I just want to talk to you, understand? I'm going to let go now." His grip relaxed as he spoke, releasing her arms.

So Susan coshed him in the balls again. This time, she did it properly.

CHAPTER THREE

It took some time before the white blaze of nauseating pain subsided enough for Templeton to uncurl from his agonised huddle on the floor. Once he managed that, he realised that the gaslight was on. Susan stood at the other side of the bedroom. She held a gun, which was pointed at him.

But she wasn't shouting for a policeman, so this was going better than expected.

"Good evening," he croaked.

"Go fuck yourself. What are you doing here?"

"I wanted to talk to you."

"Of course. I always start a conversation by putting my hand over the other party's mouth."

"You might as well do," Templeton pointed out, with heat. "The impossibility of getting you to listen for five minutes—" That was true, but not helpful. He made himself start again. "That is, I apologise. I'm sorry I frightened you—"

"You did not 'frighten' me," Susan said, pure ice.

"Alarmed. Startled. I apologise for the disruption I caused by breaking into your rooms and grabbing you. Will that do?"

"No." The gun was still levelled at him. "Why did you break into my rooms?"

"Because I need to talk to you and it's rather difficult for me to make appointments!" He heard the rise in his voice, took a breath. "I couldn't risk you—uh, making any noise in natural alarm. I'm sorry. I'm a little on edge."

"I assumed you'd fled the country days ago."

"The ports are watched." Christ, that was something to say of oneself. "There's descriptions out, and I'm too easily spotted. I wouldn't stand a chance." He could disguise many things, but not his height and breadth, not in a manhunt.

"I see. If you have come here to ask me for help to flee a murder charge—"

"I haven't," Templeton said hurriedly. He knew the sound of Susan's rage kindling when he heard it. "Not at all."

"Good, because you won't get it. What do you want, then?"

Templeton breathed out, with caution. "Can I stand up?"

"I don't know. How hard did I hit you?"

He knotted a fist until the knuckles hurt. Seventeen years ago he'd have responded like a barrow-boy to that smart-arsery, and she'd have capped it with words he didn't even know. Seventeen years ago they'd have ended up crying with laughter.

Seventeen years ago he hadn't ruined both their lives. That put a damper on things.

"Quite hard," he replied with as much charm as he could scrape together. "*May* I stand up? Or, actually, sit down?"

"You can go into the other room and pull over a chair," Susan said. "Not too close to mine. Put some more coal on the fire while you're there. And don't make any abrupt movements."

Templeton did as bid, aware of her keeping her distance, and the barrel of the gun. He pulled a wooden chair opposite the sole armchair, and sat. Susan approached, but stayed on her feet, watching him.

Templeton put his hands on his knees, palms up. "Nothing up my sleeves. I'm not going to hurt you."

"No, you're not. When did you last eat?"

That was so entirely Susan it hurt. "I don't know. Some little time."

"Obviously," she muttered. "Your ability to think has always been directly linked to your stomach. Stay."

She moved over to the cupboard. Templeton breathed deeply. He didn't want to *stay* like a dog; far more, he didn't want to hear Susan speak this way. It had been fun, once the way she'd bat back any remark, never giving an inch. It had been a game, and now it wasn't, just as he'd once been able to argue with Jerry as part of a friendship deep enough not to need acknowledgement. He really hadn't got much in his life left to ruin.

A man with self-respect would probably have left. But he was warm now for the first time in days, Susan was cutting bread, and she'd probably shoot him if he stood, so he sat, dizzy with exhaustion and hunger, shut his eyes, and tried not to think.

"How did you get in here?" she asked as she worked. "And keep your voice down, I'm not allowed men."

"Climbed."

"I'm on the second floor. It's raining. Climbed what?"

"The wall. I'm a good climber." It had been both difficult and terrifying, given the slippery fog-slime that coated the bricks. He didn't imagine he'd get much sympathy for that.

"And came in through the window? Did you break my catch?"

"It shouldn't be very badly damaged."

She growled in her throat. "What about that boy you had standing lookout? Any chance he's off to claim the reward on your head?"

"I bloody hope not."

"If the police turn up, I will hand you over without a qualm," Susan said. "Pickle?"

"It is rather," Templeton agreed thinly.

"On your sandwich."

"Ah. Yes. Please," he added.

Susan came over. Templeton opened his eyes and saw heaven on a plate—three rounds of sandwiches on thick-sliced bread, so lavishly buttered it was coming out the sides, slabs of cheese, the sharp smell of chutney—and then he paid no attention to anything except ripping into the food. The bread was a day old but the cheese was strong, the pickle spiced and tangy. He wolfed the first two halves of sandwich, not caring if he looked like an animal, and realised Susan had put a cup of beer on the table in front of him.

"Don't choke," she advised.

Templeton muttered unclear thanks, sluiced his throat, and went back to work. It had been two days and eight hours since he'd last eaten, and he felt every one of them.

He cleared the plate, and could have eaten as much again, but opted not to mention that. "Thank you."

Susan, sitting opposite with a glass of whisky and the gun, gave him a nod. Templeton tried, "Excellent pickle."

"Apple chutney. Emma makes it. Are you feeling—let's say, as close to human as you're capable of?"

Evidently food didn't constitute a truce. "Much better, yes."

"Right." Susan leaned back. "Feel free to explain why you broke into my home."

Templeton drained the last of the ale and put the cup down. "I want your help."

Her eyes hadn't changed in seventeen years. They were still blue-grey like winter sun on the sea, and they still went colder than any sea ever could. "We already discussed this."

"No," Templeton said. "I don't want you to help me escape. I want you to help me prove I didn't do it."

There was a very long silence, in which Susan's expression didn't change one jot, and then she said, "What." It wasn't even a question.

"I didn't kill the old man, or the valet. I never laid a finger on either."

"Don't tell me. You weren't even near Mortlake at the time."

He made himself breathe. Susan's open scorn was far more to be expected than Jerry's. It ought not hurt. "I was in the house. I stole the Samsonoff necklace. But I did not kill anyone, and I need to prove that."

Another long, unblinking silence, which gave Templeton time to reflect without affection on Susan's adoptive father, the reptilian Justin Lazarus, who had taught her a poker face any gambler would envy. At last she said, "Why?"

"Why would I prefer to clear my name of murder?"

"If you gave a damn for your name, you would have conducted your life differently for the last two decades."

Anger curdled in his gut again. He breathed it down. "True. I still don't want my face in the newspapers, to skulk in the shadows with a price on my head, to be an exile for the rest of my life. I have been exiled once, and I didn't like it." Her face tightened. He barrelled on. "And those are the better options. I could hang for this, and I don't want to hang, especially for something I didn't do. I did not kill anyone. I found the old man dead; I never saw the valet. That's the truth. And I don't know anyone who will—who *might* believe me except you."

"You think I'll believe you?"

"I think you'll give me a fair hearing. And I don't think you'd watch even a man you loathed hang, if you thought he was innocent."

"I wouldn't bet on that," Susan said. "Shut up and let me think about this."

Templeton waited for a few silent moments, watching her face, which betrayed nothing. She hadn't had the habit of consideration as a girl; she'd always been fast to act or decide. Sukey stopping to weigh things up was unfamiliar, and he wasn't sure he liked it.

"Some people," she said at last, "might call this a fucking cheek. Of all the detectives in London, you come to me?"

"There's only you," Templeton said. "I can't hire a private enquiry agent: they'd turn me in on the spot. The police wouldn't listen. And to anyone in my line of work, I'm a plague carrier; I'd just bring trouble to their door. I can't think of a single soul who'd so much as hear me out, other than you."

"I heard you and Crozier had fallen out over this." Susan crossed her legs at the ankles. She wore sensible carpet slippers. Templeton remembered her feet, quite suddenly and so strongly it was almost a physical experience. Prominent bones and long toes, always sharp-nailed, always cold. "If your partner in crime doesn't believe you, why should I?"

"Because you're a great deal more intelligent than he is."

Susan gave a sharp crack of laughter. "Nice try."

"In fact you are," Templeton said. "Than he or I, which is probably how we all ended up in our respective places. Jerry wasn't inclined to listen to me. I couldn't speculate as to why," he added sourly.

"If that's a dig at Alec Pyne, you're misinformed. He believes you."

"What?"

"That may be overstating it. Alec isn't convinced you would have lied to Crozier. It's hardly an expression of faith in your character, but he is an extremely perceptive man, so…" She glanced at the clock on the mantelpiece. "You've got half an hour. Irritate me and I'll call for the police."

"Christ." Templeton knew he should take the chance he was offered, but for Susan to grant him a hearing because of Alec fucking Pyne was the last insult on top of a heap of failures, self-inflicted wounds, stupidities, hurts, and calamities that made him want to punch a wall till his hands broke. "You haven't got any easier, have you? Have you ever considered giving anyone the benefit of the doubt?"

"No. Twenty-nine and a half minutes."

"Jesus Christ, Susan!"

"And counting."

Templeton dug his nails into his palms. *Calm. Calm.* She'd fed him. She might hate him but she'd fed him, and even if she was only listening because of bloody Jerry's bloody sweetheart, she was listening.

Last chance, Templeton. Throw this one away and you might as well borrow that gun and ask for five minutes alone.

He tipped back his head, stared at the ceiling. "I arrived in Mortlake around eleven that night…"

He told her the whole story, speaking into a silence so absolute that he almost wondered if she were listening. Her winter-sea eyes were unfocused, and she only moved to sip at her whisky as the tale ground on. She let him get to the end, and then said, "Again."

"Again what?"

"Tell me the whole thing again. From the start. Same level of detail."

Templeton set his teeth, and launched into the story. This time, when he reached the part where he was in the hall, she lifted a finger.

"You heard a noise. But no speech. No muffled conversation, no sounds of movement?"

"Nothing. Absolute silence."

"Explain the layout of the house to me."

"The rooms are laid out around a large central atrium, a big hall, which is double height and has a large skylight. There is a flight of stairs up to the first floor landing, and all the upstairs rooms have doors onto that landing. Think of it as a hollow rectangle with the rooms around the edge and a hole in the middle. Like a Roman villa with a roof on top."

Susan's expression conveyed her lack of a classical education without words. He pushed on. "Montmorency's room is the first one comes to from the stairs. His valet's room was next to his, with a connecting door. Then there are several guest rooms and the housekeeper's room."

"All laid out around this..." Susan drew a rectangle with her finger. "So any noise or movement from upstairs would definitely carry down to the ground floor of the hall, where you were."

"Yes."

"Whose rooms were closest to his?"

"His and the valet's rooms took up a short side of the rectangle. If you walk around the landing, the guest rooms are on the next, long side. Then various other offices on the other short side, with the housekeeper's room at the far corner. She would have to walk around three sides of the rectangle to reach Montmorency's door, because of the stairs."

"Got it. Go on."

He reached the part with the dead man before she interrupted again.

"He was definitely dead?"

"Extremely."

"How long would you say he'd been dead?"

"Not long at all. He hadn't cooled."

"How much looking around the room did you do?"

"Not a great deal. The corpse wasn't the best company."

"Don't give me bravado," Susan said wearily. "You walked into a room with a dead man on the floor. You didn't call for help for obvious reasons of self-preservation—"

"There wasn't anything to be done for him," Templeton said, stung.

"And if there had been? Never mind. You stepped over the corpse, and then what?"

"I looked under the bed and around the room to be sure I was alone. The safe-room door was open. I shone my lantern inside and saw nobody."

"Could anyone have hidden in there?"

"No. It holds some open shelves, cabinets underneath, most of them with drawers. The Samsonoff necklace was on the shelf, on a display stand. White velvet."

"And you took it."

"Well, I'd come all that way."

Susan shut her eyes. Templeton almost snarled. "I'm a jewel thief. What did you expect me to do, leave it as a sign of respect?"

"No, I wouldn't expect that at all. Have you still got it?"

He nodded. Susan looked at him and then her brows went up. "On your *person*?"

"I'm not in a position to set up a safety deposit box."

"You do realise, if you're found with that on you—"

"I know."

She let out a long sigh. "Fine. Let me see."

She held out a hand. Templeton hesitated, and got a vicious look. "If I wanted to do you over I could have shot you at any time, and I still can. Give."

Templeton forced down the skin-crawling reluctance to let anyone else touch it, fished out the bedraggled black velvet bag, and unwrapped the cloth in which the opals nestled, all dark fire. He lifted the necklace, and held it out.

"That looked like it hurt. Well." She ran the opals through her fingers. "Matched stones. That's rare, isn't it?"

"Opals are normally irregular. To have ones this size cut to shape is costly. And a shame."

"Why?"

"I prefer the natural shapes, like the centrepiece."

"The Great Nebula." Susan held up the necklace and squinted at it, as though it were a smock with a stain on it instead of a priceless gem.

The Great Nebula was of irregular shape, walnut-sized, and the most perfect fire opal Templeton had ever seen. The splash of vivid crimson at its centre was surrounded by a green, unearthly halo that faded into an intense black filled with glittering, turning rainbow colours.

"It glows," he said softly. "It shines in the dark as though it's lit from within. It holds the whole night sky."

"I've no idea what I'd wear it with." Susan dumped it back into his palm. "Can you fake opals?"

"You have no soul. No. You can put slivers of opal under glass so they look like the real thing to a casual glance, but not under a loupe."

"Have you checked this is the real thing?"

"I don't need to check. I know opal, and nobody could possibly— Why do you think it's faked?"

"Just a thought. As long as you're sure."

He made an unnecessary parade of holding the Great Nebula to the light. "I'm quite sure."

"Where was the killer hiding?"

"I don't know," Templeton said, before his brain caught up with his ears. "What?"

"If it wasn't you it was someone else, unless the old man clubbed himself to death. So I wonder where this killer could have been while you wandered around stealing necklaces."

Templeton tenderly folded the velvet cloth around the opals. "I don't know. There was a wardrobe in the room that I didn't check but I didn't hear any breathing. No sound. I didn't *feel* anyone was there."

"And presumably you would have heard someone climb into a wardrobe," Susan pointed out. "Mind you, you'd also have heard someone leaving the room, wouldn't you?"

"Yes. I would have heard anyone moving around the hallway at any point in the previous ten minutes or so, and I didn't, which makes my story of a fresh corpse in an empty room unlikely. I realise that."

"Ten minutes," Susan said. "Hmm. Would someone in the room have heard you coming?"

"I doubt it. I moved quietly. I wouldn't expect anyone to realise I was there until I was close enough to, for example, hear someone get into a wardrobe or roll under the bed. I was *listening*."

"Was the window shut?"

He thought back. "Yes."

"Had it been opened recently?"

Templeton opened his mouth to say, *How the devil should I know?*, caught her eye, and applied his mind. "I don't think so. It wasn't colder than it should have been. Or fresh either. The room stank of blood—that sweet rust smell. I could taste it."

"You can, can't you?" She wrinkled her nose. "What about the valet?"

"I don't know. The connecting door was shut. I didn't look. If I'd been thinking, I'd probably have wondered how he could have slept through someone clubbing his master to death, but I wasn't. There was a corpse on the floor."

Susan nodded. "Was anything disturbed in the safe-room?"

"Not obviously to me. There were stones out on the shelves but I understood that to be Montmorency's habit."

"He could leave them out because the safe-room door was enough protection. What was the lock on that like?"

"The door was open."

"Yes," Susan said. "Let's go back to that. How long would it have taken you to open it otherwise?"

"Perhaps an hour at most. I intended to chloroform the old man in his sleep as a precaution."

"As one would. Did the corpse have chloroform burns on his mouth?"

"Not that I noticed. No, I'm sure he didn't."

Susan nodded. "And then the housekeeper turned up. You didn't hear her coming?"

This was embarrassing. "No. I wasn't paying attention." He glowered at Susan's expression. "I suppose you've never been so absorbed in one thing that you've failed to do another. Of course you have always been sensible and logical."

"Shut up, James. To recap: Montmorency was out of bed when he was killed. The valet was murdered in his own room, also out of bed, and both were killed bloodily, but whoever was the second to die didn't raise the alarm at the other's death. The killer committed two murders and opened the safe-room door, not necessarily in that order, and either escaped without you seeing him or hid so well that he wasn't found in the subsequent search. And yet, for all that effortless competence, he didn't steal a single one of jewels that lay behind the door he'd gone to all that trouble to open. Crozier is right. Your story is ridiculous."

Templeton hadn't hoped, exactly. The opposite, in fact: what had driven him to Susan was despair. He had become an outcast in London's underworld, with all doors closed to him, and not even his closest friends on his side. Alone, hunted, accused, consumed by the injustice of being condemned for a crime he hadn't committed after getting away with all the ones he had, he hadn't been able to think of a single soul with a reason to help him, and of only one who might do it anyway.

Susan had a sense of justice that far outweighed trivia like personal feelings or the laws of the land. Susan would help him because he was being wronged. He'd told himself that again and again, as he'd huddled in filthy alleys to avoid policemen, formulating his poor excuse for a plan, and made himself act as if it was true because if she didn't believe him, he was finished.

He had to clear his throat to speak. *Plead.* Christ, he didn't want to plead to this woman. When Susan said no, a wise man accepted it the first time, but he had no choice.

"I know how stupid it sounds, but it's true. I swear to you, Susan—"

"Well, obviously it's true," she interrupted irritably. "If you'd made it up you'd have worked out something better than this."

"...what?"

"I believe you," Susan said, with patronising clarity. "Not a sentence that I pictured myself saying to you ever again, but here we are."

"But— You said—"

"I said that Crozier's assessment was correct and your story makes no sense. It doesn't, therefore we need to fit the facts into a different story. I can think of three alternative explanations that would make sense of all this, offhand."

James stared. Susan looked as unconcerned as if she hadn't just upended the world. "The question is which if any of those is correct, and of course how I can get myself into the investigation— Put your head between your knees."

Templeton did so, because he had black spots in front of his eyes and a ringing in his ears. God knew what he must look like. If he swooned like a maiden on the stage, she'd never let him live it down.

"For goodness' sake," Susan muttered. "If you pass out, you can stay where you fall. I'm not rupturing myself heaving you around the place. Here." That was a tumbler shoved into his hand, half full of whisky. He lifted his head when he was sure he could do so safely, knocked the drink back in two swallows, and spent the next few moments getting his breath back from the burn in his throat.

Susan was crouched just a couple of feet away, one hand half-extended. "Are you all right?"

"Yes. Fine. I'm just tired."

"You used to be strong as an ox."

I've been in hiding for days. I had to swim across the Thames and trudge through the freezing night city in sodden clothes, so cold I might have died. My friends have turned their backs on me. I dodged police all the way to Harwich, and back again when I couldn't get on a boat, and emptied my pockets in shorter order than I could have thought possible because every man's hand is against me. And now one woman, the last one in the world with a reason to help me, has offered to help, and I'm thirty-three years old and I think I might weep.

He didn't say any of that. He didn't reach for her hand either, because he didn't want to see her pull it away. He just shrugged, and saw her mouth twist.

"Where are you staying?"

"I've been moving around."

"The street, in other words. That explains your frankly disgraceful state. Have you other clothes with you?"

"I had to leave my bag behind at my last lodging."

Susan rolled her eyes. "So you're entirely destitute, on your uppers, and without a single resource on which to rely?"

"I still have my wits," Templeton offered, with the best stab he could make at joviality.

"As I said, destitute. God's sake."

"You don't need to tell me I've made a damned mess of things. I'm aware of that."

"It's about time you were. Have you yet taken the logical step?"

"What would that be?"

"Changing your behaviour," Susan said with something of a snap. "Ceasing to make a mess, instead of sitting in it like a puppy that couldn't possibly have predicted any of this and expecting other people to clear it up for you."

Templeton had to exhale. "You really don't get any easier, do you?"

"If by 'easier' you mean 'more inclined to pander to self-indulgence', no. You're a burglar, a thief, and a disgrace, and none of that is improved by your not being a murderer. I'll help prove your innocence of this particular crime, but if you want sympathy, go elsewhere."

In other circumstances he would have taken her up on that. Unfortunately, sympathy was the least of his current requirements. Susan was like lye soap: caustic to the point of pain, but very effective.

"I would prefer aid to sympathy," he made himself agree, as though this were a discussion rather than a pummelling. "As to changing my behaviour, I'll be delighted to consider it when my future doesn't involve a noose."

"I'll hold you to that," Susan said. "Do you have anywhere to sleep?"

"I'll manage."

"Don't be stupid. If you get picked up by the police you don't stand a chance. Oh, for God's sake. You can have the floor."

It wasn't gracious; it was openly grudging. It was still more kindness than Templeton had imagined possible.

"Are you—" He bit off 'sure'. She'd said it. "You know that I can't guarantee I wasn't seen coming here, though I did my utmost."

"I bet you did. You can sleep in here. I don't need to remind you I have a gun."

It took a second for the words to sink in to his brain, and then he rose, steadying himself on the chair-back as blood rushed around his head. He'd swallowed most of his pride by now, but he couldn't swallow this. "If you think you have to tell me that, if you actually believe you need a weapon, I'll leave now and take my chances. That was unwarranted."

"What was? Considering my safety, rather than your self-esteem?" She let that hang for a moment then added, "Oh, don't look so offended. If I really considered you a danger, I'd have shot you. You can have the floor and a blanket, and tomorrow we'll discuss next steps. Now sit down while I get some supplies. You look worn out."

He sat with relief. His head swam with exhaustion and the weakness that came in the wake of a lifted burden. Not that it was actually lifted. He was no better off than he had been, except that Susan had said she would help, and he couldn't even be completely positive about that. She might intend to lull him into a sense of security, slip out as he slept, and summon a policeman. It was what any sensible woman would do in the circumstances, with a large and dangerous man in her room and a big reward on the table. He had no problem imagining that Susan would take that route; she'd always been a ruthless liar and frighteningly amoral when it suited her needs.

But if she didn't help him he was doomed anyway, so he might as well spend his last night of freedom in a warm room by the fire, rather than huddled on the cold, wet streets.

Susan returned with a pair of blankets, plus a lidded chamber pot, all of which she set down. "Don't leave this room," she told him. "I'm not supposed to have gentleman friends in here, let alone wanted murderers. There's nobody else on this floor, but the girl sleeps above, in the attic. I'll tell her not to do the fires tomorrow."

She whisked out again. Templeton spent a few moments in the chair thinking of nothing, until he realised he was almost asleep, and got to his feet to shake off the sickening tiredness. He added a few shovels of coal to the fire, folded one blanket over the rug in the hope it might ameliorate the floorboards, and then drifted around the room, telling himself he was merely trying to stay awake until she returned.

It wasn't what you might call a feminine room. Back when he'd known her, Susan had never grasped the idea of making a house a home, with frills and pleasant details to delight the eye, or mementos and treasures proudly displayed. He'd bought her things once or twice—he recalled a little china statuette of a crinolined shepherdess whose painted hair and face had borne a peculiar resemblance to hers. She'd gone quite pink when he'd given it to her, and put it on a shelf that remained otherwise bare.

You can't have stuff that matters, she'd told him once. *That just slows you down when you need to run.*

She would be thirty-four now, with an established business as an enquiry agent and a fearsome reputation among evildoers, but apparently she still thought about running, or at least didn't want to be slowed down. There was almost nothing here except books, piles of papers, and haphazard boxes of bits and pieces. A single pencil drawing adorned one wall, of a rather lovely woman with large, thoughtful eyes who looked vaguely familiar. Actress? Artist's model? He couldn't place her. There was also a framed photograph on a shelf; naturally he went to have a look.

It was slightly blurry in the way of older photographs. Two young women, seated, two men behind them. One was Susan herself, aged fifteen or sixteen, eyes huge in her small pinched face. That was her as he'd first known her: sly, aggressive, afraid. He'd been belligerent, loud, and painfully lonely. A match made in heaven.

In the photograph she was seated next to her not-quite-sister Emma, the slow-witted girl who did the housework. Behind them were Justin Lazarus, her adoptive father, wearing a faint smile that made him look like the vicious shit he was, and the big, dark, imposing Nathaniel Roy.

Templeton hadn't thought twice about that pair at the time. Lazarus was good friends with Roy who was in turn a friend of Aunt Harriet, and they'd all been similarly interfering, dictatorial adults. Susan had referred to Roy as "Uncle Nathaniel" occasionally but not consistently. It had been many years later, when the Braglewicz & Lazarus agency had become a thorn in the Lilywhite Boys' sides, that he'd looked into the enemy and back at his memories, and realised what was going on there.

It must have required a damned lot of nerve to have what was in effect a family photograph taken, and to display it as such. He doubted Susan invited many people up here, of course, and even if she did, a photograph of two men could scarcely be considered incriminating even in the febrile climate of which Jerry had complained since Oscar Wilde had made a fool of himself. But if one knew that Lazarus and Roy were lovers, would one not be cautious of displaying the fact?

Then again, Lazarus liked to show the world how much cleverer he was than the rest of them, and Roy was rich and well-connected.

Probably neither of them particularly feared exposure, any more than the nerveless Jerry had until he met Alec. Alec, the duke's son, whose family scandal of murder and suicide had been spread over the newspapers for months and who would be newspaper fodder for the rest of his life. Jerry scaled walls, impersonated nobility, and robbed castles, but Templeton wasn't sure he would have a photograph taken with Alec.

He was lost in thought when the door opened, and jumped about a foot in shock.

"Only me." Susan kicked the door shut and locked it. "I borrowed another blanket, and here. Probably a bit stale but needs must." *Here* referred to a plate of scones, precariously balanced on top of a thick folded blanket. "I assume you're still hungry, based on years of experience. What are you—" She broke off as she saw what he was looking at.

"It's a good photograph," he said, for want of anything else.

"Yes," she said. "It is. I believe I spoke to your shitty friend Crozier regarding what I'll do if you so much as whisper a word about my guvnors."

Templeton exhaled hard. "I don't know why you think the worst of— Yes, all right, I do," he went on over her splutter of contradiction. "I know exactly why you think the worst, but I'm not a blackmailer, and nor is Jerry, for obvious reasons."

"You jest," Susan said. "Honour among thieves?"

"I am not a blackmailer."

"If you were in trouble—"

"If *you* were in trouble, you'd use any weapon to hand. You'd blackmail without a second thought, just as Mr. Lazarus would. We're not all you."

Susan's face was a picture, of shock, outrage, and an undeniable spark of repressed laughter that hurt, because he'd always liked making her laugh. "Are you taking the moral high ground with me?"

"We accuse one another of the things we know to be true of ourselves," Templeton said sententiously. "You told me that once."

"I told you to fuck off all the time, but did you listen? Yes, I dare say I would use blackmail if the need arose. Try it with me and I'll gut you like a fish."

"I'm not going to. I was thinking of other things."

Susan's eyes flickered again to the photograph. "Of what?"

"Mistakes. Regrets. Things I could have done better. There's a list."

Susan watched him for a moment, then gave a little head-shake. "Go to sleep, James. You're swaying." She moved to put the second blanket on the floor as she spoke, checked the fire with a glance, and headed for her room. "Put out the light when you're done."

The bedroom door closed. Templeton stumbled over to the chair, filled his still-complaining belly with as many scones as he could fit, and set to removing his shoes and stockings. He felt exposed, even though he knew damned well Susan wouldn't be peering through the keyhole at him. She was more likely to put a chair under the door handle.

He turned off the gaslight all the same, stripped to his drawers by firelight, lay down, and pulled the blanket over himself. It was scratchy, not very comfortable, and the floor was hard despite the thicknesses of cloth he lay on. He was used to mattresses and sheets, as he'd got used to a lot of pleasant things. That had been a mistake.

He was so tired he felt nauseous and his mind was fuzzed, but sleep didn't take pity on him at once. His thoughts kept intruding with sharp images. The old dead man on the floor; the housekeeper's distorted mouth. Jerry and Stan, furious and afraid because of what Templeton had brought on them. Susan telling him she had a gun and would use it. Susan's feet, from seventeen years ago. Susan's implacable eyes, and the feel of her when he'd wrapped his arms around her tense body and it had felt, for the few seconds before she'd hit him in the balls, as though no time had passed and none of it had ever happened.

Susan.

CHAPTER FOUR

Susan had trouble sleeping.

This was not normally the case, but normally there was nobody on the floor of her sitting room. Normally she would have been able to get up, pour herself a glass or whisky or make a cup of tea, read for half an hour, and go back to bed. The fact that she had never actually done this was irrelevant: she couldn't do it now, and therefore the desire was overwhelming.

Beyond the door, James Vane snored thunderously. Typical.

He probably needed the sleep. He'd looked awful—grimy, unshaven, exhausted, and hungry—but that was his own fault. And he'd sounded like a man close to breaking, but again, that was a consequence to be expected. Justin had been assaulted and forced to run for his life back in in his mediumship days; their house had been smashed up and Susan had spent the best part of a week in hiding. These things happened when you were in the life, and there was no point whining about it. Don't play the game if you don't like the stakes.

In fairness, James hadn't whined. He'd simply been defeated, which was unfamiliar and thus unsettling. She'd expected anger or resentment, the usual reactions of men who didn't want to face the consequences of their actions. Self-pity was the other common option, and if he'd complained about being hard done-by she'd have been tempted to pull the trigger, admittedly in the knowledge that the gun was unloaded.

She'd held him up with an empty gun, and for all his exhaustion and her training in the arts of self-defence, he was almost a foot taller and twice her width. If he'd become the sort of man she'd feared, she wouldn't have stood a chance.

She was relieved to know he hadn't, and annoyed she was relieved. It was a pathetically low threshold to apply to behaviour—*he isn't a murderer! He didn't assault me!* Well done, James, have a merit mark.

And she wasn't even all that relieved. It had been easy to think of him as an out-and-out villain for the last years. When someone you'd cared for had let you down quite so comprehensively, had been quite such a shit, had proven himself so unreliable and stupid and treacherous, it was a relief to consign him to the dustheap. She hadn't wanted to hear about light and shade, excuses and reasons. She'd just wanted him gone from her life for good.

James had left the country seventeen years ago, and good riddance. He had been gone for more than a decade, and reappeared, not with the reformed character and fortune that a spell in the colonies was meant to bestow on the delinquent upper classes, but as a jewel thief. That had proved he was exactly the shit she'd thought. She'd intended to catch him; she'd tried to shoot him. She'd been sure in her heart, had *made* herself be sure, that he was just another selfish criminal waste of air.

And now look at her. Five fucking minutes listening to a tale of woe and here she was, letting herself think of him as a person again. Worrying that he was hungry and exhausted and afraid. Angry on his behalf because of the blatant stitch-up. Taking up his cause because he needed help, as though it was her job to look after him. What an idiot.

Susan glared at the dark ceiling. She could see the problems that loomed ahead with the inevitability of moves on a chessboard. Justin, Mark, and Nathaniel would all be unhelpful at best even if they were prepared to accept James's innocence, and she wouldn't put it past Justin to lay information. He was not a forgiving man. The police had trumpeted their belief in James's guilt; she doubted they'd be interested in a difficult and potentially ugly investigation when an obvious culprit was in their grasp. She'd be on her own, she probably wouldn't get paid, and she'd need to work with James bloody Vane throughout.

And if she didn't do all that, he'd hang for a murder someone else had committed.

It didn't matter how much she disliked him, or how much he deserved to face the consequences of what he'd actually done. It wasn't about him at all, but about the simple mathematics: if he swung, a double murderer would walk free. She would do this because it was right, and if the entire rest of the world thought she was misguided, foolish, or irritating for it, that was their hard luck.

Armed with that resolution, she thumped her pillow and turned over. It still took her another hour to get to sleep.

The next morning was so full of bustle that Susan more or less managed to ignore the presence of six foot four of wanted criminal in her rooms. The papers had said taller, of course; she was amazed they hadn't gone all out for seven feet tall with two heads. She slipped the housemaid a few shillings to purchase her ongoing deafness, took his frankly filthy clothes to be washed down the street, and bought some adequate off-the-peg garments at a schmutter shop a short omnibus ride away which she'd never visited before. She also picked up a razor, a toothbrush, a basket of provisions, and a box of bullets because she didn't intend to be caught with an unloaded gun again. She sent James, huddled absurdly in a blanket, into her room with a jug of hot water and instructions to make himself respectable, and put together a late breakfast while he did that. In fact, she kept herself far too busy to think.

And then he emerged from her bedroom.

It wasn't the first time she'd seen him as an adult, of course. She'd seen him robbing a safe, and dressed as a gentleman at social events to which he hadn't been invited, and posing as a valet in a castle, and bedraggled and exhausted last night. But she'd been at work on all those occasions, mind focused so narrowly on the job that her thoughts were like the beam of a dark lantern, concentrated in one direction only. She was at home now, and when he walked out of her bedroom...

He'd always been big; now he was broad. She'd bought the largest shirt she could find but his shoulders still strained against the linen, his upper arms filling what should have been loose sleeves. He had the build of a thug, or a boxer, but he walked lightly, and took the chair to which she waved him without taking up all the room around it. That was a skill developed from thievery, she was sure; his size must be an inconvenience. If she had to have a man in her rooms, thank goodness it was one who didn't thump about as though he owned the place.

She'd remembered his eyes were blue, but had forgotten the exact shade during his long absence. It came as a shock every time she saw him. They were royal blue, even in the weak sunlight of a London November, deep and vivid and striking against his dark chestnut hair, with a deceptively sleepy look to them because of the droop of his eyelids. People always mistook that droop for insolence or indolence, when it actually betrayed powerful emotion. It had mostly been anger in their youth, and it had called to Susan because she'd mostly been angry too.

Blue eyes, strong jaw, lazy good looks, and that bulky, impressive body. Susan tended to classify men in terms of the potential threat, but the visible evidence of his strength seemed suddenly very appealing. The more so after loving a woman so physically frail she had coughed herself to death.

That was a stupid response. Anyone could fall ill. It didn't matter how strong James Vane was, because no amount of muscle would stop his neck breaking when they put the noose around it and pulled the lever that opened the trapdoor. And if strength could be given its true measure, as an attribute of character and not body, Cara could have snapped James in half one-handed.

But Cara had been dead for over a year, and James had extremely nice thighs, and Susan didn't want to think about either of those facts at this moment.

"Ham, bread, pies," she said. "Tea. Eat."

"Have you considered a career as a restaurateur?" James was already reaching for the butter. "Thank you. You'll be unsurprised to learn I'm ravenous."

"Nothing changes." Susan took her own seat, aware of his swift assessing glance. She'd put on one of her primmer walking dresses today, a high-necked grey thing that blended with her drab colouring to make her entirely forgettable. It had been intended as a clear signal that she didn't care what he thought but now she wondered if he'd realised she'd dressed with him in mind, and thus that she did care what he thought, if only in a negative way. Or perhaps he simply assumed she was as dull as she wanted to appear.

Or maybe he hadn't noticed her at all because he was too busy eating half a loaf of bread.

He swallowed. "Thank you for all this. I feel a new man, and I'm sure you'd be the first to say that was necessary."

"Does the coat fit?"

"Not entirely, but if I rip a few stitches it should do for the moment. I can get another when I go out."

"You're not going anywhere for now," Susan said. "You can't just wander up and down stairs. This is a women's lodging house and I'm not allowed male visitors. I've bribed the housemaid who sleeps upstairs not to hear you or lay the fire this morning, but she has a job to think of. So you stay here very quietly until I find somewhere else to put you, and then you're out the window again."

James took that with equanimity. "And meanwhile, there is the small matter of murder."

"That," Susan agreed. "Tell me, who knew you were after the Samsonoff? Everyone who knew, and everyone who had a decent guess."

James considered, chewing in a ruminative way. "This is under the seal of the confessional, yes?" Susan gave him a scathing look that he took as assent. "Jerry, of course, and Stan."

"And their respective other halves?"

"I've never enquired what constitutes pillow talk. Neither of them is stupid—Stan or Jerry, I mean—and I don't suppose either Alec Pyne or Stan's girl wants to see us all gaoled. But you never know."

Susan took out her notebook. "Crozier, Kamarzyn, Alec, and who's Kamarzyn's girl?"

"She goes by the name of Miss Christiana, professionally."

Susan blinked. "What, the singer?" She'd seen the travesty act a few times at the music hall managed by Pen Starling, one of her gaggle of adoptive family. "Is she in the life?"

"Not at all. She's as respectable as it's possible to be in her position. Very nice girl, if a bit sharp-tongued, and of course six inches taller than Stan, but who isn't?"

Susan didn't have a great deal of sympathy for the problems of criminal association. If you got mixed up with bad people, you should expect bad things to happen. She did, however, object to punishment for things that shouldn't be crimes. The law would consider Miss Christiana a Mr., and that would land her in trouble if the net closing around the Lilywhite Boys scooped her up, just as Alec would be threatened. She could well imagine James's partners weren't very pleased with him.

The question was, of course, how displeased they'd been before, and what they might have done about it.

"So they could all have known, and been in a position to pass on that knowledge," she said.

"Technically, yes, but you aren't seriously suggesting Stan or Jerry flapped their lips about my plans." James paused. "Are you?"

"Unless you're a victim of the world's most unfortunate series of coincidences, *somebody* did. Come on, James, think. You just happened to burgle a house at the very moment of a double murder, you and a killer just happened to creep in and out of Montmorency's rooms without meeting, he just happened to forget to steal anything, the alarm just happened to be raised in time to catch you red-handed while he got away, and your boat just happened to become unmoored? Please."

James's mouth opened soundlessly, and then he said, with impressive lightness, "Well, the Samsonoff *is* cursed, you know."

"I forgot," Susan said drily. "But that would only account for the events after you stole it."

"True, very true. You think I was set up?"

"Don't you?"

James picked up the thick slice of bread on his plate and tore it deliberately in half. "Yes. Ye-e-es. Would that I had your mind, Sukey. Well, now. Why would someone do that?"

She absolutely would not react to the old name. He probably hadn't even realised he'd used it. "To pluck a single example out of the air, the wealthy Mr. Montmorency's sole living relative was in the house when he was brutally murdered. If the housekeeper hadn't seen a blood-smeared ogre conveniently positioned as scapegoat, I imagine Mr. Stroud would have faced a lot more questions."

"For Christ's sake," James said. "In my defence, it's less glaringly obvious when you're on the wrong end of the murder charge."

"I'm sure. And I don't say it was the nephew, of course. That was merely an illustration."

"One of which your pal Alec would be proud," James said, and Susan saw the twitch on his face a second later.

She ignored it for now. "All right. Who else knew, or could have guessed, you were after Montmorency?"

"You won't like this."

"Go on."

"Francis Peevy. The murdered valet. I paid him a substantial sum to take an impression of the house key for me."

Susan hissed. James put up both hands. "I know, I know, the judge is reaching for his black cap as I speak."

"Who made your key?"

"Stan. Keep it in the family."

"The valet knew what you were up to, could presumably have identified you, and is now dead, probably with a large sum of money in his bank account or sock drawer. Bloody hell, James. Anyone else?"

"That's it. I bought the rowboat three weeks previously, in Putney. I don't think anyone else would have known what I was up to. Though, as Jerry said, the news about a priceless opal necklace might as well have been addressed to me personally."

"We'll come back to that," Susan said. "When did you tie the rowboat up?"

"Several hours earlier that evening. There were a few walkers, nobody who seemed to be watching me."

"But clearly somebody was, because they untied it." Susan shut her eyes. "Tell me again about your escape, everything from when the housekeeper turned up."

"I do enjoy this part," James remarked. "She appeared while I was distracted by the necklace, and began screaming. I, ah, got past her as politely as possible in the circumstances—"

"Shoved."

"—and ran. She was shrieking like a steam train. I heard shouts almost immediately—"

"When exactly?" Susan interrupted. "Where were you when the shouting started?"

"I think running down the stairs, but I couldn't swear to it. It was a nightmarish experience. Housebreaking at night always takes a toll on the nerves, the dead man made it particularly unpleasant, and then there was the necklace."

"What about the necklace?"

James's hand went to his waistcoat pocket, an unconscious betrayal. "It's the most beautiful thing. Opals, especially black opals, are... They fascinate me."

"Why?"

"I was in Australia, you know."

She'd seen the stamps on envelopes she'd burned unopened. "So?"

"So I spent several months digging in an opal mine. That was where I learned that you don't get rich by hard work. But when you see them come out of the rock, when you're in the dark, with the dust, and the heat and the noise—and the silence, that was the thing, the absolute echoing silence every time you stopped—and then one more blow, and the rock cracks, and you see the opal. Rainbows and lights." His eyes were focused on something far away. "Most jewels are just pretty stones. Diamonds are clear rocks, and not even terribly rare ones. If the cartel didn't restrict supply, every teacher and governess could have a diamond necklace. There are dozens of abandoned emerald mines in South America because they hold the things by the ton, and jewels by the ton have no value at all. Do you know what makes a stone into a jewel?" Susan cocked her head rather than interrupt the flow. "Scarcity. That's it. There's no intrinsic quality, no *specialness* about a red or green or blue crystal. A rough diamond is a miserable lump of dirty glass until it's cut, and the cut is all about human intervention. With a very few exceptions, those stones aren't *unique*."

"And opals are?"

"Every one," James said, almost reverently. "They're beautiful when they come out of the ground—of their own nature, not by human hand. You look into an opal and you see infinite depth and change. A black opal is a piece of the universe, glittering with stars. They glow, some of them. They eat."

"Sorry?"

"I found a possum skeleton—an Australian animal, sort of rabbity squirrel—and it had become opal. I don't know how. Nobody knows what it is that forms opals, but whatever it was, it had happened to the bones. I have the skull. It's about yea big." He held out his hand, palm up and fingers curved, to indicate the size. "Sharp teeth and empty eye sockets, shimmering and whispering in the dark."

Susan could almost see the rainbows in his eyes. "Just how long were you in these mines?" she asked cautiously.

James snorted. "Do I sound odd?"

"A little."

"Two years. Two full years in that Godforsaken hellhole, nothing but heat and dust and a handful of white drunkards trying to strike it rich in a place they didn't belong. Aren't we digressing?"

That had been Susan's intention. One could often jolt a memory loose by changing the subject to something that absorbed the respondent, so when you asked the question they'd answer freely. She was absorbed now. She wanted to ask a lot more questions, and had to remind herself that there was work to be done.

"You said you were running when the shouting started."

"Down the stairs. I'm fairly sure of that. One normally has a few moments between discovery and the hue and cry, but it seemed to come far too fast: there were already feet on the stairs as I opened the door. I ran like hell for the river. It wasn't far, but the pursuit was in full voice and coming fast by the time I reached the bank. They shot at me, which seemed rude. And when I got there my boat had gone. It's bare mud, with nothing to hide behind, so I would unquestionably have been caught if I couldn't swim. I barely had time to kick off my shoes as it was."

Susan couldn't swim a stroke. "How hard would it be to swim across the Thames?"

"It was a bloody nightmare." James spoke with feeling. "The river is about three hundred and fifty feet across at that point, which is easy in the right circumstances, but a damned long way fully clothed, freezing cold, in the dark, with the tide against one. I was done in by the time I'd made it to the other side."

"So one wouldn't expect a burglar to flee by that means. And someone who tried it would be more likely to drown than escape?"

"Quite possibly. I wasn't certain I'd make it across."

"How good a swimmer are you?"

"Very. I won a fair few races in my youth, and I'm in fair shape. I wouldn't give much for most people's chances in the same circumstances."

Susan nodded. "And how many shots were fired?"

"Five as I ran," James said without hesitation. "I counted. Then a sixth while I was swimming, which was a nasty shock because I'd thought they'd run out, and was afraid they'd reloaded."

"Drat." Susan rapped her knuckles on the table. "We should probably assume you were meant to be shot in the course of capture. That's not good."

"Are you serious?"

"They kept a bullet back as long as possible. That suggests they wanted to make sure you were dead, because dead men don't point out inconsistencies in witness accounts. Right, I'm going out. Eat everything in the basket, and keep quiet. And see if you can think of anybody we might recruit for assistance. Anyone who'll help you, who can be trusted not to turn you in for the reward."

"If I knew anyone who'd do that—" James began, and stopped.

"Then you wouldn't have come to me," Susan completed. "I realise contacting me was the resort of desperation."

"You're the last person alive with a reason to help me. You would have been first on my list of people to ask, given a choice."

"I dare say I'm the only detective you know," Susan pointed out, somewhat snidely. She wasn't sure why she felt snide, but she did.

"I know plenty. You're the only one we ever thought was dangerous. I'd prefer to have any three of the Metropolitan Police on my tail than you."

Susan felt her cheeks pink, enragingly. "Yes, well. Nevertheless, I may need extra hands, so think."

James wore a slight frown. "Have you left Braglewicz and Lazarus?"

"Of course not."

"Then why can you not look to them for support?"

Susan blinked at him. "Is that a serious question? Do I have to explain why Justin wouldn't be inclined to help you in your hour of need?"

"I assumed he'd help you, whatever his personal feelings," James said. "You used to have him round your little finger."

"I did not. And if I did, I shouldn't abuse it by asking him to do something when I know very well he'd rather have a tooth extracted."

James exhaled. "I would have thought, if you can see your way to helping me—"

"It doesn't work that way. If you hurt Justin, *he* might conceivably forgive you, but *I'd* hunt you down to the ends of the earth. He backed off you and Crozier when I needed him to, but he wasn't pleased about that."

"He always did loathe me, didn't he?"

"No, he just didn't like you. He only loathed you when you gave him reason to."

His eyelids hooded, that sleepy look that spelled danger. "Balls. My surname was enough for him to dismiss me from the start."

"That was your behaviour," Susan said. "Though I dare say he also feared you might behave like every other aristocratic shit who leaves a trail of destruction through people who don't matter."

"That isn't fair."

"Nor is life. You made a damned mess of yours and didn't do much for mine, so I'm not sure why you expect absolution."

"I don't," James said through his teeth. "I haven't asked for forgiveness. And I don't expect you to forget the past—"

"Good, because I won't. I'm not doing this because I like you, or trust you, let alone forgive you."

"Then why are you doing it?"

"I wonder that myself," she snapped, keeping her voice low with an effort. Fucking James, lurking in her rooms so she couldn't even make this a proper shouting match. "Obviously I don't want to see a murderer walk free, but I don't care *that* much, so I advise you not to push your luck. Eat, think, wait for me, and if you disappear don't bother to come back."

"Jesus," James said. "Susan, at what point can we discuss—"

"Never."

She rose as she spoke, picking up notebook, bag, and after a moment's reflection, her gun. She didn't know quite what she'd say if James continued the conversation. He didn't try.

CHAPTER FIVE

The door closed behind Susan's rigid back; the key turned in the lock. Templeton stared in that direction for a few moments, then rose, in need of something to do. He washed up the breakfast things, noting that Susan hadn't eaten much. She looked as though she hadn't eaten properly for a few days. Her appetite had always been the first thing to go when she was upset.

He'd upset her. He hadn't expected that.

Granted that he'd ruined her life seventeen years ago as part of the ruination of his own, it simply hadn't occurred to him she'd find it difficult when he came blundering back again. He hadn't thought she'd forgive or forget, but he'd assumed she'd be somewhere between contemptuous and homicidal. It seemed likely she'd tell him to fuck off, and quite possible she'd hand him to the police. He wouldn't have thought there was a chance in a thousand that she'd be put off her food, or go pink when he complimented her professional skills—which she had, a very definite tinge to her pale cheeks fighting against the sobriety of that drab high-necked dress she'd hidden in.

Did you read my letters? he'd asked her once. The circumstances hadn't been ideal, since he'd been half-kneeling in front of an open safe, blinking in the unexpected light of her lantern, and she'd had a revolver levelled at him.

No, I burned them, she'd said, and pulled the trigger.

That was Sukey all over. He threw out a distraction; she recognised the gambit and retaliated brutally. She'd explained it to him long ago as one of her adoptive father's maxims, which she repeated as Bible truth: *Hit back harder. Never let a blow go unpunished or they'll think they can kick you at will.* Whatever weapon you pulled on Susan Lazarus, you always, *always* brought a knife to a gun fight.

He was smiling, he realised, as he stood like an idiot over a bowl of dirty water wearing a fatuous grin. He forced his attention back to his work, made sure that everything was cleaned and dried and put away, then tidied the room to remove all trace of his presence in case a sharp exit should be required. He shaved again, swept the floor, and at last stood with nothing else to do but face the fact that he'd hurt her.

He'd hurt her at a time when he'd have cut off his own hand to spare her pain. He'd probably hurt her when he came back to England a criminal, as worthless as everyone except her had always said he would be. Not that any lingering sentiment had stopped her from trying to put him in prison, but that was Susan all over. And now he'd hurt her again because he'd come to her for help, which meant dragging up the past.

Or maybe he was wrong and she hadn't thought of him at all. Susan had always been good at refusing to remember things. She'd told him long stories about her childhood as a fraudulent spiritualist's apprentice and how they worked their deceptions; she'd made a hell of a story out of the time she and Emma had hidden, frightened to breathe, as a murderer pulled their house apart, and how they'd fled for their lives into the Great Fog of '73. But she had never mentioned her life before Lazarus except in the barest terms: a mother who died, no father, no shoes, no food. She didn't want to remember, therefore it didn't exist.

Had she put him into the same category, a part of her past she refused to acknowledge?

Templeton did not like that thought. He hadn't meant to hurt her. He'd wanted to do the exact fucking opposite, in fact, and if they'd been given a chance—

Of course they had not. His father, Lord Dickie Vane, brother to a marquess, might conceivably have permitted his younger son to wed a businessman's daughter, if she came with a dowry and the unimpeachable virtue of bourgeoisie on the rise. But Susan had been a feral, nameless slum-child, her adoptive father neither rich nor respectable. And in the unlikely event that one of Lord Dickie's sons could have persuaded him that love conquered all, it wouldn't have been the twice-expelled troublemaker.

James Vane had never had any business falling in love with Sukey Lazarus. It had always been impossible, and she had always been doomed to suffer for it.

He wanted to do something. Walk this off, mile after mile down the streets, or take himself up and down a few sheer walls till his fingers cramped and his arms hurt too much to think of any pain that wasn't physical. What a pity he was stuck in a room with a murder charge hanging over his head and a sick sensation in his stomach that wouldn't go away.

He'd suffered for their juvenile passion too, God knew. Most wealthy young men could interfere with a girl of the lower orders without consequence; Templeton had been transported for it. He'd written to Sukey before he was carted out of the country, and had the letter returned unopened with a biting enclosure from Mr. Lazarus. He'd written again from Australia and seen his passionate outpourings opened and publicly mocked by the overseer; he'd emptied his pockets bribing traders to post letters for him. She'd never written back, and that had fuelled his rage and resentment like oil on flames. He'd cursed her and blamed her and hated her; told himself she was probably married without a care in the world and resented it as though it were truth; vengefully imagined her miserably tied to some brute and worked himself into seething despair at the idea.

In fact, he'd been a fool. He'd had only himself to blame for the whole thing, and if she hadn't wanted any more to do with him, that was a testimony to her common sense. He'd come to realise that in time, and even to wish her well.

And then he'd returned to England and they began to clash professionally. That had been entirely fair and reasonable too. It was the way of the world, fox and hound. He *understood* Susan as his adversary. In the context of his life, a cat's cradle of bad decisions and worse outcomes, it made perfect sense.

What didn't make sense was that Susan hadn't married. She wore no ring, had no photographs except the one of her family, and no portraits other than the pencil drawing. There was no trace of a man's presence, nothing to suggest any sort of relationship. Had she been alone for seventeen years, or did she simply remove all traces of a lover once she'd concluded he wasn't worth her time?

He took another look at that single pencil portrait. The woman's face still reminded him of someone, and he still couldn't place who. He wondered what she was to Susan, reflecting that if it had been a man's portrait he'd have drawn the obvious conclusion. Was she happily content with the thoughtful-eyed woman? Were there feminine clothes in her wardrobe that weren't hers? If he went to look, what were the odds she'd realise he'd done so and throw him out?

He considered Susan happily settled with someone—a New Woman suffragist type, he'd bet—and found the idea unwelcome. That was contemptible, since he'd assuaged his guilt for years by telling himself she'd found a new love without effort. He should want that to be the case. It was disturbing to realise he didn't.

The problem was, Susan was unforgettable.

Not that most people would realise that. She *looked* forgettable. She was scrawny, or slender if you didn't want your shin kicked, of no more than adequate height, unremarkable in looks. Her blue-grey eyes didn't stand out in her pale face; her once-fair hair had darkened to a nameless light-brown-to-straw. Unobtrusive colouring, unobtrusive build, a sharp face that wasn't pretty or ugly or striking. Just an ordinary, commonplace woman.

And she had a mind like a rat trap and a razor-edged tongue, and she turned everything into a weapon, and he'd never been so happy in his life as when they'd clambered onto the roof of Aunt Harriet's house, smoking illicit cheroots, watching the clouds or the stars, talking for hours on end. She'd laughed at his adolescent miseries and given unexpected sympathy when he'd tried to brave deep hurts out, and sometimes told him things herself and accepted the squeeze of his hand as comfort. She'd taught him to pick pockets, and then locks. He'd taught her boxing and fencing, and exercises to put some muscle on her skinny arms, and helped her root out the taint of the streets from her vowels until they were as unobtrusive and colourless as everything else about her—if you weren't paying attention.

Justin says, use what you got, she'd told him early on. *I'm not big like you or pretty like a lot of girls, or important like a marquess, but people look at big men and pretty women and important people. I could help Justin because nobody ever looked at me. I reckon an enquiry agent that nobody notices would be the best kind there is.*

I notice you, he'd told her, and she'd said, *Course you do. You're not a flat.*

He'd cherished the words, holding onto them as his father shouted. He was a problem, a nuisance, a worthless waste of a son, but he wasn't a flat. Sukey said so, and she knew.

They were friends—intense, passionate, to-hell-with-everyone friends. James's seething unfocused anger at the injustice of school and family and life in general had meshed with Sukey's helpless rage at the upheaval of her comfortably criminal existence, and her growing awareness that the world would always hold her negligible unless she forced it to do otherwise. She treated him as if he wasn't always in the wrong. He saw her glorious will and stood, exultant and amazed.

And then Sukey, a late developer, settled into womanhood and James, an early one, got to grips with his fast-grown, clumsy, hulking body. The consequences were predictable, wonderful, and catastrophic.

They'd tried to take care, once the first tentative kisses and exploratory touches had turned hungry. Sukey went to seek advice from older friends, came back armed with information, and sat James down for a lecture. Trying to count days around her monthlies wouldn't work. He mustn't spend in her without a sheath; the best ones were from the new Lambert company in Dalston. If he couldn't get hold of those, he could pull out before spending, but he'd have to apply self-discipline, and remember that his moment's pleasure could bring her nine months of trouble. She'd need to be able to trust him.

And she could. She truly could, and he'd proved it. He'd found a druggists' shop where they sold him the prophylactics without question. He'd learned to use the clumsy things and secretly been grateful for the loss of sensation when faced with the joy of Sukey's skin, her small breasts just the right size for his palms, the dark blonde tangle of wet curls he was almost afraid to touch, the way she gripped his arms and cried out with rare, perfect abandon. And when they ran out of sheaths, the wild, unruly James Vane, who had never learned discipline no matter how hard and often he was beaten, hadn't failed her. Not once. The feel of her flesh around him, tight and hot and urging him on, had been the best thing in his life to date, but he'd made himself pull out before climax every time. That was how he'd keep Sukey out of trouble; that was what she wanted, so it was what he did.

She was in the family way within four months.

Templeton walked to the window of her empty room, and stared out through the dirty glass. It was fingersmeared with fog trails, but he could see the grey drizzle outside. It wasn't a day to be out, but he still wished he could walk, fast and hard and away from here. He pressed the heels of his hands into his eye sockets, as if that could push the memories back.

He'd got so much right, even then. When she'd told him, with determined lightness, that she was late, he'd uttered reassurances. She missed the second month, and he held her as she raged and cursed and kicked things. She told him pennyroyal and steel water were poisons and she wouldn't take them, and he begged her not to anyway. He never thought or said that it was her fault, her responsibility, or her problem; it was theirs, because she was carrying his child. The young James had seen his duty as clearly as though it had been written out for him. He would not fail.

He asked to go with her when she told Lazarus. She looked at him as though he were insane.

"You think that will help?"

"If he's angry with anyone it should be me," James said. "He can shout at me, not you."

"Don't be an idiot. What do you think he'll do, turn me out of doors for immorality? He'll wring your neck, though, so you'll need to stay well out of the way."

"For how long?"

"Until I decide otherwise. It's not your affair."

"How is it not my affair? I'm the father!"

"I won't be your secret family." Her voice was grim. "I'll raise this baby with Ems and Justin. I don't want my child to grow up a bastard Vane, treated like an embarrassment or a mistake. That's no way to live. The guvnors will love her for who she is, not sneer at who she isn't, and if you can look me in the eye and say the same for anyone in your family…"

He couldn't. "Do I have any say in this?"

"You got ten minutes of fun; I get nine months of growing a child. That's how much say you have."

"But," James began, and made himself think. "But I want what you want. I don't want a bastard child either."

Sukey's face tightened. "Then don't have one. Walk away."

"No," he said. "Will you marry me?"

"You fucking what?"

It wasn't precisely the response he'd expected. "Marry. You and me. Sukey—"

"Don't be ridiculous, your uncle's a marquess. You tell the high and mighty Vanes you've got some girl in the family way and what do you think will happen?"

"Maybe my father will see I'm growing up," James said. "Maybe he'll see that I want to take responsibility. Or he might cut me off without a penny, but I don't care if you don't. I love you."

She stared at him, eyes wide and wild for a moment, then shook her head. "No. If you tie yourself to me now and cut yourself off from your family, you'll blame me later."

"I will not! It's my choice."

"Bet you will," Sukey said. "Or maybe not, but this is *my* choice."

"And mine too. I shan't let you sacrifice yourself and our child for my future. I don't care if my family cut me off."

"I'm not sacrificing myself, I'm trying to stay out of trouble. I can be an unwed mother, with the guvnors behind me, and I'd rather that than make myself the enemy of a posh family. I don't want your old man calling me a scheming seductress-"

"Nobody would ever call you that once they'd met you."

She choked on a laugh. "No, well, it won't get that far. Come on, think. He won't let you marry me."

"Then we'll do it anyway."

"You're seventeen, you berk. You can't marry without consent."

"If we post banns, I can."

"If your father finds out and forbids them, you can't. I'm in enough trouble without your family prosecuting Justin for entrapment. I don't want to go up against the Vanes, understand? It would make things worse, not better."

His throat and chest were constricted. "I want to make it better."

"I know you do."

"I would marry you, Sukey. I wouldn't regret it, ever."

"I don't know that." She must have realised he was on the verge of tears, because she added, "I might risk it, mind you. Maybe. If it wasn't for the rest."

He ignored the last part, grasping her hand. It felt cold. "Really? Sukey, would you marry me?"

She let out a long sigh. "I *would*. Which is to say, I won't but it's not because I don't want to, and that's the best I can do so stop asking."

"If my father agrees," James said, intent. "If he gives his permission—"

"*James*—"

"—will you marry me?"

She snarled in her throat. "Do not ask your father. Do not *tell* your father. Do not go within fifty miles of your family with this. I don't want the Vanes involved. Are you listening to me?"

"Yes, but—"

"No *but*. I don't think you know what big rich aristocratic families do to inconvenient girls who want to marry their sons."

"My family aren't villains from the melodrama, for heaven's sake. They'll—" He couldn't voice *be reasonable*. "I'll make them see reason."

"No you will not, because you're not going to tell them," Sukey said. "I want you to promise me. You've made the offer and I know you mean it and that's all that matters."

"Not for our child. Not for a baby who'll be born illegitimate."

"Justin was a workhouse foundling and I never had a father. This one will have a family. Sounds like a step up to me."

His knuckles hurt. He relaxed the fist he'd made without realising it. "It's not enough. It's not right."

"But it's how it is, so don't make things worse. Don't tell your father. Promise me you won't."

He shut his eyes. "I promise. I won't make it worse."

And that was where he'd gone wrong, with the first promise to her he ever broke.

His hands were cold. He'd leaned against the window for God knew how long, staring out into the damp misery of grey London. Sukey—*Susan* was out in that, shouldering the consequences of his actions while he stood around doing nothing. It was all of a piece.

At least he wasn't standing around in the warm. He didn't dare light a fire, and it was damned cold. He stripped to his undershirt, and set about some exercises: Hindu push-ups, side bridges, squats, arm holds, whatever he could think of as long as it could be done without thumps on the floor, and as long as two hundred repetitions hurt enough to occupy his thoughts to the exclusion of all else.

He kept that up for an hour or more, working until his arms and legs felt like jelly, and then moved to hand exercises, lifting a heavy book with one finger after another, at a speed that demanded full concentration. It passed the time as much as anything could.

She ought to have married. Or she ought to have half a dozen photographs of the woman with the eyes, and some clothes that clearly weren't hers. She ought to be happy, so that he could demand her help and then slink out of her life again without a kick in the balls from a conscience that he hadn't let bother him in years. *I don't know why you've turned up now*, he thought resentfully at it. *Feel free to leave.*

He made himself luncheon and considered the task he'd been given. It would be nice not to fail at something, but sadly, no generous loyal friends leapt to mind. He drank with people often enough, but he wouldn't call them friends, not of the kind that would stand up for a man accused of murder, keep his secrets, not sell him for the reward.

Those friends were Jerry and Stan, or had been. They'd have helped him without question if he hadn't entirely failed to think about helping them.

"Christ, you prick," he said aloud, then cursed himself. No male voices in Susan's room. He wondered how long he'd need to stay here, silent and passive.

He *was* a prick, though. Stan had done time once, and he'd always made it clear he didn't want to do it again. Miss Chris, his girl, was frighteningly vulnerable to a legal system that would cut her hair and throw her in a man's gaol. And Jerry, that hard-eyed reliably ruthless son of a bitch, had found something in Alec, or himself, or the combination of the two, that was remaking him from the inside out. Of course he'd thought first of Alec, just as Templeton hadn't given a damn for any other obligation when he'd loved Susan. He'd have burned the world for her without hesitation, and had said as much to his father.

"I love her. I want to marry her," he'd said. "It doesn't matter where she comes from, only who she is."

"Do you have no regard for your name?" his father had demanded, knuckles white on the chair. "Have you entirely forgotten who you are? Who we are?"

"I don't care about the Vanes!" he'd shouted back. "Cut me off, you never wanted me anyway! I'll change my name if you like, I'll never be a Vane again, just let me marry her!"

He'd been too angry, too flown with high emotion and thoughts of Susan, to pay any attention to his father's face. And yet he'd thought afterwards that he'd seen shock, perhaps hurt. Even if you'd long ago decided your son was worthless, it probably stung to learn he didn't care about you either. Maybe that had played a part in his father's vengeance.

Because it had hurt when Templeton had brought matters to a choice between himself and Alec, and Jerry had picked his new lover

over his old friend. It had hurt like hell, and the reason that hurtful thing had happened was that Templeton had forced Jerry to an entirely unnecessary decision, and the reason he'd done *that*...

He sat heavily in Susan's armchair, leaned back, and put his hands over his face.

It was contemptible, stupid and, worst of all, avoidable. An unforced error, as so many of his mistakes were. He knew exactly why he'd pushed Jerry so unreasonably, and demanded a single loyalty from a man who had a complicated existence to manage. It was bloody Susan again.

He'd lost her when he'd broken his promise, then lost his chance at making amends along with everything else when his father had exiled him to Australia. He'd had nobody at all for years after that. He'd taught himself not to trust, never to rely on anyone, never ever to set himself up for a fall like he'd taken for love of Sukey Lazarus, who hadn't even written back.

It was the loneliness that had done it. He had been lonely for much of his childhood in a family that seemingly disliked him from birth; the opal mines of Lightning Ridge were far lonelier than that because by then he'd found out what it was not to be alone. He had realised that loneliness could kill you, so he had set out to stop feeling it.

And he'd succeeded. He'd escaped the mines and made a new life that was a deliberate fuck-you to loneliness and longing and everything James Vane ought to have been. He'd met Jerry, recognised his resentful defiance as though he'd looked in a mirror, and formed a bond based solely on getting as rich as possible at the expense of people like his father. He hadn't wanted the partnership to become a friendship; he wasn't even sure when it had. It didn't do to think about such things too closely, in case Fate noticed and took a hand.

He'd focused on enjoyment of the present rather than hope for the future or regret of the past. He had made himself Templeton Lane, half of the Lilywhite Boys, and that did very nicely indeed.

Then Susan and her blasted agency had begun to dog his steps, and he hadn't let himself think about that either because it only mattered what he was now, not what he'd been. She'd tried to shoot him and told him she'd burned his letters, and that was entirely in keeping with everything else.

And then, with Alec's help, she had entrapped the Lilywhite Boys into her scheme to nail the Duke and Duchess of Ilvar for a pair of twenty-year-old murders. She'd used him and fooled him, but most of all, she'd looked him in the eyes and told him they weren't even close to quits.

You owe a debt, James. Your payment is, in fact, very seriously overdue. Consider this a visit from the bailiffs.

She'd also punched him in the stomach and locked him in a cellar to await the police, but those were trivialities. How could he still owe her? Had he not paid enough in the mines? What did he not know? It had been near-incapacitating, to the point that he'd happily let Jerry finish the job, cracking the Duchess's safe as a gesture to Alec much as a normal man would offer flowers.

Months had passed. Susan's words had dug into his flesh and festered, a splinter too deep to remove. And meanwhile Jerry had visibly changed, as though a part of him that had been dead for years was coming back to life. As though years as a care-for-nobody had withered his soul, and love of Alec was working on it like spring rain.

Templeton had not wanted that to be true. It was easy to be the Lilywhite Boys. It was profitable and dangerous and fun, and it kept Susan and his past as far away as if he were still in Australia. Templeton Lane had no need to think about such things.

Every evidence of Jerry's growing attachment had felt like another blow to the life he'd constructed. Had forced him to think of other things, and wonder again what he owed Susan, and feel a deep, painful envy that he knew was contemptible but couldn't get rid of, which only made him angrier.

Stan had tried to broach the subject after an unusually heated row. *Temp, mate, anyone can see you're pissed off about Alec. Is there anything you want to talk about? Not with me, obviously, but Christiana's good at this.*

Ah, the irony. Stan thought he was jealous of Alec because he wanted Jerry. Templeton had let him go on thinking that because it was so much less embarrassing than the truth, which was that he wanted what Jerry had.

Of course he'd been a prick about it. If he'd told Jerry, *Alec comes first*, and *Some things are more important than jewels*, he'd have had to apply those principles to himself, and that would not do. Loneliness had nearly done for him in the opal mines; he'd refused to be lonely in the middle of London just because his partner in crime had found something that Templeton had spent years assuring himself he didn't need or want. Naturally he'd hit out. Anyone would have, probably.

And in that process he'd rendered himself as alone as before, except that now he had a price on his head and every man's hand against him. Which brought him neatly back to the conclusion that he was a prick.

He was sitting in the dark with his face in his hands when the door opened.

CHAPTER SIX

Susan had considered a number of possible outcomes as she returned to her rooms. James had been discovered, and her landlady would be waiting, arms folded and foot tapping. James had been discovered and identified, and her rooms would be full of policemen ditto. James had vanished as unexpectedly as he'd arrived and she'd never see him or her valuables again. The whole thing had been a hallucination. She was rather hopeful of that last; it would have solved all her problems.

She didn't expect to find him hunched in the dark. He looked utterly despairing. He didn't even raise his head as she entered, and she had the sudden, sharp thought that he was dead, that an assassin, or a heart attack—

For crying out loud, Lazarus.

"Are you all right?" she enquired, as she shook out her wet coat.

There was a long silence, then he inhaled deeply, shoulders visibly rising and falling. "Yes. Of course."

"You don't look all right."

"Let's pretend I do," James said. "I doubt you want to take on any more of my troubles."

"Or even any of them, but here we are." The fire was laid, she realised. "Did the maid come in?"

"No. Nobody so much as knocked."

"In that case, thank you for—" She indicated with her head. "Light it?"

James hauled himself out of the armchair with a visible effort and knelt by the fireplace. Susan reclaimed her chair and watched him as she unfastened her boot buttons. He looked defeated, as though he'd already lost the battle she'd sallied forth to fight on his behalf, which was a cheek considering she'd been on her feet all day while he sat around.

"If there's a problem, I need to know," she said, once he had the fire started.

"I had a great deal of time to think today and didn't much like the conclusions I reached." She raised a brow. He shrugged. "I can't imagine you approve of any of the decisions I've made over the past seventeen years or so?"

"Not really."

"Then we find ourselves in agreement. How was your day?"

Susan added that to the growing pile labelled *Let go for now*. "Extremely useful. I went for a word with the CID. I'm reasonably popular there after the Ilvar case."

"Really? I thought you embarrassed the police considerably."

"The county police. The Met loved that."

"Good point." He was making an obvious effort to sound lighter. "So, what did you find out?"

"Oh, not much. I just had a quick chat with Detective Inspector Wilby."

"Who?"

Susan rolled her eyes. "The man in charge of your case. Do you not read the newspapers?"

"I felt self-conscious about buying them, in the circumstances. You spoke to the Detective Inspector." An actual smile dawned. "Well, that's useful. Or was it?"

"Depends how you look at it," Susan said. "First things first— All right, how much of the situation in the Montmorency house on the night do you know?"

"He had his long-lost nephew staying with him, and his lawyer."

"The nephew, Harrison Stroud, was his sole relative and heir, so he would normally be the obvious suspect. I told Wilby I had a client who had been approached by an intermediary offering to sell some of Montmorency's jewels, even though probate hasn't been granted. I said I wanted to know if it was a fraud, if it might be a lead to you, or if Stroud was dipping into Uncle's estate, and asked what he could tell me about the man."

James's mouth was open. "You said that?"

"Why not?"

"It sounds very like interfering with a police investigation."

"Obviously it does," Susan said. "I am. Do you want to know what he told me?"

The spark had returned to James's eyes, she was sure. It was lurking deep, but it was there as he said, "By God I do."

Susan leaned back. "Put the kettle on, will you? Right. Montmorency had a sister who went off to India with her husband, a Captain Stroud, thirty years ago. She died there, leaving one child, and Montmorency lost touch with her widower. This didn't seem to concern him until two years ago when he suffered a serious illness and noticed that he was alone in the world. He sent out enquiries to India via his lawyer, whose agents duly turned up Mr. Harrison Stroud. Stroud came to England on Montmorency's invitation, and the old man made him his heir. That makes Stroud a strong candidate for murderer. However, Montmorency was an elderly man who had already arranged to give him a generous allowance. Nobody heard any disagreement between the two. And Stroud isn't in particular need of money—no business to support, no pressing debt. So it is isn't obvious why he would have killed his uncle when he was certain to inherit in the not-so-distant future."

"Unless, of course, he isn't Harrison Stroud at all," James said. "It's easy enough to become someone else at that distance. Is his identity proven?"

"I asked that. And so did Montmorency's lawyer and old friend Cecil Brayton. Apparently the two fell out over the matter, since Montmorency was happy with the results of the initial queries, but Brayton wanted to investigate further for certainty's sake."

"Any particular reason?"

"Just lawyerly caution, it seems. Montmorency wanted to embrace his nephew and didn't feel inclined to delay for years to have the i's dotted and t's crossed. So he steamed ahead, and Brayton took it upon himself to continue his own investigation without Montmorency's knowledge."

"And what did he find?" James hung the kettle over the fire.

"Nothing. All the evidence Brayton turned up confirms Stroud is who he says he is, the legitimate heir, with no need or reason to kill his uncle. And as if that's not enough, he has an alibi."

"Damn." James sat down.

"Yes, well, wait till you hear it," Susan said. "The thing is, Brayton remained stubbornly cautious about Stroud's identity. He wanted Montmorency to wait for more and more proof. It reached the point where Stroud lost his patience, and Montmorency demanded Brayton apologise to him. This was the night of the murder. Stroud went to bed so irritated he couldn't sleep, and, knowing that Brayton was an insomniac, went to speak to him in his rooms. There he offered to answer every question and recount his entire life over again if Brayton would only give him a fair hearing. They were together when they heard the housekeeper scream."

She gave him an expectant look. James stared at her. "In the first floor guest rooms?"

"That's right. But they didn't hear anyone in the house because they were both engrossed in conversation."

"The God-given fuck they were," James said. "By which I mean, I find that unlikely. I would have heard them, and seen a light under a door. I was *listening*, damn it, and I will swear the house was asleep."

"Yes, I thought you would." Susan grinned at him. "It may be the doors are heavy and very well-fitted, of course, but it sounds like horseshit to me. And if it's horseshit, it's being produced by Brayton and Stroud as a matched pair."

James was sitting up straight now, all trace of the slump gone. "The lawyer and the nephew are in it together?"

"Looks that way to me, because I've got your account. Wilby has not, so as far as he's concerned they can give each other an unassailable alibi."

James rose and went over to get out the tea things. "But what about this lawyer? Is he suspected?"

"He's in debt due to unfortunate investments, but he neither expected nor received anything in Montmorency's will, which he drew up. They've been friends for years, and he's a scrawny old stick, in no shape to batter a man to death. I hope you're impressed by the thoroughness of Wilby's investigation, by the way. Other detectives would have accepted the guilt of a seven-foot bloodstained ogre in the night and knocked off early. Wilby's taken it seriously. He even looked into whether the valet could have killed Montmorency and then cut his own throat."

"Could he?"

"The former, but not the latter. The doctors are sure his throat was cut from behind."

"Thorough, but unhelpful. So is Wilby open to changing his mind on my guilt?"

"He might be with new information. If he heard your testimony and believed it, that would shine a very interesting light on Brayton and Stroud's evidence. Unfortunately—"

"—he'd have to believe me." James brought over the tea tray. Tea canister, milk, teapot, cups and saucers, all arranged without a clink of china. He poured boiling water into the pot and sat. "Why do you?"

"Why do I what?"

"Why do you believe me?"

It was a question she'd have to answer at some point, especially when Justin found out about this. "Your story raises too many questions to ignore. The talking or lack of it in the night, and the unmoored boat, for a start. And you sounded credible."

"Is that it?"

"What would you like me to say? That I remember you from seventeen years ago and I'm quite sure you couldn't have grown up a murderer? Please. I've seen what people do."

"And you know what I do, so why would you believe me?"

Susan felt defensive, for some reason. "I doubt you'd come here to lie to me. If you wanted to die you'd have turned yourself in to the police."

James gave her a twisted smile. "You do realise that any observer would think you're revealing a soft spot for a lost love, don't you?"

"Is that what you think?"

"Christ, no. I'm not that conceited. I think—"

"What?"

James considered for a moment, evidently weighing his words. "I wonder if you're hoping to demonstrate, if only to yourself, that I'm not as bad as all that. That I wasn't a mistake."

"That wouldn't be possible." Susan saw him flinch at that. "I know who you were back then," she went on, annoyed that she was explaining herself. "What you've become since then is your responsibility. I don't regret the past, and if I did, this would be a damn fool way of dealing with it."

"That's certainly true. I find it hard to believe you don't regret anything, all the same. Especially given you burned my letters."

"You ignored the one thing I asked of you and exposed me to the most humiliating experience of my life. I wasn't inclined to build you a shrine after that."

"I didn't ask for a shrine! I just wanted to explain—"

"Explain what? You thought you knew better, and you were wrong. If you'd listened to me in the first place—" She bit off the words, astonished she still felt the urge to have this out after seventeen years. "Oh, who knows. It doesn't matter. But after what you did, and what you brought down on me, no, I didn't feel like reading your letters. I was angry."

"So I see."

"What did you expect?" Susan had often been told that women should not show anger. She'd concluded early on that this meant she should not emulate Nathaniel, whose rare but spectacular rages were always short-lived, but rather Justin, who was coldly vicious and could hold a grudge forever. "Do you think I should have waited for you to return from Australia and forgiven all?"

"No. No, that would have been foolish. I'm sure you had better things to do."

"I did, and still do. Is dragging up the past the best use of your time or mine right now?"

James leaned forward to pour the tea without answering, and sat back once he'd handed her the cup. Only then did he say, "Possibly, yes."

"Oh, come on."

"I'm serious. With all due respect, you're not a magician. I have run my head into a noose and it's quite possible nobody can get it out. I'd like your time not to be entirely wasted, or entirely spent on me, which amounts to much the same thing."

"Are you sure you're all right?"

James grimaced. "I dare say you'd call it a dark night of the soul. I need to resolve some of the mess I have made with people who might have once cared for me. I want to understand the debt I owe you, and how I pay it."

The words made no sense for a moment, and then she remembered. The confrontation in a guest bedroom in Castle Speight.

Alec shaking and white-faced next to her, Crozier's hard features raw with pain. And James, standing there, trying to bluff it out.

She'd been so angry—that he was a criminal, that their lives had come to this, that he *dared*—that she'd almost raised her voice. But she was Susan Lazarus, who never lost control. Men could rant and rave all they chose; if a woman did the same, she showed herself a slave to her emotions.

So she hadn't shouted. She'd just hit him as hard as she could in the softest place she could think of.

"You don't owe me anything."

"I remember what you said. Let me put this right, Susan, as far as that's possible. Please. I don't regret nine-tenths of what I've done, but I will always regret that."

"What part? The part where I conceived your child? That was my doing as much as yours."

"The lie I told. The stupid mistake I made. I thought I was acting for the best, but—"

"For the best? You thought what you did was for the *best*?"

"Of course I did. Noble self-sacrifice is all very well—"

"It might be," Susan said furiously. "But since that doesn't remotely resemble what you did—"

"It was what *you* did!" There was annoyance in his voice now. "I didn't want to sacrifice you—"

"But you did," Susan said over him. "You threw me, and Justin with me, to the wolves to make yourself look better."

"That is a gross distortion!" James said, too loudly, and brought his voice down to a hiss. "I wasn't trying to impress you. I wanted to marry you!"

"Horseshit. You ran away. You all but told your father I was forcing you into wedlock, and left us to face the music while you lolled about in bloody Australia, and you have the *balls* to paint it as anything but a piece of cowardly—"

"*Susan!*" he hiss-shouted. He had been trying to get a word in for some time. "What the devil do you mean, I said you were forcing me? What?"

"You told—" Susan stopped, holding up her hand for silence. James jabbed a ferocious finger at her in return, but managed not to speak. They glared at one another.

"Right," Susan said at last. "Tell me, clearly, step by step, what you did."

"I promised you that I wouldn't tell my father. I then went straight to him, and informed him that you were with child and I wanted to marry you. I said I would renounce my name and never darken his door again. He told me I was a damned fool, and confined me to the house. I offered to do anything: take up any post he liked, reform my behaviour. I begged him with every argument I could muster for three days, to no effect. So I climbed out of the window and came to see you. That was the night that you—the baby—"

"I miscarried."

"Mr. Braglewicz answered the door. He wouldn't let me in, told me to come back later. I went to Aunt Harriet's house, since I didn't know what else to do, and found three of Father's footmen there. They manhandled me home and I was confined to a room, of which the shutters were now nailed closed. The next day they put me in a carriage and took me to the station, and I found myself in Southampton under close guard for several days. I had a gold watch, which I exchanged with the potboy for his services as a postman, and I wrote to you. Mr. Lazarus returned my letter unopened along with one of the nastiest notes I have ever received, informing me that you had lost the child. That was discovered, so the potboy was sacked for his efforts and nobody else would take a letter for me. And then they put me on a ship to Australia."

Susan breathed in and out, deeply. "I...see. I see."

"That was what happened," James said. "What did you think happened?"

She wasn't sure she wanted to answer that. "When you spoke to your father, after you came to see me—"

"I didn't. I haven't set eyes on him since I climbed out of that window. He didn't give me so much as a goodbye."

"Before that, then. What did he offer you to stay away from me?"

"Nothing. I was the one pleading; he merely had to refuse. And to have me shanghaied onto that damned ship, of course."

"To Australia. What did you do there?"

James smiled without mirth. "My father wrote me a letter, which I was given in Southampton. He told me he was sending me to the colonies for my own good. It was to be a new beginning after all the trouble I'd caused, a chance to start again. I was furious, of course, but I was also stuck, and after a few days' raging I decided to give it a try. I thought I'd write to you and explain, throw my back into the work, make Father proud. By the time I'd got there I had persuaded myself you'd wait for me, or even come out to marry me. It didn't quite go to plan." His voice was mocking. "I was taken to the mines, under the impression I was to learn the opal trade, and found myself serving as indentured labour. Father had ordered his property manager to put me to 'the hardest menial work possible in order to break my spirit'. His words. The letter had been a ploy to keep me from jumping ship when we stopped in port. A deliberate lie as he packed me off to hell."

Susan realised her mouth was open. She shut it.

"I have never felt so alone in my life before or since," James went on. "A damned dusty oven of a country on the other side of the world, stranded hundreds of miles from anything like civilisation, under the lash of a drunken brute who treated me almost as badly as he did the natives, and his dog better than any of us. And he kicked his dog. I learned to deal with isolation and not to care about what I had to do, and I took those lessons to heart. Probably not what my father had intended me to learn, but there we are. And opals, of course. I learned about them."

Gilded Cage

"What did you do?" she managed.

"Raged and swore and fought for months, then started thinking. Father had said he wanted me broken, so I broke. I crept about, as cowed and humbled as that bastard of an overseer could have wished, and laboured without complaint for a year or more until he considered me quite negligible. That eventually gave me an opportunity to steal the strongbox, which I did, along with a horse. I made my way to Brisbane with saddlebags full of coin and pockets full of opals, and took the first boat out."

Susan nodded slowly. "I…did not know that. Any of it."

"You would have done if you'd read my letters."

"Do you blame me?" she demanded.

"For what?"

"That I didn't read them. That you were sent there. That I was—I don't know, the last straw. The insult too far to your noble name for your father to overlook."

"The latter two, no," James said. "I cursed you in the mines, but if it hadn't been you, it would have been something else. My father had already decided I was bad to the bone, and subsequent events bear him out. I wish you'd read my letters, though. May I infer you had a reason for not doing so?"

"You may, yes."

"What don't I know?"

"We could be here for some time," she said automatically. "Oh, hell. All right. You made me that promise and then I didn't hear a word from you for three days. Miss Rawling told me you were at your father's house. I waited for you, and then I began to have pains, and realised I was bleeding. It hurt, and I knew it was for the best, but it didn't feel like the best. And you weren't there. Mark told me you'd come, that you'd promised to come back the next day. It was over by then and I needed you, but you didn't come. Your father did."

"Oh Christ."

"He sent a footman first, in livery, to command Justin's immediate attendance. Mark told him to sling his hook. So your father came to us. He told Justin, with me in the room, in my *home*, that I had preyed on your youth and misguided chivalry to ensnare you and it was all clearly a scheme to extort money from the family. He said you had broken down in tears, told him how trapped you felt. That you'd agreed to make a new start overseas managing some Vane holdings, to get away from your mistakes, and I should be aware that I would never get my hands on Vane money, or have any future brat acknowledged. And he threatened us. He knew about Justin's past, he said he'd ruin the firm's reputation, he called us frauds and me a whore— Oh, you know what he said. Or at least you can guess."

"Jesus Christ." James had gone red. "Jesus Christ, Susan, you couldn't believe that I was part of that. You didn't."

"I'd lost the child, I hadn't slept, you *didn't come*, and it was as much as I could do not to burst into tears in front of him. And Justin— I've never seen him so humiliated. He couldn't risk telling Lord Dickie Vane to go to hell, not then. So we just took it. We sat there while your father called us names, and we took it."

The lines of James's throat stood sharp. "He never gave me a choice and he never told me he'd seen you. Christ, Sukey, you must have hated me."

"Oh, it was worse than that," Susan said grimly. "I didn't blame you. I looked at the situation and I decided that yes, of course you would have wanted to escape once you'd had a few days to think, because you'd always been weak and unreliable and all the things your father said of you. I didn't blame you: I blamed myself for believing you in the first place. And I made sure I wasn't fooled again."

"Shit." James stretched out a hand towards her, stopped himself. "Sukey, I am so sorry."

"It's not your fault." She paused, tasted the words, and repeated them. "It is, genuinely, not your fault. I was in a lot of pain, or I'd have come looking for you, if only to rip your balls off. I was…unhappy." She always hid when she was unhappy. She'd curled up round her clawed-up belly and aching heart, too young and fearful to get up and fight. "I think your father told Miss Rawling a tale too; she was livid with you for running away from your responsibilities. That convinced me of course, because I knew she wouldn't lie to me. And there was a notice in the paper that Mr. James Vane was sailing out on the Whatever-ship-it-was to take up a position on his father's properties. It all fitted. None of us said, 'No, James wouldn't run away and put the blame on you and look after himself'. We all thought you would do exactly that, because it's what any young man of your class would."

James opened his mouth, shut it again, tipped his head back, and stared at the ceiling. "I'd like to assert here that I wasn't just 'any young man of my class', and of course I wasn't. I was worse."

"Define 'worse'," Susan said. "Would you have married me if you could?"

"Like a shot. I swear it."

She exhaled hard. "And I never saw you hide behind your station."

"But when my father said I had, you believed him. Because when it comes down to it, I was a toff, and that's how toffs behave."

"I knew what I thought about aristocratic young men." And apparently she'd let that outweigh what she knew of him. She hadn't trusted him, or her own judgement, or a world that she knew bloody well didn't give fairy-tale romance to girls from the gutter.

"There's a certain irony here, isn't there?" James remarked. "My father called me a traitor to my name and class, while you refused to believe that I would be anything of the sort."

Susan was still holding her cup and saucer. She put them down, carefully. "Irony is one word for it. I think I should…" Oh God. "Apologise."

"I don't want to watch you choke on your own tongue," James assured her. "And no, you shouldn't. It is grotesque that my father should have lied to you. There are obligations attendant on our station in life, which include scrupulous honesty at all times."

"I'd almost think you meant that."

"Considering how often my father barracked me for my moral failings, it would be extraordinary if I couldn't catch his tone. The hypocritical old fuck."

"Marvellous, isn't it?" Susan said. "The lofty denunciation of my and Justin's characters while he lied through his teeth. Have you ever considered robbing him?"

"Frequently."

"I'll help." She shook her head, angry yet almost laughing, almost light. "You didn't change your mind. You didn't let me down."

"I did, but I didn't choose to. Does that make so much difference?"

"It means I wasn't wrong," she said, and James's face lit with a laugh so familiar it felt like a blanket round her shoulders.

"God, yes, of course. *That* must have been a thorn in your side."

"Seventeen years and counting. Ha. I wasn't wrong. At least, not about you, and that's what counts. I was misled—by a toff, which is embarrassing, and Justin will spit—but not wrong."

"And only because of circumstances," James said helpfully. "Under other conditions you'd have seen him a mile off, I'm sure."

He was laughing at her. She didn't care. That gross, stupid error of judgement for which she'd kicked herself so often, the bitter self-recrimination because she'd been so easily fooled—it was all based on a lie. She'd judged the core of him just right.

"I *knew* it," she said aloud, victorious, and he clamped his lips together. She grinned back at him, stupid youthful merriment bubbling in her chest. She wasn't good at being wrong, and she'd thought she'd been wrong about James for so long. And she hadn't!

Which, apparently, she could have found out for herself. Damn.

"I should have read your letters," she said. "I burned them because I thought it would be excuses." Because it would have hurt to read them. It was far easier to be angry than hurt, and easier still to insist it didn't matter and never had. Not her problem, not her pain. "If I had read them—"

"I don't know how much good it would have done, given I had no idea what Father had said. And I was mired in self-pity at that point, so I doubt they were worth reading."

Susan narrowed her eyes. "You seem very forgiving about this."

"Am I?" James paused, thinking, then spoke slowly. "When you ignored my letters, I concluded that you hated me, but I thought it was either because I'd put you in the family way in the first place, or because I'd been fool enough to speak to my father against your express wishes, or both. Am I right that you hated me for what my father said I did, rather than what I actually did?"

"I hated you because you cast blame on me in order to rid yourself of an obligation I never asked you to take on. And if you didn't do that—"

"Then you don't hate me now?"

"Let's not get ahead of ourselves."

He gave her a look. "I want to be clear on this. You said that I owed you a debt. Is that still the case in the light of this information?"

She exhaled, breathing out old, stale, poisonous air. "No. You don't owe me anything."

He shut his eyes. "Good. Thank you."

"You owe society a debt for years of larceny," she added in case anyone had been in danger of forgetting that small point. "And I owe your father, and I will pay him back with *interest*."

"Christ, I missed you." James's eyes met hers, and something inside Susan twisted so hard it hurt.

"I," she said, and had to start again. "I didn't miss you. But…I might have done, if I'd known. So it's probably good I didn't know, under the circumstances."

"I'm not sure that follows."

"We are where we are," she said briskly. "Which includes you being a thief who's wanted for murder, so can we get back to the point?"

"No, I like this digression," James said. "I am almost certainly absolutely screwed and going to hang. Let me enjoy such vindication as I am likely to achieve."

"Are you doubting my ability?"

James sighed. "I'm not an idiot, Sukey. If all we have to go on is my testimony, that's not worth a damn. And even with it, all we have is suspicions of the lawyer and the nephew colluding. We don't have a motive, a witness, or any evidence of who actually killed him."

"The money will do nicely for motive. I have a witness right in front of me and I'll find a way to use you. And as for evidence, we'll get that at Sorley House when we go down tomorrow."

James tried out a few words and settled on, "I beg your pardon?"

"Wilby isn't happy. He knows something's not right even if he can't put his finger on what. He gave me his blessing to ask some questions: I think he hopes I'll shake something loose. So you need to—"

A knock rattled the door. Susan hissed an obscenity and swung around. "Who is it?"

"Harriet, miss."

James was already up and moving like a ghost, impossibly silent. Susan cast a very fast glance around for evidence of male occupation—she'd brought back his cleaned clothes but they were in a wrapped parcel. She scooped up the second cup and saucer and tiptoed to put it at the far end of the room. There she opened a jar of Emma's pungent cucumber pickles, splashed some vinegar onto the floor, called, "Coming!", and took her time going to the door.

Harriet was the maid of all work who slept upstairs and had taken two guineas to be selectively deaf. She gave Susan a jerk of the head, pointed sharply downward, and announced loudly, "Evening, miss, only Mrs. Hewson is worried because Miss Thivett on the first floor said she heard a man in the house."

Damnation. She'd been culpably careless talking to James, and distraction was no excuse. "Does she want me to have a look round for her?"

"She's having a look herself, miss."

Mrs. Hewson read the *Illustrated Police News* avidly, and had been overjoyed to rent to a genuine enquiry agent because it soothed her anxiety about anarchists under the bed. She'd be outraged if she discovered a man in Susan's rooms, and all too likely to identify the Mortlake Opal Murderer if she saw him.

Susan shrugged. "Well, there's no man in here."

"I should hope not, miss," Harriet said firmly, voice pitched to carry down the stairs. "Nobody would stand for such a thing, this being a respectable house. I only wanted to know if you'd heard anyone."

Mrs. Hewson came up the stairs then, in a bustle. "Miss Lazarus! Miss Thivett downstairs has reported the sound of a male voice—"

"So Harriet tells me," Susan said. "I heard nothing, but I had the window open and there was quite a bit of noise from the street. I wonder if that carried."

"The window open? In this weather?"

"I spilled some vinegar," Susan said unblushingly.

"Miss Thivett was quite positive. I am obliged to look around."

"Naturally. Do you want me to come with you? I have a revolver."

Mrs. Hewson's mouth opened. "A revolver! Is—is that necessary?"

"It depends whether you suspect an unlawful intruder or just an unlicensed guest."

"Yes. I see. I wouldn't normally—but one reads such terrible things, and with that dreadful murderer on the loose—"

"I'm sure it's an unnecessary precaution," Susan said, with a very small twinge of guilt at playing on the woman's fears. "I'll just fetch it."

93

"Please do." Mrs. Hewson stepped into Susan's room without asking, and took a swift look around. She might be fearful, but she was thorough and responsible, a fact Susan both respected and resented at this moment.

The room smelled pungent, thanks to the vinegar. Mrs. Hewson gave a startled sniff, but didn't seem to detect the odour of male presence. Thank heavens James wasn't in a position to use eau de toilette.

"My gun's in here, if you'll excuse me," Susan said, going to the bedroom. Mrs. Hewson followed at her heels, evidently determined to do her duty. Ah well; James hadn't avoided arrest for years because he was stupid. Susan opened the door wide, and gestured her landlady in.

Her bedroom appeared entirely devoid of jewel thief. Susan collected and loaded her gun, wondering where he was. The wardrobe was both small and creaky; the bed was reasonably sized but had no blankets hanging over the side. She'd doubtless find out.

"Right," she said. "Shall we go?"

It took a good twenty minutes to check the house with sufficient thoroughness to allay Mrs. Hewson's alarm. Susan returned to her own room at last, locked the door behind her, and looked round. There was no sign of James anywhere.

She considered that. Then she opened the bedroom window, stuck her head out, and gave a soft whistle.

"Thank Christ," an equally soft voice murmured from above, and a long pair of legs appeared. Susan stepped back, allowing him to manoeuvre through the gap. He landed silently, and stuck his hands under his armpits with equal silence, a pantomime of extreme cold.

Susan pointed. "Reach me that suitcase."

James lifted it off the wardrobe. "Are you off somewhere?" His voice was pitched so low she could barely hear it.

"So are you. Needs must."

James blinked. "Needs must what?"

"Your clean clothes are in the parcel in the other room. Get them for me, then can you get down to the ground without making a mess of yourself? Via the window, I mean."

"I expect so. What are we doing?"

"Starting our honeymoon," Susan said. "Every lodging-keeper and hotelier in the city will be on the look-out for a very large man, but not a married couple. I'll bring down the case and meet you in the alley, and we can find a hotel for a late-arriving pair of newlyweds. Think of a false name, will you? And put on your hat and coat. You look chilly."

CHAPTER SEVEN

Templeton clambered down the building to the alley below, conscious of every tiny noise. He had no idea how long it might take Susan to emerge; in the event it was about twenty minutes, by the end of which his fingers were icy and he was convinced that the policeman who had strolled along the street would be back at any moment to accuse him of lurking with intent.

But at last she was there, in hat and coat, with the suitcase. She lugged it a few paces until he slid out of the shadows and took it from her hand.

"About time," they said simultaneously, and Templeton had to bite back a laugh.

"Is your landlady not suspicious?" he enquired as she set off at a brisk pace.

"I told her I was going to catch a night train and would be away for some days. Do we have a name?"

"As a married couple? How does Ranelagh suit you? John and Sarah?"

"Could anyone link that to you?"

"It's my great-grandmother's maiden name."

"I'll take it," Susan said. "Thank you for not suggesting Smith or Peters. It would be tiresome if I had to throw something at you and go home."

"The first rule of aliases: never use a first name or a place name," Templeton said sententiously.

Susan turned to look at him. "Did you—*you*—say that?"

"I was young."

"'Templeton Lane'? Nobody's that young."

"Young and also stupid."

"It was your *address*."

"Do you hear me trying to justify myself?"

Susan snorted and strode on, sensible shoes clacking on the pavement. It was, at least, not raining. Templeton kept up without effort despite the weight of the suitcase.

Templeton Lane, number twenty-two. That was where he'd lived with Aunt Harriet Rawling, where he'd met Sukey and known the only companionship and happiness of his adolescent years, without reproaches and anger and frustration. He'd needed to come up with a new identity as he sought a berth on a ship away from Australia, and when the purser had asked him, "What's yer name, and where'dya want to go?", *Templeton Lane* had seemed a good answer to both.

They walked for some fifteen minutes, a middle-class gentleman and, he saw as they passed under the halo of street lights, a very nicely dressed woman to match. Susan had changed her clothes and looked smart—not pretty, because she wasn't, but self-possessed and confident. A practical type, not in the first flush of youth, but what sensible woman of the middling sort married young? She looked like she'd made a considered decision to accept the fictitious Mr. Ranelagh and would become an indispensable partner in his work. And, he thought, she looked like she'd expect her marital rights too. No separate rooms for Mrs. Ranelagh, no mealy-mouthed prudery or fear. She'd got to thirty-four unmarried by choice, and now she'd chosen a husband and she'd have *expectations*.

God, he wished he were Mr. Ranelagh.

Susan evidently knew where they were going. She led the way to Frederick Street where she slackened her pace to drop back a fraction. "Thurgood's Hotel, Mr. Ranelagh," she informed him, slipping an arm through his. "I think this looks perfect."

"So it does, darling." He'd have liked to pat her hand for effect, but was hampered by the suitcase, so he simply beamed at the doorman as they passed. Thurgood's was clearly a hotel for the Mr. Ranelaghs of this world, smart but not lavish, suitable for those who had money to spend but didn't like to waste it. He handed the case to an attendant with a smile, but no tip because he didn't have a penny on him, and they went together to the reception desk.

"Do you have a double room?"

The clerk's eyes flicked over them. "Do you have a reservation, sir?"

"I'm afraid not. We, ah, found ourselves changing our plans quite suddenly." He shot Susan a wink.

"Oh, John," Susan said, with laughing rebuke, then smiled at the clerk. It was a glorious smile, brimming with excitement that had to go somewhere, and Templeton felt his gut twist. "You see, we were married today." She tightened her grip on Templeton's arm, a tiny movement that said as much as a wiggle of pleasure on a young girl.

He beamed down at her, then returned his attention to the clerk. "I don't suppose you have a honeymoon suite."

"John!"

"We'll have one in Paris, Mrs. Ranelagh," he assured her. "Why not tonight?"

"There is the Edmonton suite, sir," the clerk suggested. "Our best rooms."

"Perfect," Templeton said. "We'll take that—I think for two nights, but I will confirm that tomorrow."

"Certainly, sir. And if I may offer my congratulations?"

"Thank you so much," Susan said. "Do you know, you are the first person we've told? Oh! John, we really must—"

"Telegrams tomorrow," Templeton said firmly. "Tonight is for my wife."

She looked at him with delighted admiration, which Templeton memorised as an expression he'd probably never see again, and they headed upstairs arm in arm, the very picture of a modern romance, with the clerk smiling benevolently after them.

It was warm in the hotel. Susan stripped off her gloves as they entered the lift. Templeton glanced down, and saw without surprise that she already wore a plain gold band. She slipped her hand into his with a little confiding smile, and Templeton felt the cool, hard sensation of coins in his palm.

You are, in fact, the perfect woman.

He passed on her largesse to the bellboy without even looking, and received an appreciative bow in return. Susan said, "We'll want to eat."

"There is a dining-room, Mrs. Ranelagh, ma'am."

Susan glowed at the title. Templeton had no idea how, but she actually glowed, as though her entirely fictitious happiness had to spill out. "Thank you, but do you know, I should like to eat here. To be private and enjoy this lovely room."

The bellboy admirably restrained his smirk. "I'll bring you a menu, ma'am."

He departed. Templeton turned to Susan. She had hung up her hat and coat and was looking around the room, hands on hips, so he allowed himself a moment's contemplation.

She looked good. The dress wasn't new but it was smart and well fitted, in a grey-blue shade that suited her eyes. More flattering than the drab don't-look-at-me garments she'd put on this morning by some way. Her hair was pinned up differently—he couldn't quite say how, except that it framed her face rather than being pulled back. She wore ear-rings too, silver drops set with red stones, and he stepped forward to look.

Susan didn't spin round, because that would imply she was startled, but she did tense, muscles snapping alert, chin tilting a fraction. Templeton, carefully not thinking, even more carefully not touching, put a finger under her ear and lifted the ornament, angling it to the light.

"Do they pass muster?" Susan enquired.

"They do. Burmese?"

"I have no idea."

"From an admirer?"

"Nathaniel. Thirtieth birthday present."

"Hmm. I wouldn't give you rubies."

"Of course not. You'd steal them from me." Susan was very still, head up. His fingers were half an inch from her earlobe. He could straighten them and touch the point where the curve of her jaw met the line of her neck.

"If I were to give you jewels, they wouldn't be rubies," Templeton said patiently.

"What then? Diamonds?"

"Sapphires. Or rainbow moonstone. Do you know those?"

"It sounds like a bad poet named a racehorse."

"Milky stones that glow blue from within, like moonlight on water. They're not considered precious, but we discussed the worth of that." The silver teardrop rested on his finger, cool and smooth. "You can't pin down rainbow moonstone. It's impossible to see quite how it contains the blue, where the sheen comes from. They aren't showy; they don't glitter. But they glow." He moved his finger a fraction closer to her neck, let the earring fall and swing. "You could wear them with anything. Hardly anyone would notice at all."

"How well you know me." Susan's voice was tart and sardonic, but he was sure she'd made an effort at that. He could see the pins in her hair from here, the dull brass heads. If he pulled them out…well, she'd probably resort to violence, but if he pulled them out with her permission, the loops of mingled flax and ginger and gold and chestnut that only looked indeterminate if you weren't paying attention would drop and uncoil over her shoulders in tendrils.

"One could set hairpins with moonstones," he said softly. "Perhaps strong sharpened pins that would serve for self-defence. The wives of the samurai—Japanese warriors—have those."

"So do Englishwomen," Susan said. "Don't underestimate my hairpins. What are you doing, James?"

That was a hell of a question. *Regretting the past* seemed too obvious, as did *Wishing I had a future*. He was saved from answering by a knock at the door. Templeton called, "Come in," and saw her posture soften and her smile widen as though she wanted nothing more than his touch, so the waiter would see a newly-married pair in a moment of intimacy. He gave it a second and stepped away, taking the menu with a word of thanks.

"You order, John," Susan said with a smile. "You know what I like."

Templeton had no idea, but she'd never been fussy, and he was hungry. He ordered soup, fish, the beef Wellington, and a bottle of champagne, and received a sunny smile from Susan that dropped off her face as the door shut again.

"You have lavish tastes," she remarked.

"We're on our honeymoon."

"So we are. Are you paying?"

"I can pay you back," Templeton said. "If and when I can get to my cash reserves."

"And in the meantime...?"

"I assume you thought ahead. You usually do. If you haven't got the money, I'm sure you've already planned how to leave without any trace except the spectacular bill—which, needless to say, we will remit later by post."

"Is it needless to say?"

That stung. "I'm not a sneak thief. I don't take the cost of a meal from the waiter's pocket. I'll have it from the lady dripping with overpriced ornaments for which the workers who dug and cut and set the jewels were paid a pittance."

"Makes all the difference."

"It does, yes," Templeton said. "I wouldn't state that you agree with me as fact, but only because I'm afraid of the consequences."

Susan choked. "Yes, well. Notwithstanding."

"Notwithstanding what?"

"Just notwithstanding. No, actually: notwithstanding, what do you mean, you think I've already worked out how to do a runner? Are you implying I don't pay *my* bills?"

"Not at all," Templeton said. "I just don't think you've entirely given yourself over to respectability. You might not put the cross on any more, but don't tell me you've forgotten how. Or that the urge doesn't bite occasionally."

"*Excuse* me?"

"Oh, come. You're clearly enjoying yourself. The very first chance to perpetrate a fraud and you seize it."

Susan's mouth curved, just slightly. "Deception is a perfectly legitimate tactic, when done for a valid reason."

"Of course."

Sukey had been brought up a kiter, taught by the best. It was in her blood. He had no doubt she enjoyed the enquiry work—it would slake her fierce need to know more than other people, to weave traps, to be always one step ahead. All the same, he doubted it had the dark, unhealthy thrill of a true con game.

He knew the feeling well. It was why he stole opals instead of trading them.

"Some pleasures have to be lawless," he said aloud.

For most people that would be a non sequitur. Susan followed it effortlessly, but then, she knew how his mind worked.

"Some *people's* pleasures," she said. "I'm sure your friend Crozier gets half his fun from breaking the law, but Alec certainly doesn't. Or Nathaniel."

"Whereas your guvnor…"

"Has been a model citizen for twenty years."

"Took the pledge and hasn't touched a drop since?"

"Justin wanted to change." She sounded serious. "Not just to stop kiting. He wanted to be someone else because he thought that's what Ems and Nathaniel and I needed."

"Did you?"

"No, which is lucky, because he hasn't changed at all," Susan said. "He's exactly like he always was; he just makes different choices. And some of them aren't very different." She gave a sharp smile that was all too reminiscent of Lazarus senior. "But it's in a good cause."

"A knight in shining armour, fighting for the right."

"Something wrong with that?"

"Not at all. I just assumed…"

"Go on. What did you assume?"

"I don't know. Possibly that you'd have your own criminal empire by now. I didn't think the law was important to you."

"It's not," Susan said. "The laws are a pile of shit, written by rich men and the Church for the benefit of rich men and the Church. To hell with the law. I wouldn't be a policeman if they'd have me."

"Then why—"

"Don't be obtuse, James." She went over to the suitcase, opened it, and started to unpack with economical movements. "I do what I do because it's a job I can do, where nobody asks me to sit behind a typewriter or a till. I do it because I'm good at it. And I dare say I do it *because* the laws are a pile of shit."

"Another knight in shining armour, then. Redressing wrongs."

"Hardly. I solve problems for money."

"What did Alec Pyne pay you to see his father and stepmother hang?"

Susan paused, her back to him. She was entirely still for a moment. "They didn't hang."

"Only because they acted first." The Duke of Ilvar had killed his duchess and himself rather than face the humiliation of a murder trial. "What *did* he pay for that? I'm interested."

"Nothing, except that he ran into your pal Crozier, which cost him plenty. That business was my idea. Alec wanted to see his father in hell, but I made it happen, and not for money."

Templeton took that in. "Why?"

"Because the duke of Ilvar killed someone I loved." Susan couldn't possibly have anything left to unpack, but she still didn't turn around. "By omission—no court could have convicted him, and that's what I mean about the laws being shit. She was ill, and he didn't help, didn't support her. Didn't care. There was a sanatorium in Switzerland that offered a new treatment, but she didn't want to spend months alone there, or to put her brothers and me into debt. We were trying to find a way round that when she died. And all the while, her father draped his wife in jewels."

"Lady Caroline Pyne-ffoulkes," Templeton said. "Pyne's sister. That's the woman in the drawing, in your rooms, isn't it? She looks like him."

"A little, yes. Alec did it. He's very good."

"So that was vengeance. For your…?"

"My what?"

"You tell me. If you loved her enough to bring down a duke, I'd hate to use the wrong word."

"It's hard to put a name to it. I loved her, and I miss her. If she hadn't been so ill…but she was, and she didn't want to leave a widow. That was important to her."

It sounded like she'd done that anyway. Susan's voice was steady, but the note in it was unmistakable and made him wish he could hold her, that she could lean on him and be comforted. "I'm very sorry."

Susan breathed out hard. "It was a year ago, and we both knew she wouldn't make old bones. But she—we—could have had longer, and the life she did have was tainted by her shit of a father. So I brought him down."

"Did that make you feel better?"

"It passed the time."

Jerry had explained the miserable Pyne-ffoulkes family as an excuse for dragging them both into Alec's mess. Templeton wished he'd paid attention. "The duke had fallen out with his children, yes?"

"If by that you mean he murdered their mother and Cara witnessed it."

"Ah."

"It damaged her," Susan said. "So did spending her life watching the duke and his new duchess untouched by what they did. So did knowing that her father put his pride before her life."

"I imagine it did. I'm sorry."

Susan turned then. Her eyes looked wet, but her voice was all brisk professionalism as she said, "Anyway. Have you been in touch with yours?"

It took him a second to adjust to the conversational switch. "With my father? Christ, no. What would that achieve except to prove he was right all along?"

"Under the circumstances—"

"The best possible outcome of speaking to him, and it is not a likely one, would be that he treats me as his prodigal son and forgives me. I would not take his forgiveness if it came on a silver platter with a bottle of champagne and a signed affidavit from whoever killed Montmorency. Therefore, I shan't trouble myself."

Susan gave him a narrow look, then swung round as a knock sounded at the door. "Talking of champagne."

Templeton put his 'fond husband' expression back on, and watched the instant softening of Susan's stance as the waiters came in. The table was swiftly set up and laid, an ice bucket produced, and they took their seats. Templeton reached for Susan's hand across the table, and felt her fingers entwine with his so naturally that she might have wanted to do it.

The maitre d' beamed at them and uncorked the champagne with a celebratory pop. He filled their glasses while an underling dealt with the soup bowls, made complimentary remarks, and whisked his staff away.

"We'll be constantly interrupted, won't we?" Susan said, untangling her hand. "How trying."

"It would probably be more trying if we were on our honeymoon."

"If we were on our honeymoon, I wouldn't be wasting time with"—she sniffed at her spoon—"cold soup?"

"Vichyssoise, beloved. It's meant to be cold."

"It's leek and potato, is what it is." Susan took a sip, and tipped her head in reluctant acknowledgement that it might be tolerable.

Templeton spooned up his own soup, and restrained the impulse to ask about what she might envisage them doing on honeymoon instead. He'd overstepped already this evening and she had closed that conversation down in short order.

She will let you know in the unlikely event that she wants you, Mr. Hunted Murderer Jewel Thief.

They ate in silence except when observed: soup, fish, then the beef Wellington. Templeton watched her, watched the way her throat moved when she swallowed, found himself irritated by the man who had given her rubies. They were so obviously wrong for her, it was exasperating. Nathaniel Roy probably didn't have much experience buying women jewellery, but even so.

"You were thinking about possible help."

Templeton's thoughts had been entirely on how opals would look against her skin. "I was, yes, but without success. I'll have to ask Jerry, and hope his newfound spirit of forgiveness stretches to me."

Susan raised a sceptical brow. Templeton shrugged. "It might. And even if it doesn't, I owe him an apology."

"Can you contact him?"

"Probably."

"Do that. Set up a meeting for tomorrow. Evening," she added. "We're off to Mortlake first."

"You mentioned that earlier. I thought you'd gone briefly mad."

"I have Wilby's authorisation to look into the business. I'm going to do that, and you're coming with me."

Templeton contemplated that. He cut off a corner of beef and pastry, chewed it carefully, washed it down with a mouthful of champagne, and finally said, "No, sorry, still doesn't make sense."

"You can be our new man at Braglewicz and Lazarus. It would be extremely useful to have you there, and you can't stay here all day, still less wander around London."

"Do you not feel," Templeton said with restraint, "that this might be a tad—just a *tad*—on the risky side?"

"It's the last place anyone would expect to see you."

"Because I'd be mad to go back."

"Only the housekeeper got a look at you, and she won't remember your face. And you've shaved since. No-one will recognise you. Or if they do, we'll have found our conspirator."

Templeton put down his knife and fork with emphasis. Susan sawed at her meat, apparently unconcerned. "Are you serious, woman?"

"Of course I am. We need to know the exact inconsistencies between what you saw and what the witnesses told the police. You have to be on the site for that, and I also want you to have a look at the jewel store. I'm no expert. Will you need to get one of those lenses?"

"Jeweller's loupe. Yes, but—"

"Don't tell me you've lost your nerve."

"I have not, nor am I open to crass attempts at manipulation." Susan just grinned at that. Templeton sat back and thought. "What if the police spot me?"

"Been and gone. The house has been examined and cleaned up. Stroud, the nephew, is staying there. Otherwise there's only staff, and the only one of those who could have identified you is the dead valet, yes? I can't see a problem."

"None at all. A completely reasonable course of action." He picked up his cutlery and turned his attention to his plate again. "Absolutely unexceptional. I hope you realise, if I get nabbed, it will confirm that story about how murderers always return to the scene of the crime."

"That would be tiresome," Susan admitted. "Did I ever tell you about—" She caught herself. Templeton understood how she'd made the slip, because he was feeling the sense of familiarity himself, as if the seventeen years apart barely counted. "That is, I once worked on a case that went wrong, in that by the time I'd tracked the culprit down, someone had beaten his head in. He was a quack doctor, you understand, mostly cures for marital failure. Took a hands-on approach to his work." She raised an eyebrow meaningfully. "The investigating officer was a chap named Hayward, none too bright but quite relieved to have a woman around to explain what all the euphemisms were about. He didn't get anywhere in the first couple of days of the investigation, but then there was a breakthrough: two separate letters from concerned members of the public identified a suspicious couple who had been seen several times. Obviously an outraged husband and wife, and both letters offered a similar description of a dark thuggish man and a light-haired woman of suspect demeanour. Hayward put out an alert for what was clearly a pair of murderers who'd returned to the scene. It took another two days for it to dawn on him." She paused invitingly.

Templeton considered that with dawning joy. "Please tell me this policeman was dark and thuggish?"

"He's still known as the man who put out a bulletin on himself."

"Superb. That reminds me…" Templeton launched into a peculiarly absurd tale from his time in the United States. He wouldn't consider the prospect of tomorrow, and the grim reality of his situation, not now, because he was dining with Sukey Lazarus, laughing with her as though half their lives and half the world hadn't intervened, watching the way a single ringlet had escaped her hairpins and was curling over her shoulder. He'd never expected to have this again.

When the next knock sounded, he took her hand, interlacing their fingers. He kept hold of it while the plates were removed and the unseasonal, expensive ices were put out. This time he didn't let go when the waiters left.

CHAPTER EIGHT

Susan was not quite sure what she was doing.

No, that wasn't true. She knew exactly what she was up to professionally, and had a headful of ideas that she was itching to test. She was also thoroughly enjoying her role as Mrs. Ranelagh, newly married and bubbling with joy. The staff had swallowed it whole, and London hotel staff were among the most suspicious, uncharitable, and sharp of beings. She felt an intense satisfaction in duping them to which she wouldn't have admitted at gunpoint because that was what bad people did.

The only question was at what point her dinner with James Vane had turned into this. She wasn't even sure what *this* was. A reunion? A truce? A new friendship built on the ashes of an old affair? All that sounded very reasonable; none of it explained why she'd let her hand rest in his for several silent moments after the waiters had gone.

She'd pulled it away of course, made some comment about eating their extremely expensive pudding before it melted. They'd consumed the ices in silence, and were now waiting for the staff to return and remove the dinner things. She wasn't quite sure what they'd do then.

Well. They'd go to bed. That was the point.

Susan had had two small glasses of champagne and could feel them both. James had drained the rest of the bottle and it didn't seem to have touched the sides. She suspected he would normally have ordered a second bottle; it was good to see him show a bit of sense. It was good to see him at all. Unfortunately.

He was busy charming the maitre d'. Susan leaned back in her chair as the waiters bustled to remove the evidence of the meal and pack up the accoutrements, and attempted to take an impersonal survey of her friend turned lover turned thief turned petitioner.

He was an intimidating man, when one looked objectively. His blue eyes offered laughter and understanding, his smile was irresistible when it wasn't too obviously practised, his bulk might be comforting or protective in the right circumstances, but when his mouth hardened and his eyes chilled, Susan could easily see why Alec found him frightening. There was no sign of that quality now, but it wouldn't be far under the surface. You learned ruthlessness in his game.

He didn't look like the huddled, despairing figure of earlier. That had been unnerving because she'd seen Justin like that a few times, paralysed with bleak self-loathing. Nathaniel treated those moods as though they were a physical ailment, providing endless cups of tea, quiet affection, and gentle, non-combative companionship until Justin was ready to fight again.

Susan wasn't much good at gentle companionship, and in any case it seemed to her that James's darkness was of a different kind, the sort that you got by doing damn fool things and which could be driven away by useful work. He'd perked up enormously at the prospect of a bit of wall-scaling and some elaborate deception, and while she could imagine it might be unpleasant to return to Mortlake after his ghastly night there, she was quite sure he'd thrive on the bold-faced lies they were going to tell.

The waiters took away the final oddments, and at last they were alone, looking at one another, champagne and laughter gone. His eyes were royal blue in the gaslight, very serious.

He raised a hand, slowly, and looped a long tendril of fallen hair over her ear. "There. That's been distracting me."

"I thought it was the rubies."

"Both. I will buy you moonstones one day. Thank you, Susan." His hand still cupped her jaw, not touching, but close enough that she could feel the heat of his skin.

"I haven't done anything yet."

"Oh, you have. You always did. If the police came for me first thing tomorrow, you'd still have done more for me than anyone." He stood another moment then lifted his hand away. "Sleeping arrangements. I presume I'm on the sofa?"

"Is there one in the bedroom? You can't sleep in this room; the maids will be in at God-knows-what o'clock to do the fire and it would look odd to say the least."

James threw open the connecting door. The bedroom it revealed was dominated by a very large bed with a golden coverlet on which lay a red rose. There were many more roses in a vase. There was, however, no sofa.

"Damn."

"I'll take the floor," James said.

If he'd complained she wouldn't have offered. If he'd sounded martyr-like or sorry for himself…but he didn't, and Susan needed him looking like an enquiry agent, not a sleepless fugitive. "You take the bed. I'll have the floor."

"Nonsense."

"Don't be chivalrous. You're bigger than me and you need the sleep."

"*You* need the sleep. I'm depending on that razor-sharp mind of yours to save my neck." James glanced at the obvious honeymoon bed. "Look, it's big enough for two of me, or four of you. If you want to share, you have my word of honour I will behave as a gentleman."

"I've met gentlemen."

"Good point. I will behave as a gentleman ought to."

Susan had few illusions about men, and James's interest was clear. But he was offering, not pushing, and he'd backed off when she'd wanted him to. It wouldn't do to pretend he was still her James, her steadfast ally and first lover, but she was pretty sure she could trust him this far.

"I'll take your word," she said, and refrained from threats as to what she might do if he broke it. He already knew. "So. It's past ten."

"Bed, then."

"Best."

"Shall I…?" He indicated the other room.

"I'll just get my night-things."

It felt ludicrously exposed to find her hairbrush and tooth powder under James's eye. There was nothing intimate about carrying a nightgown through to a bedroom. James had seen a lot more than her nightgown in the past.

Of course, in the past they'd both known what they wanted and it had seemed like an indisputably good idea.

She got ready for bed as quickly as she could, and slipped under the covers. "All right, you can come in."

James entered. He looked slightly self-conscious. "You may wish to revoke permission. I realised I don't have night-clothes."

Of course he didn't; she hadn't bought any. "Oh, for heaven's sake," she said tartly. "Get on."

She rolled over on her side, facing away. He put out the lights anyway. She heard him moving around—still quiet, even though there was no need for quiet. Maybe it was ingrained habit by now, or an effort not to be large in order not to intimidate her with his presence.

He pulled back the sheets very carefully, only lifting his corner, and got in. The mattress dipped considerably. He shuffled around, adjusting his position with the tiniest possible movements.

"If you're trying to be imperceptible, it's not working," she said after a moment. "I know you're in here."

"I'm *trying* to be considerate and respectful."

"But you're actually wriggling like a two-year-old. Just make yourself comfortable and have done."

He snorted, but shifted more noticeably. "Do you have much acquaintance with two-year-olds?"

"Emma has two children. And a husband," she added, somewhat as an afterthought. "They live at Robin Hood Yard."

"Why don't you?"

"Why don't I have a husband and two children?"

"I meant, why don't you live at Robin Hood Yard."

Susan looked up at the ceiling. The curtains were good and thick but a little light seeped in from the street all the same. "I work there. I grew up there. I could live and work with Justin all my life and have Emma and Nathaniel and Mark around every day and the Moretons dropping by, and everyone else. If I lived like that I dare say I'd be happy, but my happiness would be dependent on them."

"Is that bad?"

"People die," Susan said. "They leave. They let you down and change things, and—" She didn't want to talk about this. God damn the champagne. "The point is, you have to take responsibility for yourself, not sit back and wait for other people to make you happy. I need to run my own life, not just enjoy the one Justin gave me. Same for my work. I've got a career because Mark and Justin let me have one. Nobody else would have taken me on as an enquiry agent because I'm a woman, and plenty of people who engage the firm still don't want me on their cases. I've earned my place but that's not enough. I need to do it myself."

"You want to start on your own?"

"I think so." She hadn't told anyone this since Cara, but it felt like old times, the pair of them lying together on their backs, staring up to the sky. "I think I have to, or I'll always feel as though I'm getting by on Justin and Mark's name."

"If it helps," James said, "most of the underworld is terrified of you. I certainly am."

"Unfortunately, yours are not the opinions that matter."

"I don't see why not. They're a great deal more informed than the opinions of decent people, because we're the ones who can assert the value of your services. In fact, you ought to put criminal testimonials in your advertising. Susan Lazarus, Lady Detective. 'If she's on your track, you're scrobbled!' says Mr. SK, receiver of stolen goods. 'Oh Christ, not that bloody woman'—Mr. TL, jewel thief, London."

Susan whooped aloud. "I'll do it."

"When they hang me I'll give you a deathbed endorsement, in rhyming couplets. What about the husband and two children, or lack of? Is that down to Lady Caroline?"

She felt her smile fade. "Not just her. I never wanted the first, and I took more care not to put myself in the way of the second."

"You've never considered marrying anyone else? Marrying anyone," he corrected himself hastily. "Anyone who wasn't Lady Caroline, I meant. Which of course you couldn't."

Susan gave him a sardonic look, completely wasted in the darkness. "Have you seen what happens to married women?"

"In what sense?"

"Marriage means absolute surrender of my money, my future, my body, my name. Mortgaging my life to a man and hoping I haven't guessed wrong. If he decides to make me miserable or spend every penny I earn, there's no way out but an endless trudge through the law-courts with no guarantee the judge won't decide he hasn't treated me quite badly enough. A wife is *property*, James. Why would I give away my humanity for a ring?"

"That's…quite a strong view," he said cautiously. "Isn't Emma happy in her marriage?"

"She is now. Her first husband hit her."

"Ah."

"I'd have seen him off the first time he did it, but she wanted to give him another chance. The next time, she was three months gone, and he beat her so hard it brought on her bleed. I wonder how many women have died giving men a second chance."

"Christ," James said. "I trust he didn't get a third?"

The process of removing Emma's husband from her life had been lengthy. Mark had thrown him out of the house while Nathaniel helped her embark on the long process of legal separation and prosecution, but the bastard wouldn't leave her alone. Emma was his wife to do with as he pleased, he'd said, with the righteous anger of thwarted ownership. He'd hung around the house, followed her in the market and hammered on the door at night, and after three months of that Justin and Susan had stopped waiting for the law to take its course.

"No. He didn't, and he won't."

"Good. May I ask—?"

"It was a funny thing," Susan said. "He passed out in a pub, and woke up in a goldsmith's shop with his pockets full of loot, surrounded by policemen. He couldn't explain what he was doing there and the judge wasn't convinced by his claim that someone had drugged him and set him up. He got six years, and Emma got her divorce."

"Nicely done. When does he get out?"

"Next year. I'll be waiting at the gates, and we'll have a little chat about what his future might hold."

"I'm sure he'll find it informative. All right, I see your point about marriage, though I'm convinced you could pick a reasonable specimen of the male sex if you wanted."

"I don't know why you say that," Susan remarked. "Your experience of my taste in men is you."

"Ouch. Do you have anyone currently?"

She hadn't tried. She missed Cara far too much; the thought of missing someone else in the future was not inviting. She'd have liked a casual bed partner, someone to whom she could bid farewell without regret, but not enough to actually go out and find one. "Too busy. What about you?"

"Nobody for a while. Don't ask how long a while; it's somewhat embarrassing."

"I'd have thought you'd be fending the ladies off with a stick."

"Ladies who would like to be draped in unlawfully obtained jewels, yes. Unfortunately, that's the fastest way to the Old Bailey I know. Ladies who don't know my profession—well, it would be unfair to involve them."

Susan considered that and found it good, not that she had any intention of telling him so. "So, any woman who chooses to be involved with you must by definition have dangerously poor judgement?"

"That is a very characteristic interpretation of my words."

"There must have been someone." She wasn't sure why she was prodding at this.

"Yes, of course. I was particularly fond of a young lady in the States who handled a gun with remarkable skill. And there was a professional gambler who could fuzz cards so beautifully it would bring a tear to your eye."

"The sort of people who move on."

"*I'm* the sort of person who moves on," James pointed out. "You always said, you can't have stuff that slows you down when you need to run away."

"And that includes people?"

"You're the one who isn't living at home with the family."

"I'm not the one trying to flee the country."

"That isn't by my choice. If I get out of this mess…" He paused, long enough for her to wonder if he knew how to finish the sentence. "Well, we'll see. Stan can retire at any time he likes, and I know Christiana would like him to. I don't know what Jerry wants. I could probably find out by asking him."

He didn't sound like a man devoid of personal ties, a fact Susan chose not to point out. She had something else on her mind. She chewed it over a moment, wondering if it was too raw, but the hell with it. They were in the same bed, it was dark, and if she wanted to know what he thought, this was her chance.

"If it hadn't gone wrong," she said. "If your father had approved, or just cut you off, and I'd had the baby, and we'd got married. Would it have worked?"

"I've wondered that. Sometimes I've felt cheated of the life I should have had. Then I wonder if I'd have been fit for it. I was a damned fool of a boy; you were the sum total of good sense I ever displayed. Would I have pulled myself together to be a father and husband? I meant to, but I recall a lot of promises that I meant when I said them. And would you have handed the baby to a nurse and become an enquiry agent? What would I have thought about that? What else might you have done?"

"I don't know."

"It's possible we'd have been extremely bad for one another," James said. "It's also conceivable that you'd have turned me into a model citizen and I'd be Chancellor of the Exchequer by now. I'd have liked— No."

"No what?"

"I was going to say I'd have liked the chance to find out, but I'd probably have made the same damned mess with you as I did everything else. I wouldn't want to have let you down any more than I actually did. I'd rather be where I am."

"Wanted for murder?"

"Apart from that."

"I think I'd have made a mess of it too," Susan said. "I'd have given you a hard time, and you'd have started to see me as another adult nagging you to behave and telling you what to do—"

"Oh Christ, don't. What a callow little tit I was."

"You weren't little. And I didn't want to be a wife, or a mother. Still don't. I wanted to be an enquiry agent, and that was all."

"No, it wasn't."

She turned to give him a blank look in the dark. "Eh? Of course it was."

"No," James said. "What you wanted was to be Susan Lazarus. Not Mrs. James Vane, and certainly not James Vane Junior's mother, just as you're chafing at being part of Braglewicz and Lazarus when it isn't the right Lazarus. You wanted to claim your name for yourself."

"Because I wasn't entitled to it." Her throat felt dry. "Because Justin gave it me when I was twelve. God knows what my real name is, if I have one."

"It's Susan Lazarus. You've worked for it. I wouldn't give that away either."

She took a couple of breaths, for control. "And what about Templeton Lane?"

"That saved my life, I think," James said. "It meant I did things differently, for good and ill, and left a great deal behind me that I couldn't bear to bring along. Templeton Lane wasn't lonely, because he had nobody to miss, and he had no regrets because he had no past. Templeton Lane was a blank slate."

"In my old trade, a blank slate was a lie. I'd write on it with onion juice, then Justin would wipe it with a chalky handkerchief, and there you are, a message from the spirits. The flats fell for it every time."

"Perhaps the invisible writing is always there, whatever you do," James said. "You were always Susan Lazarus. It was just a matter of the rest of the world learning that fact."

Susan turned on her side, an aggressive motion, and felt the mattress undulate as James turned too, toward her. She reached out, hand landing on his bare shoulder, and gripped it as she pulled him close, and their mouths met.

It was a motionless kiss for a moment, both of them stiff and still, lips pressed against lips. Susan's fingers relaxed without her conscious will.

James made a low noise in his throat. His hand came down on her back, warmth perceptible through the linen of her nightgown, and his mouth moved against hers almost savagely. Hungrily. Susan was hungry herself. She slid her hand across his shoulders, feeling their strength and some thin ridged scar-lines, as his hand moved downward.

They were devouring each other, as though kissing now could make up for all the embraces they'd lost, all the love that had gone wrong. Susan tried to get her other arm out from underneath her, and found herself trapped by the sleeve of her nightgown. She cursed in his mouth, and James pulled away.

"Sukey?"

"Sodding arm's—just a second—" She attempted to lift her hips and pull at the same time. Her arm came free more easily than she expected, and she bumped James's chest. "Sorry."

"Don't apologise." His voice was a rasp. He'd always loved it when she touched his chest, hadn't he? She ran her hand over the expanse, feeling unfamiliar muscle and hair, and wondered if she wanted the gaslight on. Possibly not.

She found a nipple and circled it with a fingertip. His intake of breath suggested nothing much had changed. "Christ. Can I touch you?"

"Within reason."

"Reason doesn't come into it." His hand slipped over the curve of her bottom, and he cupped one buttock through the linen, thumb brushing back and forward. "Ah God, Sukey. Please."

He leaned in as he spoke, meeting her lips. Susan tasted toothpowder and a tang of the wine they'd drunk, felt the prickle of stubble against her skin. They were lying on their sides, face to face, like a pair of youths. She shifted a leg—the voluminous skirts of her nightgown at least let her move—and hooked it over his hip to lean into him. His drawers and her gown did very little to muffle the pressure of his stand.

Funny what you forgot. The taste of a mouth, the press of a prick.

"Jesus. Sukey." James sounded hoarse. He still had his hand on her arse. He urged her forward and shifted himself so that her quint was against his hip. Susan couldn't help a noise in her throat, and James must have heard it because he pressed her closer, intention unmissable.

And why not? She rubbed against him, felt the pleasurable tension build. James's fingers were flexing, urging her on without exploring further. His other hand brushed against the cloth over her breasts, sending shudders through her.

"God. Yes."

He was half lying on that arm and this was a stupid position, but the pressure on her arse wasn't losing any urgency. She had always come easily this way, rubbing against him, and he'd loved it. She had his hip more or less locked between her thighs now; she could feel his rigid stand, and shifted to press against it. James rolled his palm over her breast and squeezed gently, the way he'd known she liked. "Christ, you wonderful witch. Your tits. Ah God, I want to see you come. Is there any chance that you'd care to have the light on, or the nightgown off, or both? I would do—not murder, but certainly a great deal to see you."

Did she want to be naked in his view? She was older, but so was he, and she wanted to see the way he'd filled out.

Oh, what the hell. This couldn't get any more foolish.

"You do the light, and I'll get this thing off."

James found her lips and kissed her gently. "No, I'll do the lights and then I shall remove the...thing with all due care and attention."

"Will you indeed?"

"I'm virtually a condemned man. This is a last request."

"Hmph. When I prove your innocence, you'll have to pay me back."

"Done."

She rolled off, and shoved the covers down as James stood and lit a single gas-lamp. Susan shut her eyes as it flared to life, and opened them to see him standing by the bed, looking down.

He really was a lot bigger. Youthful lankiness had been replaced by extremely solid shoulders and a burly chest, sprinkled with dark hair. His upper arms were stained blue with tattoos. He looked huge in the dim light, his eyes shadowed. The drawers against which his stand strained were not an aesthetic touch, but Susan liked that they were still on, in principle at least.

"What I would like to do," James said, deep and low, "is to work my way under that frankly unflattering gown and remove it from the hem upwards."

She stretched her arms above her head, a deliberate motion. "I didn't pick it for its attractiveness."

"I'm glad to hear that. I should have started to question your judgement."

"If you dislike it so much, you'd better hurry up."

He put a knee on the bottom of the bed, which made it dip notably, and crawled over to her. Susan watched him, watched the muscles of his back and shoulders, waiting. He cupped her foot in one big hand and stroked up the sole with a thumb, making her shiver.

"Your feet are still cold."

"I could wear bedsocks."

"Is that a threat?" The pad of his thumb rubbed against her toes. It felt surprisingly good. "You have such…Susan feet. Utterly characteristic."

"Bony?"

"Sharp, and highly practical. Long toes. Helps for climbing."

He slid his hand around, up, over her ankle. Susan let her head drop back, and felt him tug at the hem of her heavy, plain, sensible nightgown. She ought to have brought a lacy thing of the French sort that actresses wore, if only she'd owned one. She crooked her knees up a little so he could push the folds of material out of the way, and felt a hand slide up her calf, then the warmth of a kiss.

"Mmm."

"Mmm," he agreed against her skin. He was kissing his way up, she realised, above the knee of one leg and then the other, slow and careful, as if she were someone to be worshipped. A hand came to rest on her thigh. "Can I move this gown up further?"

"In your own time."

A ghost of a laugh, and then, unmistakably, the swipe of a tongue over her inner thigh. Susan breathed, in and out, feeling herself quiver. He pushed the acres of cloth up further, exposing her, and she heard a very definite and heartfelt moan.

"Oh Christ." He shifted, and she opened her eyes to see him sit up, with a pained expression. His gaze met hers, and he ran his hands up both thighs at once, gentle but firm. "God. You're twice as beautiful as I remembered."

"Doesn't add up to much."

"You must be joking." One thumb was right at the top of her inner thigh, just brushing against the curls. "This is… I will die happy. I want to touch you."

"What's stopping you?"

"Vivid awareness of the eight-inch steel hatpins within easy reach."

And that did it. *That* was joy. A man who asked was good, a man who touched her so worshipfully was better, but a man who noticed her precautionary weaponry and appreciated it—that shot straight through her nerves with a tingling glee that reminded her of the old days, and the wicked pleasure she and Justin had taken in their fraud. Kindred spirits.

So she lifted one leg, rested her foot on his broad shoulder, and said, "Permission to carry on."

"Oh, Jesus." James dived in. He kissed her curls, breath warm against her, and then gave a long slow lick, and Susan dropped her head back, wound her fingers in his hair, and let him work.

He was good at it. Very good. Susan's best experiences with this had been with women, but clearly someone had talked him through it at some point, because this was just right. His tongue moved steadily, concentrating on the nub of pleasure with relentless application, no veering about. Susan grunted appreciation, focusing on the feel of it, and almost jumped as a finger probed at her slick entrance.

"No?" James asked, so close she could feel the vibration of the sound.

"Yes." She parted her legs a little more and couldn't stifle a moan as he slid one thick finger inside her. "Oh, God, yes."

He moaned against her quint, but his tongue moved steadily, caressing, devouring her. His finger slid in and out and his thumb brushed her skin, and Susan came in his mouth, thrashing against him, clutching his head, hips jerking without restraint.

"My God," she managed after a few moments. Her clitoris felt raw with sensation, and she was soaked. "That was…very acceptable."

"I'm glad to hear it." James pushed himself up to sit on his knees, with some care for what looked like a rampant stand. "I'd have said glorious."

"It was better for me," she assured him.

He rocked a hand from side to side. "And we still haven't got rid of this gown. I would very much like to see your tits again. I've missed them."

"I'm not the only overdressed one. I don't suppose you have any johnnies, at all?"

"All I have in the world is an opal necklace; I didn't stop for prophylactics. I regret that more than I can tell you, but here we are. Sit up?" He stretched out a hand as he spoke. Susan took it, letting him pull her up because her muscles were excessively relaxed, and wriggled the gown out from underneath her. James tugged it up, over her head, and tossed it to the floor without ceremony. "Oh, God."

She'd never had much in the way of bosom and the situation hadn't improved. He seemed happy with what he saw, nevertheless. She sat a little straighter, pulling her shoulders back a touch, for posture. "Ahem. Drawers?"

James pushed them down. His stand was impressive, in proportion to the rest of him, and glistened at the tip with damp. He looked really quite good, she had to admit.

"On your back."

James kicked the drawers off, crawled up the bed, and rolled to his back as ordered. Susan knelt up, and slid her hand through the coarse hair over his chest, thumbing a nipple. His lips were slightly parted and he looked dazed, which was reasonable considering the amount of blood currently unavailable to his head. She flattened her palm over a pectoral muscle and dragged her fingers down.

"You've filled out."

"Honest toil."

She grinned, knowing it would look wicked, and saw the answering light in his eyes, so she dropped her head to his chest and gently bit at one nipple.

"Christ!"

He'd always been sensitive there. Susan teased at the nipple with her tongue, felt it harden. James had a hand in her hair, holding it loosely, and his chest vibrated with a deep and barely audible groan. She moved her attention to the other nipple, enjoying the way his sounds turned to pleas, until she felt it was time. She pulled away, sat up, and wrapped her hand around his prick.

"Jesus." That was rather high. "I'll be seconds."

"Exercise self control." She let go and swung a knee over him, sitting astride his belly. She was wet against his skin. His eyes were hooded.

"Susan. Christ." He ran both hands up her sides and cupped her breasts. "Whatever you want."

She arched her back, loving the way his lips parted, like the unguarded boy he'd been when the world was young. "Have you got a grip on yourself?"

"That's your job." His thumbs circled her nipples. "These are still wonderful."

She bumped her bottom against his stand. "This isn't bad." She pushed herself up and over it to sit on his thighs, with some regret. It was a few days since her last monthlies, not worth the risk. She took hold of his thick erection instead and began to stroke it, watching the way James's mouth opened in silent pleasure, his heavy-lidded eyes almost shut.

"Susan. Sukey. Fuck me."

She wished she could. It would be so easy to straddle him now, and he looked so vulnerable for all his size. So easily manipulated, so slaved to desire, so lost in it. She ran her hand up and down his length, slicked the head with her thumb, and then leaned forward and took him in her mouth.

"Christ! Oh Christ, yes like that. Yes. I won't last."

Susan grunted to indicate that was all right, sliding her lips up and down. His fingers scraped her scalp, flexing desperately. He was in his mid-thirties and it felt like the first time all over again, with the astonishing thrill of power it gave her. She'd forgotten how grateful he'd been when they fucked, as if every encounter had been a gift, and she'd been a miracle.

"Going to spend. Sukey!"

Susan let go with her hand and gripped his hips, working him with lips only. He gave a strangled groan, bucking and spilling into her mouth, and she held on, tonguing his prick until he gasped surrender.

She pushed herself off him and went to the bathroom to spit and wash. When she returned he was on his side, watching her. He looked like a statue, naked and impressive, member slack but still long.

"What are you thinking?"

"You look like that thing, what's it called. The Dying Gaul."

"I feel it," James said. "Shall I turn out the light?"

"I'll do it."

She did so, and made her way cautiously back to the bed. A heave of the springs suggested he'd shifted to make room. She climbed next to him, and had a brief, absurd thought that perhaps she ought to have put on her nightgown again, but discarded that. She lay instead, facing away from him, as pleasure slowly ebbed away and doubt rushed in to fill the gap it left.

James pulled up the covers, then his arm came over her. She didn't particularly like being held at night, but she could always push him off later. His breath was hot in her hair.

"Sukey," he mumbled.

Susan, she probably should have said. "What?"

"Still glorious. Glorious witch."

"Same to you. Go to sleep."

He did, snoring within seconds, which was entirely to be expected. She didn't shrug him off all the same but lay, with his body warm against hers and his arm heavy on her side, staring into the dark.

CHAPTER NINE

When Templeton woke, the bed was empty.

He took a moment to work out where he was, and several more to decide if last night had in fact happened. The dried patch on his belly suggested it had, and anyway, his imagination wasn't nearly that good.

Sukey.

He was not sure at all why she'd kissed him, and had a sudden spasmodic thought that it might have been an attempt to control the situation by giving what she feared would otherwise be taken. No, that had definitely not been the case, he decided, after a frantic check of his memories. She had unquestionably given permission, not to say orders, and also she hadn't killed him in his sleep.

So where had she gone, and why, and how would she want him to behave now?

He didn't delude himself they could slip back into their old relations easily. Susan had always been guarded and prickly and she'd honed her defences over the years. She hadn't given an inch, verbally at least. She'd chosen to bed him for her own reasons; he would not be fool enough to assume that entitled him to anything else, even civility. Today would almost certainly be a field of mantraps.

Still, if he'd wanted an easy life, he'd have done as his father told him.

He washed and dressed, taking care because today, like every day since the murder, might be his last day of freedom. If he'd just had his last night of freedom, it wasn't a bad way to go.

He emerged into the main room of the suite, and was relieved to see Susan. She sat by the window with a notebook on her lap, glaring out with an expression that threatened the fog.

"Good morning," he said, and swallowed *Mrs. Ranelagh* as too provocative.

"Mph," Susan responded, adding, "Morning," a moment later.

"Shall I order breakfast?"

"Tea. Kippers."

Templeton pressed the bell, and gave the order. Once the man had gone, he said, "So. Mortlake?"

"Contact Crozier first. I want to get hold of him this evening if possible."

"I'll do my best. What's my role: your assistant?"

"Too much trouble. Everyone will assume you're my superior anyway."

"Colleague at most," Templeton said firmly. "I'm unqualified to lead."

Susan scowled at her notebook. "Where do we get you a jeweller's loupe?"

"We can pick one up on the way to Waterloo. You look annoyed. Can I help?"

"There's a number of things I'd like to know, but I doubt you know any of them either. We didn't finish talking about your father."

"I'm fairly sure we did. What else is there?"

"What if you went back?" Susan said. "Presented yourself as the black sheep made good?"

"I doubt he'd care."

"He's old. He might want to know you're still alive."

"He'd probably accuse me of hoping for an inheritance. I could never do anything right in his eyes, just as Neville could do no wrong.

And when Neville was at fault, of course, he blamed me." It had always been the case. He'd tried and tried to please his father, and never understood why he failed. In the end he'd stopped trying and started misbehaving. It hurt much less to be dismissed, belittled, or punished if one had done something to deserve it.

"I remember," Susan said. "I don't suppose you ever found out why."

"I'm unquestionably his son, and my mother didn't die till a few years after my birth. I don't recall a time when he found me tolerable so if I did anything offensive to start it all off, it was at an age so young one might think he would have got over it. As far as I can tell, he simply didn't like me. He never deprived me of food or clothing, but he made it clear that everything I ever did or said was wrong. I dare say I was trying to him. He was approaching fifty when I was born and probably found a boisterous child tiresome."

"He should have thought about that before he spawned one. Isn't that what you people have governesses for, and nurseries at the other end of the house?"

"Well, that was another sore point, the lack of a vast house. He spent his life waiting to inherit Great-Uncle Richard's home and fortune, and the old fellow lived to almost ninety. I dare say Father would have found me more tolerable if he hadn't been so irritated by that."

"People who spend their lives on the scrounge for inheritance deserve what they get. Particularly if the will is changed and they get nothing."

Templeton couldn't argue. He had adored his great-uncle, a marvellous, trenchant old bachelor who laughed at noisy boys, and had welcomed the young James to his sprawling home north of London for the duration of every holiday. His father had barely managed to conceal his resentment at the old man's long life. "I don't suppose it would do anyone good to spend their life in anticipation of a grand house and a lot of money but not get it until they're sixty."

"He could have filled the time with something. Work, perhaps."

"But he was the son of a marquis, so he preferred to live on his position and expectations. Which he could do because Great-Uncle was extraordinarily generous, and kept his promise about the inheritance as well. It's more than I'd have done in his place. He died when I was thirteen and Father didn't even pretend to be sorry. Too busy spending his money." That was when the boy James had really started to go wrong, when his feelings for his father had turned to angry resentment, and a contempt he hadn't troubled to hide. He wondered if things would have been different if he'd had the old man's love and guidance for longer. "I missed Great-Uncle dreadfully, you know. He always stood up for me."

"I remember," Susan said. "You talked about him a lot."

"I expect I did."

"I used to—" She stopped herself, brushed that away.

"What?"

"Oh, nothing. Stupid. You talked about his house a lot, with all the trees to climb and rooms to explore, and growing up playing there."

It had been the best playground in the world for an active boy, and he'd run around the grounds acting out endless games of pirates and soldiers while Susan, just a year older, had defrauded people for a living. She'd lived in a cramped little house in a sordid little alley and counted herself lucky, while he'd had an estate to play in. He wondered now just how much he'd mourned his lost Eden to a girl who'd barely seen a tree, how thoughtless he'd been. Had she wished for a childhood playing at Arrandene too, or had that been unthinkable? Had she ever played at all?

Neither of them spoke for a moment, then Susan shook her head and Templeton cleared his throat. "Anyway, I don't have any desire to speak to my father now, and I don't see what I'd gain by it. Why?"

"Just thinking. Never mind. Get on and contact Crozier, would you?"

That was all she had to say until they were on the train to Mortlake. They shopped on the way to Waterloo station, purchasing Templeton a smart new hat, a notebook, and a jeweller's loupe. He'd sent Jerry two messages by circuitous routes, and was aware how much he hoped he'd get a reply. He was also aware that he didn't want to return to the dark and nightmarish house by the river. The prospect made him twitch.

He kept his hands very still and relaxed, his face calm, and didn't think it fooled Susan for a minute. Not that she paid him any attention: her eyes were focused on a point somewhere above his shoulder, as though she were trying to stare a hole in the wall. He knew that look. Susan was scheming.

Mortlake was a pretty little village on the river with which he was entirely too familiar, having visited three times in the weeks before the robbery. He'd sported a sizeable moustache then, which was now gone, but his size wasn't conducive to anonymity. He made sure he kept his face and posture relaxed as he engaged a hansom cab; the driver gave a sharp whistle when he requested Sorley House.

"Press, are you? Because that young chap isn't talking to the papers. Which is to say, I'll take you there but you'd best engage me to wait or you'll have a walk back."

"Not press, but thank you for the warning," Templeton said, holding the door for Susan. He climbed in after her, and grabbed a strap as the cabbie set off. "I didn't think the newspapers would still be coming here."

She shrugged. "Nobody else has been interestingly murdered in a week. What's your name for this? No previous alibis, no first names as surnames, and—"

"—no streets, I know. What about Harry Rawling, in tribute to Aunt Harriet? I find actual names have a conviction that ones you make up often lack."

"As long as they don't belong to someone famous," Susan said. "There was a housebreaker round our way taking a look at a property, and when a constable asked what he was up to, he gave his name as Charles Dickens. He'd heard it somewhere and thought it sounded good."

"Marvellous." He squinted out of the window. "Not far now."

"How would you know? You haven't been here before, Mr. Rawling."

"True. Are you getting cold feet?"

"My feet are always cold. You complained about that often enough."

Are we going to acknowledge last night? Templeton decided not to ask. They had a job on, one to which Susan was giving her full attention. He needed her formidable powers to prove his innocence, not soothe his self-esteem. All the same, a mention would have been nice.

The cab trundled on, out of Mortlake village and along the winding lanes past Pink's Farm to Sorley House. They turned up the drive and came to the gates, which were frankly inadequate: he'd scaled the walls without any trouble on his way in and out. Of course, they hadn't had a man on duty then. One was at his post now.

The cab stopped, and Susan poked her head out, along with a hand and a folded paper that served as their introduction. They were allowed through, and shortly found themselves in the main hall of Sorley House. It was significantly less sinister in daylight.

They were conducted in to a sitting room, and a few minutes later, a young man arrived. He was sunburned in the way some white men went, baked red rather than brown.

"Good day," he said, shaking Templeton's hand and then, since she had extended it, Susan's. "I'm Harrison Stroud. I understand you're private enquiry agents?"

"That's right. My name is Rawling and this is Miss Lazarus. Our condolences on your tragic loss." He went for charm, since it seemed the area Susan was least likely to have under control.

"Thank you, but I don't see any need to engage a detective. The police are working hard on the case."

"So I should hope," Susan said. "We aren't touting for work, Mr. Stroud. I'm here on behalf of a client whose case may relate tangentially to yours."

"Tangentially, eh?"

"Detective Inspector Wiley authorised us to come and ask a very few questions and examine the scene. I have a note here, and I believe he's written to you."

"Yes, yes, he has." Mr. Stroud took the letter she held out and scanned it. "He requests I extend assistance to Miss Susan Lazarus. I suppose that's you. Eh—"

"Mr. Rawling is working with me," Susan said. "May I ask you a few questions first? And then we'll take a look at the upstairs rooms."

"Yes. I suppose. Eh, do you want to speak to Mr. Brayton too? My uncle's lawyer. He was here on the night. I could go get him—"

"Please don't trouble yourself." Susan shut the door as she spoke. "We'll talk to him later."

Mr. Stroud's brows drew together. "I'll just order tea?"

"Not on our behalf. Do sit down." She kept her eyes on him till, reluctantly, he seated himself. "How long did you know your uncle, Mr. Stroud?"

"Just a few months. I only arrived in this country in August, in response to his letter inviting me. I knew my mother had had a brother, of course, but they lost touch long before she died."

"You were in India, is that right?" Templeton asked.

"Yes, I was born there. Do you know the country?"

"I'm afraid not. I was in the United States for a few years, though. Travel broadens the mind, doesn't it? Have you lived anywhere but India?"

"No, not at all, never. I came to England direct."

"Good journey?"

"Not bad. It took just twelve and a half days, can you imagine? Steamships are a wonder."

"Aren't they," Templeton agreed heartily. He could see Susan's nostril flare at the chit-chat, the tiny movement conveying all the annoyance of folded arms and a tapping toe. "So your uncle tracked you down, and wrote to ask you to come to England?"

"That's right. I wasn't sure at first, as I had to leave my post, but it was an adventure, and he paid my passage. I thought, if nothing else I'll have a chance to see the homeland, eh? So I came and he met me in London, and it was as if I'd known him all my life."

"You hit it off?"

"He felt like the grandfather I'd never met. Marvellous old man." A long flat *a* to the adjective, like a sheep's bleat. "I felt as though I'd come home. He made me an allowance at once, and intended to help me find an occupation here in due course. He wanted me to make my home in Sorley House with him. And then it was all snatched away." He pressed his lips together.

"Dreadful," Susan said. "Mr. Brayton wasn't so welcoming, I understand."

"Cecil was very protective of Uncle Monty," Mr. Stroud said. "I think he'll admit that he had a bee in his bonnet about me."

"Are you getting on better now?"

"Murder puts other troubles into the shade. I understand why he wanted to be sure of me—he was a good friend to my uncle. It got tiring after a while, but it's all one now, eh?"

"Not really," Susan said. "Since, if you weren't the real Harrison Stroud, you wouldn't inherit."

"Well, that's true, but I am." Mr. Stroud gave her a smile.

"You were discussing the matter with Mr. Brayton at the time of the murder, I believe? I wonder that didn't alert the murderer as he came in."

"We were speaking very quietly, so as not to disturb Uncle Monty. Or maybe he heard us and thought we'd be distracted by our conversation?"

Susan nodded. "And you were together when the housekeeper raised the alarm?"

"That's right."

"Dressed, not in your night clothes?"

"It wasn't a discussion I'd have had in my nightshirt. I beg your pardon, ma'am," he added hastily.

"Mmm," Susan said. "Had you come to an understanding or were you still at loggerheads?"

"I wouldn't say loggerheads. I had told Cecil everything I could. I was pretty fed up—seemed like he wouldn't believe me whatever I did. I said to him, straight out, 'Do you have anything else to ask?' and he said he didn't. I said, 'Well, then.' And that was when we heard the screams. I ran out and saw Mrs. Hendrick with her hand to her heart, and a man running down the stairs."

"Did you get a look at him?" Templeton asked, for form's sake.

"It was too dark. A big brute, he was, bigger than you, Mr. Rawling. Mrs. Hendrick gasped out, 'Murder!' and I looked into the room and saw Uncle Monty on the floor."

"That must have been a terrible shock."

"I can't tell you, Miss Lazarus. My uncle, who'd been so kind and taken me as his own—an old man, and in poor health—and Mrs. Hendrick gasping and screaming. Cecil took her away at once."

"Did you try to help your uncle?"

"It was all I could think of. I went down on my knees and took hold of him but I saw at once that the only thing I could do for him was pursue the swine who did it. A man learns not to stand around waiting where I've lived. We chased the fellow, but lost him when he plunged into the river."

"You didn't try to swim after him?"

Mr. Stroud shook his head. "Swimming the Thames at night, in this weather, was the act of a desperate man. It wouldn't surprise me if his body was trapped under some bit of lumber, somewhere in the depths of the river."

"A well-deserved end," Susan said. "Who shot at him?"

"Me. When you've lived in dangerous places…" He let that tail off.

"I quite understand. What was your job?"

"I was a clerk in a shipping office."

"Is that risky work?"

"Well, India, you know. The cobras, the tigers. I shouldn't want to alarm you, Miss Lazarus."

"Thank you for your consideration. Was Cecil Brayton a danger to you?"

"What's that?"

"You went from a conversation in his room directly to Mr. Montmorency's room and then immediately chased after the murderer, yes? I wondered why you had a gun with you."

Stroud's mouth tightened. "I didn't have it with me. I fetched it from my room when I realised my uncle was dead."

"Oh, I see. So you keep it loaded?"

"Of course not. I never imagined I would need it here. I loaded it quickly and went in pursuit of the villain."

Susan nodded. "And what happened when you returned to the house?"

"I found Cecil in grave distress. He'd discovered poor Peevy, the valet. We sent for the police, and then we just had to try to come to terms with what had happened."

"Very distressing. And you are your uncle's sole heir?"

"Except for the usual bequests to servants."

"He was a rich man."

"I would rather have had another ten years with him than all his wealth," Mr. Stroud said. "And for all we didn't get on before my poor uncle's death, I believe Cecil will tell you that too."

"I don't doubt it," Susan said. "It's fortunate you were with him. Nobody can suspect you, whereas under other circumstances…"

"Oh, I'd doubtless have been suspected all my life. Funny to think I should be grateful for Cecil's doubts, eh?"

"Very funny. May I look around? See the room?"

Stroud shifted. "You didn't explain what your case has to do with my poor uncle."

"It is an extremely sensitive matter. I'm sure you understand," Susan said. "I think Inspector Wilby has expressed his full confidence and requested we be given all assistance?"

"Yes…"

"There you are, then." She rose. "Shall we begin?"

Stroud looked dubious, but conducted them upstairs. Susan asked to see around the first floor before entering any rooms.

"My uncle's room is the first door," Mr. Stroud explained, as they walked round. "The valet had a room with a connecting door, here. My room is the next, on the corner, and here is the one Cecil Brayton always uses. He's here for a couple of days to go through papers. Then there are two more guest bedrooms, my uncle's study, a lumber room, and the housekeeper's room."

"All the way round the landing." Susan surveyed the layout. "And you didn't hear anything of the valet having his throat cut, or a heavy blow to your uncle's head? Violent death is rarely neat or quiet."

"It was not neat," Mr. Stroud said. "It was ghastly. As to quiet, this is an old house, surrounded by trees. It's noisy at night, when the wind blows. For all I know I did hear some thump or creak, some sound of my uncle's death, and disregarded it. The thought haunts me."

"I dare say," Susan said. "You said Mr. Brayton was here: I'd like to speak to him now. Perhaps Mr. Rawling can look around while I do that."

Templeton took that hint. He headed for Brayton's room, shut the door gently, and pulled the curtains.

He had his answer at once. Light spilled across the floorboards from the brightly lit hallway through the gap under the door, and he could hear the sound of Susan's voice, and Stroud's lower response. This was not a tightly fitted door. He'd have heard the men speak.

That was heartening. He opened the curtains and, since he was here, carried out a rapid search of the room and the lawyer Brayton's possession, finding nothing of interest. He had no trouble hearing when a set of footsteps came up the stairs. He emerged, and met Mr. Stroud on the landing.

"What were you up to in Cecil's room?" Stroud asked, sounding decidedly hostile.

"I needed to check the sightlines and windows. A matter of triangulation, you understand, on what can be seen from outside." Templeton put his hands together at angles in a demonstrative way.

"Tri—?"

"I need to check the same in Mr. Montmorency's room. Shall we?"

He took the heir by the arm and urged him gently into the master bedroom. Stroud said, "You still haven't explained what you're doing here."

"Following up. Miss L. leaves no stone unturned. I say, stone, that's jolly good. Like jewels, you know." He adopted a jovial, all-men-together tone, and thought he saw Stroud relax a fraction. "I'll have a quick look, and we'll be able to leave you alone."

He walked around the bed, right over where Montmorency had died. The door set in the wall on the far side of the bed was papered over, so its outline was just visible in daylight. It had definitely been shut, and the other side dark. "Is that the valet's room?"

"That's right."

"Poor chap. He hadn't been with Mr. Montmorency long, had he?"

"A few months only. Uncle was very happy with him."

"He was presumably killed to stop him raising the alarm. In his room? And you didn't hear a thing." Templeton shook his head. "The murderer must have been very competent."

"The Inspector suggested that he might have killed Peevy first, to prevent him interfering, and only then gone in, forced Uncle to open the safe-room, and killed him."

"Well, well." Templeton walked back to the window and squinted out at imaginary sightlines. "Do you intend to take up your uncle's trade?"

"I don't think so. My uncle talked about teaching me the business, but there was no time, and my heart isn't in it since he was killed for their sake."

"Very understandable. So you'll sell the stock, in due course."

"What else can I do? I've no other use for sapphires. Jewels."

"Indeed not." Templeton had no idea what to do here, but his role was presumably to keep Stroud busy while Susan did whatever she was up to. "May I have a look in the jewel room?"

Stroud opened it, not without some uncertain looks. It was as Templeton recalled, a windowless store, filled with half-height cabinets under shelves. "Did the police look over this room when they came?"

"Yes, of course."

"I hope they were careful. I've seen the aftermath of police investigations where they've done more damage than the burglars."

Mr. Stroud gave a startled laugh. "No—no, they were very careful."

"Jolly good." Templeton looked around, at the shelves. "May I open the drawers?"

"I suppose so. What are you looking for?"

"Nothing I expect to find." That was the sort of annoyingly gnomic way detectives spoke in stories. It seemed to work now. He went through the drawers, which held enough in the way of stones, set, loose, and uncut, to fill a man's pockets several times over.

"Remarkable that the killer didn't help himself to more. Is this all?" He shut the last drawer.

"I believe so."

"Have any stones been taken out of here, sold or stored or given away, since the murder?"

"Of course not. Probate has yet to be declared."

"Naturally. Do you have a list of what your uncle held?"

"I'm not sure I should give that to you. I've answered your questions to the best of my ability, but you said yourself your investigation is not to do with my uncle's death and I don't see I have to cooperate."

"Well, you don't," Templeton said reasonably. "Nevertheless, if you—"

Mr. Stroud wasn't listening. He went to the door and called, "Cecil? Cecil!"

The lawyer, a prickly old gentleman, came up the stairs. He already looked pinched around the mouth, and Templeton and Susan found themselves on the doorstep in short order after that.

Susan accepted her hat and coat from a frosty servant. "Well, it's a nice day for a walk. Along the river?"

Templeton followed her, down the path to the Thames that he'd run on the night of the murder. It had seemed significantly further in the dark, with men on his tail and bullets flying. Susan's sensible buttoned boots crunched on the stony mud. They could see all around, along the bare banks of the river and across its gently swelling grey-brown expanse to the faint lines of buildings on the north side.

"Go on," she said. "You're bursting with news."

"Damned right I am. I don't know where to start."

"With the guest room. Was it sound-proof or could you hear me in the hall?"

"I could hear you, and see light under the door. I will swear to it that there was no light when I was there in the night, and no voices. I would have heard them, I am sure of it. They're lying."

"Yes, dear. That much has been obvious from the start," Susan said. "What else?"

"Stroud's accent, that's bloody what."

Susan frowned. "He didn't speak with an Indian accent or intonation, but I've met British men brought up there who keep to the Queen's English as though their lives depended on it. He did have a couple of odd vowels—"

"Not odd," Templeton said. "Australian. It wasn't continual, but there were moments when his concentration slipped and I would stake my life on Australia."

"Would you indeed. And you got him to say that he hadn't travelled, too. Nicely done, James."

"Moreover," Templeton went on, trying not to feel puffed up at a crumb of praise, "I got a look in the jewel store."

Susan gave him a look. "What for, old time's sake? Did you see anything useful?"

"It's what I didn't see. A very fine sapphire bracelet that I noted on my previous visit was gone. Stroud insisted nothing had been removed or sold and that the police hadn't robbed them, but it wasn't there."

"Are you sure of that?"

"It was on the shelf when I took the Samsonoff. Eleven graduated cabochon sapphires set in a Russian gold curb chain; I'd estimate the central one at a trifle over one and a half carats."

"All right, you're sure."

"I went through the safe-room looking for it," Templeton said. "Stroud declined to let me see his uncle's inventory. He also happened to mention sapphires in a casual way earlier, as an example of jewels he had no use for but to sell. Possibly that was coincidence—"

"Or perhaps he had sapphires on his mind. Interesting. Anything else? However small."

"I don't think so," Templeton said. "Except that Stroud made a point of his theory that the valet Peevy was killed first—got out of the way so the killer could force Montmorency to open the safe."

"I bet he did," Susan muttered. "Well."

That was all she had to say, it seemed. Templeton waited as long as he could, which was about thirty seconds, and was forced to ask, "And how about you? What did you get?"

"I asked Brayton to explain why he'd been so suspicious of Stroud, and his reply was in effect an assurance that he'd examined Stroud's credentials to the letter and they were impeccable. I pressed him on the problem, and he eventually said that he finds returned expatriates intolerable. That seems to me a bit thin."

"Oh, I don't know. If you ask me, the most suspicious thing about that entire visit was a supposed Anglo-Indian returnee who mentioned tigers without twenty minutes of hunting anecdotes."

"God." Susan made a face like a wet cat. "Those dullards really are India's revenge, aren't they? But you're right, Stroud's cobras and tigers were pretty thin. Of course, he might have been embroidering because life as a shipping clerk in Calcutta isn't a matter of exotic Eastern wonder—"

"Or it could be because he's an Australian who's never set foot there."

"Quite. Brayton also made a point of noting that Stroud had been with him at the time of the murder, courageous in the aftermath, and devastated by the death—all in grudging tones."

"Do you deduce something from that?"

"It barely needs deduction. Brayton is giving Stroud an alibi while making it clear that he's not doing so out of friendship. And he was in charge of checking Stroud was the right man. The scepticism makes his endorsement more convincing."

"Montmorency was famous for his stubbornness in the trade," Templeton observed. "He'd always dig his heels in rather than back down."

"So Brayton provided a false candidate, plus the opposition that would cement his position. It was a fraud, and the fraudsters are giving one another alibis for murder."

"Even so, though, why would they kill the man? He'd given Stroud a generous allowance and made his will in his favour. Would you not wait for him to die?"

"Start at the other end," Susan said. "It was a double murder. Why kill the valet?"

"Stroud suggested it was in case he came to help or raised the alarm," Templeton said dubiously. "But Montmorency could just as well have been woken by the noise of a man having his throat cut in the next room."

"For heaven's sake, James, he was in on it with you," Susan said. "He got you a key. Did he know when you were coming?"

"Yes. He left the door unbolted."

"He was in league with Brayton and Stroud, who set you up to take the blame for the murder. It's obvious he killed Montmorency."

Templeton stopped still. Susan didn't. He stared at her back for a couple of seconds, then extended his stride to catch up. "The *valet*?"

"He was the one man who wouldn't have to cross the hall to gain access. That's why you didn't hear the murderer moving around: he wasn't. He waited for you to come in, slipped into the next room through the connecting door, and killed the old man ready for you."

"So who killed the valet?"

"Stroud, I expect," Susan said. "Peevy set you up, waited for you to arrive, and killed Montmorency. He then lurked in his room waiting for events to unfold. Stroud sent the household to chase after you while Brayton took the housekeeper to lie down. I think that's when Stroud killed Peevy, in the moments while he was supposedly loading his gun. Maybe Peevy was told to let himself be knocked out, to allay suspicion? And instead Stroud cut his throat, which would explain any blood on Peevy's person."

"Whereas blood on Stroud could be explained because he had hurled himself on his uncle's body."

"It would be easily done. The housekeeper was in hysterics, and everyone else was off after the fleeing villain. That's you."

"Yes, thank you." The smell of the river mingled with coalsmoke was very strong here, reminding him of that ghastly swim. "Why would Stroud and Brayton kill their ally?"

"With him gone, who could testify against them? I don't think you were meant to survive the night, but if they had been forced to take you alive, what use would your claims of innocence have been with the necklace in your pocket and an eyewitness to you standing over the corpse? Once they were rid of Peevy they were home and dry."

"Christ. So now Stroud can inherit Montmorency's fortune, and Brayton…what does he get?"

"A split of the profits, presumably."

"Would that be enough to kill his old friend and client for?"

Susan shrugged. "People murder for shillings if they need them badly enough. This sapphire whatnot that's missing, would it be easily sold?"

"If it hasn't been reported stolen. I wouldn't have thought it wise of them to start selling the goods before probate is granted, though, particularly not identifiable pieces. I'd wait."

"It suggests an urgent need for money. Hmm. The question is, did Brayton come up with the idea for the whole thing and recruit Peevy and Stroud to play valet and heir respectively? Or did someone else give Brayton his orders and provide Stroud and Peevy as accomplices? Peevy was relatively new to Montmorency's service, wasn't he?"

"About four months, I believe."

"So he came in not long before Stroud turned up. Well. I wonder what happened to the previous valet."

"It's a conspiracy," Templeton said. "An actual conspiracy, against me. Christ."

"You look surprised. I did try to tell you."

"Yes, but..." Templeton wasn't sure how to express the combination of shock, fear, and affront that someone he'd never met had sat down to plot his entrapment and death. He'd plotted to relieve people of their prized possessions often enough, but three killings?

"This is a fucking outrage," he said. "But surely the police can look into all this now. It won't be hard to take Brayton and Stroud's accounts apart."

"James," Susan said patiently. "We have nothing to give the police. Everything we know is based on what you witnessed when you were on your way in to steal the necklace. Wilby won't hold off on prosecuting an obvious murderer caught red-handed if all I have to give him is the suggestion that Stroud's accent is a few thousand miles adrift. Which is the more plausible story, a lone burglar committing murder, or a complex conspiracy?"

"But this is where we started," Templeton said. They were approaching Mortlake now, with several houses visible. He took Susan's arm and tugged her to a stop on the riverbank. "We began with the fact that nobody would believe me except you, and we're still here. If we can't give any of this to the police—"

"It is *not* where we started." She scowled up into his face. "We've found the cracks in their stories; all we have to do is apply a crowbar. We need to discover who Francis Peevy was—I wonder if Wilby will let me have a photograph of the corpse—who sold this sapphire bracelet, who 'Harrison Stroud' really is, and the location of the real nephew. Find any of those, particularly the last, and the whole tower of lies comes tumbling down."

"And how will we do that? What are the odds we can do any of it before the police catch up with me?"

"Fuck the odds," Susan said. "Are you fighting this or not?"

Her eyes were set on his, alight with fierce certainty and a kind of urgent determination, willing him to believe. She stood foursquare on the muddy bank of the reeking river in her sensible boots, with her sensible high-necked blouse and plainly pinned hair looped under her sensible hat, and Templeton could have gone to his knees there and then for wild wonder.

Instead he kissed her.

He felt her little intake of breath, and a fraction of a second's stillness, as though she were deciding how to react. Then her lips parted and softened against his, and he slid his hands onto her shoulder and down her back, astonished again that this was possible. Susan in his arms, her hands around his waist, her mouth on his.

She pulled her head away, an abrupt motion, but left her hands where they were. "James…"

"A gentleman would normally offer some sort of reassurance in this situation," he said. "I wish I had some. There's no benefit whatsoever to you in all this, is there?"

"Not much. There's every chance you'll be arrested and hanged, and even if you do survive, you're a professional criminal. Association with you is liable to ruin my reputation on so many levels I can't even count them, including with my guvnor."

"It's lucky I've learned not to expect polite reassurances from you." She was still within the circle of his arms, resting her hands on his waist. "I'll go if you want. I shouldn't have dragged you into—"

"I was not *dragged*."

"I shouldn't have humbly requested your help in the first place. I had no business asking you. Another stupid, selfish act. I'd rather vanish and take my chances than cause you more trouble."

"Excuse me," Susan said. "Do you think I'm bottling it?"

He gave an exasperated sigh. "Of course you're not: I am. I've made a bloody mess of your life and mine once already. I will not do it twice."

"You didn't kill him. We can prove it."

"For my benefit. What's in it for you?"

"Wait till you get the invoice," Susan said. "You aren't a murderer, and that matters. Two men are dead, at least one of whom didn't deserve to die, and the killers are liable to get away not just scot-free but a great deal richer, and *that* matters. I want to straighten this out because it needs straightening, and I don't need your permission to continue any more than I would to stop. You can give up and run away if you like, but I'm not."

Templeton hadn't realised it was possible to feel worse. Clearly he'd underestimated himself. "I won't run. As long as this is what you want to do."

"I want you to clear your name." Susan's hands tightened on his waist. "I want *you* to want that, James. It's about time."

"Templeton Lane is not a name worth clearing. Certainly not worth risking yours for."

He felt her stiffen at that, and she stepped out of his arms. "I'll do as I please, and I dare say so will you. Are you with me?"

"If you want me there."

"Then don't let me down. Come on, hurry up. We have murderers to catch."

CHAPTER TEN

They lunched at Waterloo on meat pies bought from a stall, and returned to the hotel in silence. Susan had a lot to think about. So, apparently, did James. It was about time, if so.

Templeton Lane is not a name worth clearing. That was true, and she had no interest in clearing it. The question was, did he?

The staff were all smiles and goodwill; the lavish suite even more luxurious than she remembered. Women could come here with lovers, luxuriate in baths, drape themselves in satin, and lie around looking alluring on the chaise longue. Susan couldn't find a way to insert herself into that picture.

"What is it?" James asked as she hung up her coat.

"What's what?"

"You look unhappy."

"I'm not. There's a conversation we haven't had, and need to."

"So we do," James said. "May I start? Whatever you choose to do, I'd like you to know you are utterly glorious, and last night was magnificent. If you want to give up on the detection and spend the remaining period before my arrest in carnal pleasure, I'd be as happy with that outcome as any. However, if you need me to pretend it never happened, I'll do that. I don't want you to regret me if you can help it, so let me know how you want to proceed and I will do my best. Is that fair?"

"I," Susan said. "Uh. What?"

"Were you not listening? Last night was wonderful," James said, with exaggerated clarity. "You are wonderful. I want to fuck you as much as is compatible with your interest and convenience."

"Uh…good?"

"Thank God I'm used to your unbelievable lack of social grace; a lesser man might feel snubbed. Clearly you have something else on your mind. What did you want to say?"

"I was planning to talk about who wants you dead."

"Oh." James paused. "I see why you were preoccupied."

"Sorry," she felt compelled to add. "I mean…" What could she say? *We don't have to discuss that now*? Of course they had to. She very much doubted there was anything he actually wanted more than survival.

Although, given he didn't believe he had a future, maybe she was wrong about that.

"We don't have to talk about last night at all," she said instead. "Or if we do, yes, I enjoyed it too and no, you needn't pretend it never happened. That's a ridiculous way to go on."

"So is not talking about important things, *Susan*. And before you say it, personal matters *are* important. It's important that you're in my life again. It's important to me to discover if, and how, I can be in yours."

"That'll be a very short conversation if I can't get you off the gallows. No, listen. I want to get this sorted out first, before we get mired in personal—" She bit back *nonsense*. It was nonsense but if she said so he might look hurt and then they might have to talk about it and…no. "Things. I'm not going to have you caught because I stopped to lounge on a chaise longue."

"Or vice versa."

"So yes, we ought to talk about you and me, but not now, because you're in danger. And you might not care what happens to you, but I do."

"Do you indeed?" He moved closer and took her hand, strong fingers engulfing hers. "Really?"

"Moderately. Don't get excited."

"Christ," James said. "Some women would give a fraction of an inch after a fellow confessed his ongoing lust and adoration."

"I didn't hear adoration."

"Well, you should have, because I adore you. I always did and you haven't changed a bit, you glorious witch."

"You called me that at Castle Speight." Susan had a squirmy feeling in her stomach. "And I punched you."

"In the solar plexus, with some force. Excellent left hook."

"Strike from the hips." The old lesson came to her lips with ease. "You weren't expecting it."

"I should have been. You keep a fellow on his toes."

His thumb was moving, tiny circles over the side of her hand. It sent spangles of sensation up her arm. She'd forgotten how overwhelming he could be in his desires, and not just physical ones. When James wanted, he did so powerfully. It was overpowering to be wanted this much.

Emma's husband wanted her, a voice in her head pointed out. Susan had no interest in being an object of someone's obsession. She was plain, abrasive, and entirely unsuited to words like *adoration*. Even so, James's focus made her feel dizzy, and tingly, and very much as if she could let the rest go and bring their existence down to this. No past, no future, no crimes or consequences, just herself and James and a bed and four walls.

"What's that thing about being in a room?" she found herself asking. "You used to say it."

"Infinite riches in a little room." James lifted his other hand to her face, and slid his fingers up her cheek and into her hair. "Marlowe, I think, unless it's Shakespeare. May I pull out your hairpins?"

"We should—oh, fuck it." They could afford an hour. He oughtn't go out again until after dark, for safety's sake. She wanted this. "If you like."

James's fingers skimmed her hair, selected a pin, pulled. She felt the weight of her hair shift slightly, a precarious sensation before the fall. He pulled out another pin, and a cluster of loops tumbled down her neck.

"God," he said. "Your hair is wonderful."

"It's nothing special."

"It's everything special." He scooped up a tendril and bent to kiss it. "Have many people told you you're beautiful since I left?"

"Almost exactly none."

"I should have come back earlier. This country's gone to rack and ruin." He slid another pin out, slowly and carefully. Susan felt coils of hair unwind and drop around her shoulders, until it was all down and James stood with a handful of pins, looking at her.

"If you put those down, one of us might not get stabbed," she suggested.

"Where's the fun in that?"

James bent his head. Susan went to tiptoes, regretting the sensible buttoned boots, and met his mouth. Strong arms wrapped around her back, one hand on her bottom. She snaked her arms around his neck, pulling him to her, and kissed him open-mouthed, hard and hungry. James grunted, dropped the hairpins on the carpet, and scooped her up off the ground to bring her face to his level. Susan clamped her knees on his waist, kissing wildly, and squeaked as he strode through to the bedroom, where he deposited her unceremoniously on the bed.

"Brute."

"Entirely." He sat on the edge of the bed, and took hold of one foot. "Allow me."

He was unbuttoning her boots. Susan let herself lie back, propped on her elbows to watch, absurdly aroused. The gentle pressure of his fingers over her ankle could have been between her legs. "You make a good lady's maid."

"It's a pleasure. A privilege, even." He eased the boot off, and stroked the sole of her foot, through her thick stocking.

"James," Susan said. "Take the other one off."

He shot her a glance. "That sounded like an order."

"It is one."

His lips curved. "Yes, ma'am."

Another row of buttons, his big, deft fingers working over the black leather. He slid the boot off her foot and paused, waiting.

"Stockings," Susan said. James inhaled audibly, then he ran his hand up her calf, under her skirts, and Susan couldn't help a moan.

"Jesus." His voice was gravelly. "The feel of you." He was working blind, but still unsnapped her stockings with impressive dexterity. Susan extended her leg to let him roll them down, one after another, and then crooked her knees as his hand slid back up, a finger probing under the edge of her drawers.

"Get those off," she said, and heard the catch of his breath. Yes, he did like her in charge. "And then I suggest you put that tongue to better use than arguing with me."

"I wouldn't dare argue," James said. "Particularly not about this." He pushed her skirts up and back. "Why women have to wear quite so much clothing—layers, ribbons, buttons, it's worse than getting into a safe."

Susan lifted her hips so he could slide her drawers down. "But worth it, surely."

"Diving for pearls is far preferable to stealing jewels," he assured her, and tossed the drawers aside. She lay, bare to the waist, legs apart, and felt like a monarch because he looked at her as though she were one. "Christ, Susan. Tell me what you want."

"Make me come. And then I'll decide what else I want from you."

"Oh Jesus," James said, and crawled between her thighs.

Christ, she loved this. Susan let herself go, concentrating on the feel of his agile tongue, the slow, arousing strokes, the way his hands gripped and flexed. He was breathing hard as he licked her, with a telltale rasp.

"Are you enjoying yourself?" she managed, and got a grunt in reply. "Ah, God. I want you in me."

That elicited a pained whimper. She grabbed the back of his head and pushed it closer, mostly for the shudder of response she felt go through him. James worked a hand underneath himself to stroke her curls, then pressed in. One thick finger slid in and out of her slick flesh, and then a second, stretching her now, and it was so good that Susan didn't think about anything except the peaking pleasure and the steady working of his tongue, until the sensation crested and she cried out, bucking against his mouth with joy.

"God." James sounded ragged as he sat up on his knees. "Christ, Sukey. I could do that forever."

She nudged the bulge against his trouser-front very carefully with a toe. "This suggests otherwise."

"If you think I'd let a little thing like that stop me…"

Susan spluttered, and reached out for his hand to sit up. She felt damp, bare, and ready to remind herself of how the dance went. "I think you should take those off. Your clothing is constricting you. You might faint."

"It's a medical necessity." James kicked his shoes off with the carelessness of a man who could afford more. Susan went out to the other room, and returned to see him barefoot and stripped to the waist, braces hanging down. She still wasn't used to the tattoos.

"See anything you like?" he enquired.

"You're a big man."

"The Great Detective at work."

"With a big mouth. Do I need to give you something else to do with it?"

"Yes, please." He didn't look away from her face as he kicked off trousers and drawers. Susan met his gaze and held it as she unbuttoned her blouse. Even his jutting stand seemed less urgent than the hunger in his eyes.

She hung blouse, skirt, and petticoat over a chair back, with elaborate care, and wasn't at all surprised when he came up behind her, big hands clasping her waist. "May I help you with the rest of it?"

"Impatient?"

"Extremely."

"You may." She turned. James took a deep breath and cupped her breasts through the undergarments. "Sukey. God, you're wonderful." He pulled at a lace to loosen the chemise. "You don't wear a corset."

She didn't have much in the way of curves to tame or exaggerate, and very little bosom to support. Mostly, though, she liked breathing. "If I want to be imprisoned, I'll rob a bank."

"Very fair. Damn fool things. Arms up, my sweet." He lifted the chemise over her head so she stood bare. "Good God, you're beautiful."

"I'm not."

"Why do you say that?" he demanded. "You bloody are. You look like…you. Like a statue of yourself made by the best sculptor who ever lived. How is that not beautiful? Stay there."

He strode over to his coat pocket, delved in it, and straightened with his fingers full of glimmering fire.

"What the hell is that?" Susan demanded, as if she didn't know.

"Face the mirror."

"That's the Samsonoff! You had the Samsonoff in your pocket when we went to Mortlake!"

"If you'd seen the inside of as many hotel safes as I have, you wouldn't trust them either," James assured her. "Face the mirror, Sukey. Please."

A sensitive woman would recoil in horror at the very thought of touching a stolen, bloodstained necklace. Susan wasn't sensitive, and she had precisely three pieces of jewellery in the world, of which the ruby earrings James had dismissed were by far the most expensive. She turned and lifted her hair.

James laid the necklace over her chest. The metal was cold against her skin. He fastened it and stepped close, hands brushing the sides of her breasts, breath warm on her neck, and Susan looked at herself clad in nothing but thousands of pounds worth of fire opals.

"You said you didn't know what you'd wear it with," James murmured. "This is what. This is exactly how it should be worn." He slid his hands down her sides. "And I was wrong about moonstones. I want you in opals, so everyone can see the fire and light within."

She wanted to make some sarcastic rejoinder, to cut through the entangling lover's knot of his words with a sharp edge. She couldn't. She turned instead and kissed him, body to body, his stand pressed hard and hot against her belly, tasting herself on his mouth, until he lifted her off her feet again and carried her to the bed.

"Shouldn't we take this thing off?"

"No."

She was on her back, the opals cool around her neck, James on all fours over her. He looked huge.

"I have something for you to wear too," she managed.

James took a second, and then his eyes lit as though she'd given him a gift of far greater magnitude than a thin rubber pouch. "You bought French letters?"

"Someone had to."

"I did," James said. "In hope rather than expectation, but I did. I can't tell you how delighted I am that you did too."

"You're easily pleased."

"Not really. The woman of my dreams is under me wearing nothing but opals, telling me she was thinking about fucking me all day—"

"I did not say 'all day'."

"—and has even bought the wherewithal to do it. I'm the luckiest bastard in England. Where are they?"

"I put them on the side table. I'm surprised you didn't notice."

"You were undressing," James pointed out as he clambered off her. "I was hardly going to notice much less than the invasion of a megalosaurus." He was back in a moment with the rubber, which he tossed onto the bedside table.

"Excuse me?"

"In a minute." He leaned down to take a nipple in his mouth, splaying a hand to cover her other breast and, she noticed, the opals on her chest. Oh well. Some people had a taste for leather, some silk; she could live with opals.

Susan ran her hands over his back and chest, spanning muscle with her fingers, and reached down to his waist. She couldn't get far enough. "Come up here."

"Jesus." He made his way up on his knees. Susan stayed on her back, giving her lips a meaningful lick. James groaned, a heartfelt sound, and braced himself over her, his thick cock bobbing against her mouth. She ran her tongue around the tip and heard him whimper; wrapped him in her hand and lips and felt him shudder. He was leaking already, hard enough that the ridges of his cock were firm against her palm. "Oh God, Sukey. Don't overdo it."

She pulled her mouth away. "Sensitive?"

"It's been all but two years since I fucked anyone, and seventeen years since you. Give me a chance." He moved back, and shifted a hand between her legs. Susan squirmed pleasurably. "My theory is that if I get you nearly there, I've a reasonable chance of pleasing us both." His thumb moved lightly over her clit as he nudged a finger into her. "God, you're wet. Is this good?"

"Don't fish for compliments," Susan said through her teeth. Her hips were rocking, more or less of their own accord. "I'll let you know if I have complaints."

"I bet you will." He curled the finger inside her, grinned at her gasp. "I love how much you like to fuck. Tell me when you want me."

"I will." She gave it a moment more out of sheer perversity, just to let him be sure who was in charge. "Now. You, in."

"Always hearts and flowers." He sat back over her thighs, donning the French letter with reasonable competence. "Like this?"

He meant with her on her back. She wanted his weight. "Yes."

James moved into position, prick nudging at her entrance. She angled her legs around him, resting her feet on his calves, and breathed out as he eased in. He was big. She shifted under him, watching him watching her.

"All right?" He sounded as though he were trying not to breathe.

She hadn't been with a man in a good few years, or missed them either, but every sort of body had its pleasures and she liked his. The warmth of him, over her and inside her, the bulge of his biceps as he took his considerable weight on his blue-stained arms, the play of muscle in his chest, and yes, the way he filled her, because it was done with such care, and with a look on his face that suggested he was undergoing a religious experience.

The woman of my dreams. She could almost believe he meant it.

James was moving a little faster now. He slipped a hand under her bottom, urging her hips up, and bent his neck in an effort to kiss her. She'd forgotten the inconveniences of a significantly taller lover. Susan wrapped her legs around his back to make that work, and felt him lift her clear off the bed.

But she never came in this position, and she wanted that. "From behind?" she suggested.

"God, yes." James reared up. Susan rolled over onto her knees, and helped him get the angle right, his prick hot and sticky against her hand, and now it was good, now the thrusts were so deep they almost hurt, the fullness so intense that she felt goosebumps rise.

"Christ. Keep doing that."

"Doing—my best." James sounded strained. "So good like this."

"Perfect. Oh God, keep going, I'm close. Jesus!"

His hands closed on her shoulders, and he was pounding into her now, so that the opal necklace shook and bounced against her skin. The sensation was overwhelming, and rose steadily, not to the intense joy his mouth brought but a more diffuse, shivery pleasure that crested and left her gasping, slumped down on her forearms as James, behind her, cried out wordlessly. He thrust twice more and collapsed forward over her back, bracing himself enough that he didn't break any of her ribs.

They lay together for a moment in that inelegant posture. "My God," he said at last. "My God. Susan."

"Yes."

His hand groped, found hers, held it, and she let her fingers curl into his. That was better than words. Words were untrustworthy, and made promises, and confused matters, and opened up vast imaginative vistas of things you were best off not hoping for, because dreams were dangerous. Half the cases in the newspapers came down to someone who had a dream once. Two bodies together and the touch of hands was true at this moment, so she'd take that.

They lay a little longer, until James's chest stopped heaving and he pushed himself up on his arms. "Hold still, I need to get this thing off."

He extricated himself and the scumbag, and went to dispose of it, then returned to the bed. Susan had managed to roll onto her side instead of lying with her arse in the air, but that was about it for effort. James lay down next to her, and if his weight on the mattress meant she rolled towards him, that wasn't her fault. He wrapped an arm around her shoulders, so that it was only sensible to adjust her position and rest her head on his chest, and they lay together in a silence she didn't want to break with the conversation they had to have.

He sighed at last, ribs rising and falling enough to make her seasick. "Damn."

"Regrets?"

"For more or less everything I've done with my life up to about fifteen minutes ago. However, the last fifteen minutes were perfect."

"It's a start," Susan said. "We have to talk."

"I know. Thank you for the reprieve."

Susan sat up. The necklace shifted against her chest, and she attempted to unfasten it, cursing as she realised her hair was tangled in the clasp.

"Let me," James said. "Go on."

"Someone set you up," Susan said as he worked the fastening. "Perhaps they simply needed a scapegoat, but any thief would have done, and less competent ones would have been easier to catch. We cannot rule out the possibility that this was personal, and that someone decided to kill two birds with one stone by involving you. So who wants to see you dead?"

James carefully lifted the Samsonoff from her neck. "I dare say there are a few people who don't like me. Actively wanting to kill me, though?"

"What about Crozier?"

"Balls."

"He's ruthless. You haven't been getting on. He thinks you've put him and thus Alec at risk. Is there a scenario in which he'd deal permanently with you?"

"Not like this," James said. "If he actually wanted me out of the way for good, he'd do it himself. And, before you ask, Stan isn't a killer, even by proxy. No, I am fairly sure my closest friends haven't conspired to kill me."

"It's a wonderful thing to be popular. Who else? Someone who dislikes you and has an interest in jewels?"

"When you put it like that: Kammy Grizzard."

"That sack of shit?"

"Ah, you've met."

She knew Grizzard by sight: a jowly man with the sad eyes of a disappointed bank clerk. She could also, and vividly, recall the vitriol-burned face of the woman he'd exploited and who'd tried to give evidence against him. Kammy had been one of the bigger rats in the London sewer for a good few years. His star had been on the wane recently but he was still a bad man to cross. "What did you do to upset him?"

"A number of things, but the main one would be—did you hear about Kammy's protection scheme to get a cut of all receivers' dealings? He pushed a few people into line, then he tried it on Stan, who sent him off with a flea in his ear. Kammy decided to make an example of him and had his thugs snatch Stan off the street. Fortunately, his girl was there to tell me and Jerry what had happened, so we went after him, and to cut a long story short, I ended up dropping one of Kammy's lieutenants out of a window."

"That *was* short," Susan said. "How high a window are we talking about?"

"Second floor."

"For God's sake!"

"We'd heard Stan screaming all the way up the stairs." James's voice held a note she hadn't heard in it before. "I kicked the door open, and there was Kammy sat in comfort, Stan tied to a chair with one foot on a stool, and this fucker standing over him with a mallet. Kammy had ordered his ankles broken."

"Ah."

"He's a vicious bastard. Jerry had put down two of his men and had a knife on Kammy. I had my chap dangling by his ankles, yelling for help. But Kammy just looked at me and said, 'You don't dare let go.' As if it was nothing but a battle of wills. Perhaps it was." James smiled without mirth. "He lost."

Susan was fairly sure she'd have done the same, given the physical ability, but she gave him an incredulous look as a matter of principle. "And the man you dropped?"

"Defenestrated. Did you know there was a word for turfing someone out of a window? The man I defenestrated broke both legs and his pelvis. He won't walk again, still less take a mallet to anyone else's ankles. And he can count himself lucky, because if he had landed a blow on Stan I'd have gone to fetch him, carried him upstairs again, and thrown him off the fucking roof."

Susan believed that. "Does this chap have a name?"

James sighed. "Grizzard. Geoffrey. Kammy's nephew."

"Oh, marvellous. Why didn't I hear about this at the time?"

"Neither we nor Kammy wanted to advertise for obvious reasons, but you would have heard if you were a fence. Stan put the word out, so that when Kammy's men came round to other fences demanding their ten per cent, what they mostly got was window jokes and threats to call us. He lost face badly. It all happened in whispers, but it reached everyone who needed to know."

"Well." Susan slotted that into what she knew of Grizzard's activities, and that odd recent slide in his reputation. "So you damaged his nephew and his profits. That's a considerable motive for vengeance."

"And Kammy holds a grudge well."

"He goes to the top of the list, then," Susan said. "Anyone else?"

"Not that I can think of. I dare say there are dealers who resent our activities, but I can't see any of them ordering Montmorency's murder. And we haven't made a big haul since the Cyrus-Price job in spring, except the Ilvar job, but we gave that loot back."

"What was that about?"

James rolled his eyes. "Jerry's bit of stuff, of course. Once the Duke and Duchess were dead and the Ilvar estate had descended to Pyne's older brother, it was too much like stealing from the in-laws."

There was a sardonic note in his voice. "Why don't you like Alec?" Susan asked.

James blinked. "Why would I? He entrapped us in summer."

"I did that. If you dislike Alec for his part in it, you ought to loathe me."

"Yes, but entrapping us was your *job*."

"And I recruited Alec to do it. What's the difference?"

James started to answer, then his shoulders sagged. "Nothing. There's no difference. And I don't dislike him personally. I dislike the way he's disrupted my extremely comfortable and effective arrangement with Jerry, but that's hardly his fault. I…" He paused for so long she wasn't sure if he'd continue, then let out a breath. "If you must have it, I found myself painfully envious of him."

"Because of Crozier?" She hoped to hell not. If James harboured an unrequited passion for his partner, it could be awkward.

"Not the way you're thinking. Do you recall that encounter with the four of us in a room at Castle Speight, when Jerry and I realised you and Pyne had entrapped us?"

It would be hard to forget. Aside from that two-sentence exchange by the light of a dark lantern, it had been the first time she'd spoken to James since his return, and it hadn't been pretty. "Yes."

"You—I'd say you hated me but it was worse. You were contemptuously indifferent. You didn't care at all. Pyne at least looked as if he regretted what he'd done—as if he'd flayed himself alive, in fact, and the next thing you know he and Jerry had forgiven one another. They were all April and May again while you despised me, and the truth is I was jealous as hell. That's contemptible to admit so, naturally, I didn't admit it and behaved like a petulant idiot instead."

"Naturally," Susan said. "I…wouldn't say I was indifferent then. I mean, mostly I was. You deserved everything you got. But I didn't enjoy that meeting either."

"That's good to know."

James reached for her hand again, linking their fingers loosely. This was a hell of a conversation to have naked on a bed. "Anyway," she said briskly. "Any other names to add?"

"I can't think of anyone."

"What about your family?"

"What?"

"You were sent to Australia when you were merely an embarrassment. Now you're a criminal and Crozier's been using the Vane name to pass as a gentleman. Are the family aware of your existence, and if so, would they want it put an end to?"

James winced. "Lovely thought. No, I can't see that. I hardly matter: I'm only the current marquess's first cousin once removed. That said, it wouldn't be the first attempted murder in the family. My great-grandmother was confined for beating my great-grandfather's head in with a candlestick, and there's a story a great-uncle tried to have an unsatisfactory nephew removed. My grandmother used to say that there was a distressing streak of instability in the Vanes."

"Well, look at you."

"Quite. But Cousin Roddy, the current marquess, always struck me as a terribly nice chap." He was silent for a moment. "We're carefully not naming my father, aren't we?"

"Yes."

"Granted he had me unofficially transported, but I don't believe he would want me arrested and tried."

"And if you weren't meant to survive the night?" Susan said. "Your death would have left Templeton Lane as villain of the piece, no further questions needed, no danger of your true identity coming out."

"But as with the jewel dealers, my death would have been part of Montmorency's murder," James said. "It is...conceivable, I suppose, that my father might want me removed from the world, in the unlikely event he knows I'm on this side of it, but I can't imagine him getting entangled in this rather sordid fraud."

His voice was easy but his fingers were tense. Susan squeezed them, not really noticing she'd done so until he looked up at her with a tiny smile. "I'm sure you're right. I just want to cover all the options. It's still possible that Montmorency was murdered for his own sake and that you were cast in the role of villain by chance."

"It is. But Kammy Grizzard is a nasty bastard. He'd know how to set this up, too; he could find men to act as expatriates and valets. I think it's him."

"Perhaps, but don't persuade yourself it's true or you'll start shaping evidence to fit the theory. An investigator should always keep an open mind."

"Noted. But what do you think?" James asked. "If you had to place a bet, where's your money?"

"Kammy on the nose, so let's nail the fucker. It's time to call in the troops."

"Do we have troops?"

"Justin will help, like it or not. So will Mark, and Nathaniel might be extremely useful."

"Ah, your endless uncles," James muttered. "Ironic, isn't it? I come from a vast aristocratic line and have dozens of relations, you came from nowhere and have none, and yet only one of us has ended up with a family."

Susan couldn't argue. She'd gone from orphanhood to Justin's care to finding herself with a frankly absurd number of self-appointed responsible adults, none of whom had ever let the foul-mouthed, abrasive, terrified girl she'd been push them away. James had been unwanted by his parents for no reason at all; Susan didn't think she could do anything that would lose the love of her family, although she foresaw extensive recriminations from multiple directions in her near future.

Which she should probably set in motion. She wrote a brief note to Justin advising him that she needed to meet that evening, and added, "The spirits are murmuring," their old code for when something was going wrong in a seance. It would keep him on his toes.

James gave her letter to a bellboy for delivery while she dressed, and ordered tea while he was at it, and they ended up seated across the tea table from each other, just like a respectable couple.

"So what's next?" he asked, once he'd consumed several teacakes.

"I'll dig into the various aspects of Brayton and Stroud's story. You need to keep your head down now. If you get arrested it'll be a lot harder to persuade Wilby of our case, and the odds are you'd be gaoled for the burglary even if you got off the murder charge."

James gave her a quizzical look. Susan said, "What?"

"I *ought* to be gaoled for the burglary. I committed it. Not that I'm volunteering, but you don't have to save me from the consequences of my own actions."

"I don't have to do anything at all," Susan pointed out. She was playing for time, and they both knew it. "Confess if you want."

"Susan." He put his elbows on the table. "Would it be fair to say you would prefer me not to go to prison?"

"It's not up to me."

"No, it's not. Would you prefer it?"

"What happens if I say I don't care? You volunteer for hard labour?"

"Under no circumstances." He reached out and she left her hand where it was, so his fingers closed around hers. "I am not asking you for anything except one piece of information: would you prefer it if I didn't end up in gaol?"

"Arse," Susan muttered. "All right, yes, I'd prefer that. If you must know."

His eyes lit, as though she'd offered him some sort of gift. "I didn't realise how much I missed you. I didn't imagine you missed me too—and yes, I am aware you haven't said you did. I'm extrapolating."

"Well, don't. What do you want from this conversation?"

"To feel I haven't entirely wasted my time on this earth. Tell me one more thing, please. If I get out of this damned tangle—if you get me out of it, rather, and if I stop repeating the damn fool mistakes that brought me here—may I buy you opals?"

Susan blinked. "Why?"

"Because they suit you. It doesn't have to be opals. I could arrive with flowers, interesting cases, or helpfully apprehended villains. Whatever you want, as long as you want it from me."

"You want permission to…?" *Court me*, she thought, but couldn't voice the words. They belonged to pretty women in expensive dresses who didn't swear so much.

"Call it permission to hope."

Susan shoved her free hand into her hair. "I don't believe in people reforming themselves for other people's sake. I told Alec that about Crozier and I'm telling you now. If you want to do things differently, that's up to you, but I'm not making promises."

"I'm not asking for them," James said. "I'd like, shall we say, your minimum standards. If I were not wanted for murder, and promised not to be arrested for burglary—"

"Those are the most minimum standards I've ever heard."

"—could I take you to dinner?"

He caught a tendril of hair as he spoke and wrapped it round his finger. Susan's chest felt constricted. It was easy to fall into bed, to do things without words and keep them separate in her mind. This was brutally hard work, and she was damned if she'd make any demands of him. He might meet them, and then where would everyone be?

Oh.

"Who's asking?" she enquired.

"Sorry?"

"I want to know if you're asking as James Vane or Templeton Lane. Because I'm not interested in Templeton Lane. If you ask me, he's done any good he'll ever do and a great deal of harm besides."

"James Vane isn't worth much either."

"James Vane was my best friend," Susan said. "James Vane bought me a china shepherdess and taught me to box and broke my heart. Templeton Lane is a larcenous shit, but James Vane could buy me dinner, if he wanted to. Maybe. If he got himself in order first."

"I haven't gone by that name in fifteen years." James sounded more unsettled than she'd ever heard him. "I'm not that man. If you want a different name—"

"No. That's just another way for you not to face up to things—to your father, or me, or what happened. It's *your name*, and if I can use it, so can you. I'm not going to be the one woman in the world who knows you, James. I've no time for that nonsense. Put your life back together in some sort of sensible shape, and if you still want to bring me flowers when you've done that, you know where I live. *And* you can come through the door like everyone else."

James looked unsure whether to laugh or choke. "I...can't say I expected that particular stipulation."

"You should have." *Templeton Lane* had been a splinter that she couldn't dig out for years. "You talked about me owning my name last night, didn't you? What make you think you can walk away from yours?"

"Perhaps I wanted to choose my own."

"But we already agreed it was a terrible choice."

"Sukey." His fingers tightened on her hand. "Does this really matter to you?"

"It matters to you, otherwise you wouldn't have used an alias this long." She met his eyes. "And yes, it matters to me. I missed James Vane. I think you did too."

James released her arm. His eyes were very wide, and very blue. "Would you take him back? No, that's not fair, forget I said it. All right, I've heard you. I can't wish the last seventeen years away—"

"I don't expect you to. Do as you choose, but you wanted my opinion so there it is. More tea?"

James exhaled. "Speaking to you leaves me with a powerful fellow feeling for carpets."

"Trodden on?"

"And beaten for their own good."

Susan couldn't help a smile. James smiled back. "You mentioned the china shepherdess."

"What about her? It. What about it?"

"Did you keep her?"

Of course she had. She'd loved the shepherdess so much that the astonishing fact of ownership had been hard to encompass. She had passionately treasured the fragile, feminine thing, the first frippery she'd ever owned, the only object in her life with no purpose except to make her happy. Justin had given her whatever he could afford or think of but he'd been a painful novice at joy too: he hadn't known she wanted a pretty china figurine any more than Susan had herself. After James had gone she'd twice snatched the ornament up to throw at a wall but couldn't bring herself to let go, and eventually she'd wrapped her in tissue and put her in a box. Not on display, never to be seen now, but safe all the same.

"I…might have," she said. "I dare say I could find her if I looked."

She poured the tea. James's hand brushed hers as he took the cup, and Susan thought, *To hell with it*.

"On second thoughts, put that down." She went round the table, reached down for his head, and pulled it up to meet her lips. James grunted, arms coming around her waist and bottom in a way that was pleasantly familiar, and kissed her with an urgency that suggested a man running out of time. Susan wriggled onto his lap as best she could given her skirts, pressing herself into him, biting at his lips.

The blood pounded in her ears, between her legs. James's big hands moved over her with tender force and Susan kissed him wildly, lost to everything except the urgency of his mouth, the restraint that quivered through his fingers. He wanted to sweep away the tea-things and throw her onto the table, she was sure, and he wasn't doing so, which was very decent of him and also a fucking travesty.

"Bed," she snarled against his lips in lieu of kicking over the furniture, and grabbed on to his shoulders as he stood.

CHAPTER ELEVEN

"Oi. Wake up."

Templeton blinked. He hadn't expected to sleep, but then he hadn't expected Sukey to make love to him like a starving wildcat either. They'd fucked twice more, fast then slowly, and he could feel the marks of her sharp nails on his back. He didn't intend to complain about that. "Sorry. Was I snoring?"

"Yes, but you also need to get up." She was already dressed. She arranged her hair as he watched, remaking herself into the unremarkable person she pretended to be. "Where are you meeting Crozier?"

"I told him to come here, unless he wants to arrange another venue, or ignore me. I don't want to go to any of our old haunts. Too likely I'll be recognised, and a hundred pounds is a large temptation."

"That reminds me, I want to know who offered that reward," Susan said. "All right. As long as you think he'll be discreet."

"Please. Jerry was born for hotels."

She nodded. "Meanwhile I need to go and see the guvnors. Did you have a time set with Crozier?"

"No."

"He can leave a message, I suppose, if you want to come with me."

Templeton could imagine nothing he wanted less than to face Justin Lazarus. "I will if you think that's best. Or even if you don't but would like me there anyway."

Susan made a face. "The odds of him being a prick about this are high. I'll talk to him and you stay here and wait for Crozier. I'll eat there and meet you back here. If anything goes wrong, get a message to Robin Hood Yard."

Templeton nodded. "And, just to keep our stories straight, you're going out alone on the second night of our marriage because…?"

"Good point. Call it family obligations." She scooped up the gold ring she was using as a fake wedding band. It had not escaped his notice that she'd taken it off before they fucked. "We should leave here tomorrow, as well. Honeymoon."

"I'll ask for boat-train timetables and whatnot."

Susan nodded briskly. He had a feeling she wouldn't be receptive to any suggestion that they actually take the boat train and spend the next week in a Paris hotel bed. "What do you want me to arrange with Jerry, if he turns up?"

"If there's any chance he or Kamarzyn could find out about the sapphire bracelet, that would be good. Any word about what Kammy Grizzard is up to. And I want to know who the valet, Peevy, really was. I'll see if I can get you a photograph of the corpse."

"Understood."

"Tell him to put his back into it. Once we get a purchase on any one part of this, we can make the whole scheme come apart. I'll see you later." She took up her hat and left without a goodbye, still less a kiss.

Templeton hadn't expected more. All the same, he sat naked in the large bed for a few minutes, looking at the door without seeing it, before he made himself get up and face the evening.

He completed another round of exercises, then read the newspaper from cover to cover, and could not have described the content of a single article once he put it down. He ordered sandwiches and a bottle of wine rather than a full dinner, having covered a few sheets of paper in scrawled notes so that he appeared to be working in his wife's absence, and discussed boat trains and Paris hotels with the waiter. After that, there wasn't much to do except wait.

He was holding the Samsonoff necklace, staring into the infinity of the great opal at its centre, when there was a knock on the door. It was gone nine o'clock. Templeton pocketed the necklace, answered the door, and saw Jerry, in brown suit and bowler hat, clutching a document case. He looked exactly like a harried clerk except for the expression in his eyes.

Templeton stepped back to let him in. Jerry closed the door with a precise click, locked it, dropped the case, crossed his arms, and said, "What the fuck do you want?"

"You've calmed down, then."

Jerry's eyes narrowed dangerously. Templeton held up a hand. "All right, sorry. Thank you for coming."

"You said I needed to talk to you. I'm waiting to find out why."

"For a start, I have an apology to make." Templeton hadn't wanted to launch into this without preamble, but Jerry didn't seem in the mood for chit-chat. "Do you want a drink?"

"No."

Templeton picked up his own glass, for Dutch courage. "An apology to both you and to Alec. I've been a prick and I'm sorry for it. I'm particularly sorry to have landed you in this miserable tangle when you specifically told me to stay out."

"I did, repeatedly. I'm not sure why you couldn't listen."

"A lifetime's habit of bad decisions, combined with jealousy." Jerry's brows shot up at that, but it was time for honesty. Time and past, as Susan had once said. "You've found something remarkable with Alec and the truth is, I was bitterly envious and played the fool accordingly. You needn't tell me it's contemptible. I'm well aware."

"Oh God," Jerry said. "If you're planning to confess to unrequited love, can I strongly request you don't."

"Why the devil does everyone think that? Don't flatter yourself. I..." He wasn't sure he wanted to admit this, but he owed it to Jerry, and he needed to talk to someone. "I told you why I left England in the first place, didn't I?"

"Your father had you removed because you wanted to marry the wrong girl, blah blah. So?"

"So it became apparent to me this summer that I still want to marry her. That I always have, and I still can't. Which made it particularly grating to be faced with your marital bliss, so I was an arsehole about it. That's an explanation, by the way, not an excuse for making bloody stupid decisions in order to punish myself and everyone around me. I should have listened to you, and I'm sorry I failed you as a partner, and as a friend."

"Jesus," Jerry said. "Have you been drinking long?"

"It's an apology, you sarcastic shit. You may not be familiar with the concept."

"You'd be amazed." Jerry exhaled. "It isn't an excuse, and it's not much of an explanation. Why can you not just marry the damn girl?"

"Because she's a private detective."

Jerry stood completely still for a second, then his brows arched so steeply he looked like a caricature. "Are you taking the piss?"

"I'm afraid not."

"Your long-lost love is *Susan Lazarus*?"

"Quite."

"Susan Lazarus? And you never told me?"

Templeton shrugged. Jerry stared at him. "You absolute arsehole! What the—but—I—fucking *what?*" He waved his hands in lieu of the words he couldn't find, then gave an explosive bark of laughter and doubled over.

Gilded Cage

He was probably entitled. Templeton made an offensive gesture anyway, and waited for him to regain control.

After a few minutes Jerry calmed down and wiped his eyes. "This is a thing of beauty. I always knew you were an idiot, but my God. And here I thought my efforts to romance a duke's son were ill starred. Susan Lazarus!"

"Yes, all *right*."

"Not that I'm an expert in the way of a man with a maid, but you realise this is a disaster, yes?" Templeton didn't reply. Jerry's eyes sharpened. "Oh, now you *are* joking."

"I have no comment about Susan's thoughts on the matter." As if he knew them. "But she's working with me."

"She what?"

"Or, rather, I'm attempting to assist her. She's looking into the murder. She's going to clear my name."

Jerry stared at him, then shook his head briskly, as if to clear it. "I'll have that drink now."

They took the two armchairs by the fire, wine glasses in hand, and Templeton launched into the story, from its calamitous beginnings to his appeal for Susan's help, the visit to Mortlake, and her deductions. He left out the personal parts, as if Jerry hadn't noticed he was in a luxury suite for a married couple, and concluded with the question of whether the whole business was chance, or more than that.

"Susan thinks it likely I was set up for this. Their plan depended on a scapegoat, of course, so it wasn't necessarily personal. But if it was—"

"Kammy Grizzard," Jerry said.

"That's what I thought."

"He's got the grudge, the manpower, and the funds. Might he have bought up the lawyer's debts? He'd have had to set this up a while ago, though, well before Montmorency got hold of the Samsonoff necklace."

"I assume that was serendipity. Kammy was going to set *someone* up; when Montmorency bought the opals, he had a wonderful chance to make it me."

"I told you you were walking into a trap."

"Yes, you did."

"Well," Jerry said. "*What* an interesting state of affairs. Do you know, I'm annoyed with Kammy. This is, frankly, rude."

"It lacks charm, I agree."

"Along with finesse, and that indefinable quality that marks a gentleman. Are we kicking his arse or what?"

"I did hope you'd say that," Templeton remarked. "I have tasks for you."

"I bet you do. I've worked with the divine Miss Lazarus before. Never felt so much like a housemaid in my life. What's my role?"

Templeton gave him a description of the sapphire bracelet. "I think it's been sold. It would be useful to track down to whom. Any word about what Kammy Grizzard is up to would help. Most of all, this character Peevy, the valet. We need to link him to Kammy. There can't be that many men who can act convincingly as a competent valet but are also willing and able to beat their employer's head in."

"If I were a valet, beating my employer's head in would be my main ambition in life, but I take your point."

"Excuse me," Templeton said severely. "A superior gentleman's gentleman takes unobtrusiveness to an art. You couldn't even hear my great-uncle's valet walk; he would never have approved of a violent murder."

"What about a discreet one?"

Templeton cast his mind back to the slender, elderly man who had taught him the art of silent footsteps. "Oh, discreet murder would have been fine. Obviously Peevy was *not* a superior valet, but he was good enough to keep Montmorency happy, and that's a skill that might help identify him. I also want to know what happened to the previous valet to create the vacancy, but I imagine Susan can take that to the police. Meanwhile, if you can dig anything out…"

Jerry grimaced. "I'll try. What did he look like?"

"About forty, brown hair, a long, slightly concave sort of face. Five foot eight, nine? Thin. Susan will get a photograph of the corpse, although I suspect that won't encourage people to admit they knew him, what with the cut throat."

"I wonder if Alec could draw him from it."

"That is a damn good idea if he'd do it. Though I'll understand if he doesn't feel any obligation to help."

Jerry waved a hand. "He's as keen for this business to go away as any of us, and I'm sure he'll be ready to do Miss Lazarus a favour. You really are a lucky bastard if she's on your side."

"I know."

"So what are you going to do?"

That was the question. Templeton reached for the bottle, topping up both glasses. "In the short term, whatever she tells me. She's the expert. In the long term…" He held his glass up against the fire, and stared into the red heart of the wine. "Probably whatever she tells me."

"Templeton," Jerry said. "Are you reforming for the love of a good woman?"

"I fear I am. Which makes me even more of a prick that I didn't sympathise with your own situation."

"Alec has *never* asked me to reform," Jerry said, a trifle smugly.

"You haven't been up for work in months, and nor should you have been. We have enough money, and if we'd called it quits in summer we'd be a damned sight better off now. We always said we'd stop before we got caught. It's my fault if we don't."

"Not entirely," Jerry said. "You were right that I've been marking time. I knew I had to get out—and not because Alec asked me to, either. I can see for myself he deserves better." He sighed. "The truth is, I was putting it off. I *enjoyed* the Lilywhite Boys, damn it."

"So did I. It's been a good run."

"Not bad, you anthropoid ape. Not bad at all." He gave Templeton a smile, a little rueful perhaps, but real. "Ah well, needs must. I have to say, though, if I retire on my ill-gotten gains now, that will make my bit of stuff a happy man. Is yours quite so ready to let bygones be bygones?"

"If you never call Susan my bit of stuff again, we might both live until Christmas. No, I doubt she would be. I don't think I can just retire from thievery. Something will have to change."

"What are you thinking of?"

"Death."

Jerry's brows angled. "A bit drastic?"

"Templeton Lane disappeared in the river that night at Mortlake and nobody's seen him since. I've reached the conclusion that he drowned. End that story, start a new one."

"With a new identity."

"No." Templeton found he was lifting his chin. "With the old one."

"Really?"

"It's what Susan wants. God knows why, but she said she missed James Vane. It may even be what I need. I've had a grudge against the world for years and it's time to redress the situation instead of sulking about it."

"Nice work if you can get it."

Templeton knew very well what that meant. Jerry's own grudge against the world stemmed from its refusal to allow him to love as he chose, and there was no redress to be had for that. He shrugged, since there was nothing useful to say.

"It's not a bad idea," Jerry went on thoughtfully. "You're going to need a clear space between Templeton Lane and your new life, and being someone who undeniably exists is a good way to do it. Yes, I like it. Return from the colonies, reconcile with your estranged father, marry your childhood sweetheart. You might as well get *some* use out of your family, since we never did rob them."

Templeton scowled. "My father had no interest in me seventeen years ago. He won't care now."

"Who cares if he cares? You just need a wealthy family to agree that you're James Vane and always have been. That should keep your bird happy."

"Do you place *any* value on either your or my testicles?"

Jerry grinned evilly. "It's perfect. Get your arse over to America, come back with your honestly-earned fortune for the girl you left behind, tell your family you're tying the knot. I demand to be best man."

"Susan thinks marriage turns women into property."

"Of course she does. What does she want, then?"

"Damned if I know. It doesn't matter."

Jerry's brows rose. "No?"

"I mean, she doesn't want me to do this in the hope I can win her back. She wants me to change for my sake, not hers, so I need to do this for myself in order to be acceptable to her. If you follow me."

Jerry blinked. "God, I'm glad I'm a sodomite."

"Because things went so smoothly with Alec?"

"Fuck off."

"Anyway, I'm not assuming her interest, or her help, far less her enthusiastic acceptance. I took you and Stan too much for granted. I will try to learn from that."

"Oh, stop apologising, it's embarrassing," Jerry said. "So is it James now?"

"I think so. Yes. It is."

"Doesn't suit you. Jim?"

"James, you bastard."

Jerry grinned, that wicked conspirator's grin that he was going to miss from his daily life. "If you insist."

He had gone by the time Susan returned, near half past ten. She looked tired as she hung up her hat and coat, and James didn't think: he just came up to her, arms open. Susan walked into them as if she'd been doing it all her life and put her head on his shoulder.

"Long evening?"

"*God.*"

"Drink?"

"Yes."

He stood with her for another moment anyway, then stepped back and poured her the last of the wine. She flopped into one of the chairs by the fire. "It's cold outside."

"I'm sure." He knelt to unbutton her boots. She began what he assumed would be a protest, then stopped herself. "How was it?"

"Full house," Susan said. "Justin, Nathaniel, Emma, Mark, and Pen—Greta Moreton's twin—and all of them with strong opinions on the subject of James Vane And Other Bad Ideas. *You* get a word in edgewise with that lot, the guvnors especially. It's like arguing with…" She searched for a simile. "A bunch of bastards."

"Ah."

She eased her foot out of the first boot with a grunt of pleasure. "I don't like making explanations, or justifying myself. It's not up to anyone else what I do."

"No. I'm sorry."

"Not your fault."

"It is, though."

"I was trying to be kind, but yes, it is." She knocked back a mouthful of wine as he worked on the second boot. "It was all very personal and irritating and you're going to go and see Justin tomorrow."

"Am I? Good. Excellent." James pulled off her other boot, this time catching her foot, and ran his thumbs over the stockinged sole. Susan made a throaty noise. "Can't wait."

"Thought you'd be pleased. Unf. God, that's good. Harder."

He cupped her foot in both his hands and dug his thumbs in. She purred with unrestrained pleasure. It was spectacularly arousing.

"Jerry turned up," he said, mostly to distract himself.

"Mmm?"

"He thinks Kammy's behind this as well. He'll do some digging as requested."

"Settled your differences?"

James nodded. "We agreed it was time to end the Lilywhite Boys."

"Alec will be pleased."

He didn't ask, *Will you?* He rolled her big toe between his fingers instead, enjoying the noises she made. "I also told him Templeton Lane is dead. Drowned. I told him to call me James."

She went still under his hands. "What did he say?"

"That he prefers Jim. Typical."

A tiny relaxation. "You never could stand that."

"I'm too large for diminutives." He let her foot go, took up the other one to massage. "We spoke about ways I can reclaim my name. A trip to America will be in order, and, as I suppose you anticipated, I'll have to see my father when I get back."

"You think he'll acknowledge you?"

"My face is my fortune. I could simply stand next to Great-Uncle's portrait and put paid to any question of identity. Of course, that wouldn't prove I wasn't *also* Templeton Lane—"

"But it would take a forward-thinking policeman to link James Vane the marquess's cousin to a dead jewel thief."

"That's my hope." James ran his thumbs up the middle of her foot. Susan made a throaty noise that he wanted to hear again. "Thank you for not giving the police my real name at any point on the last few years, by the way. I do realise you could have."

"It would have been unsporting," Susan said. "And embarrassed Lady Cirencester. Greta wouldn't have liked that."

Two explanations where one would have done, James noted, and kept the thought to himself. Some people might find it alluring to have their foibles pointed out; Susan was not among their number.

"Jerry is going to drop off my clothes tomorrow, to Robin Hood Yard unless told otherwise," he said instead.

"You were confident I'd get my way with Justin."

"Of course I was. You always get your way, and he'd do anything for you."

"You don't know that. You've barely met him."

"I heard you talk about him. There was so much you were afraid of back then, but you were so certain of him that you didn't even notice it." Susan had been painfully prickly, suspicious of almost everything, but she'd trusted her guvnor. James had envied her that faith. "I dread to think what he'll have to say to me, but I suppose I have it coming."

She bent to put down her empty wine glass, then cupped the side of his face in her hand. James met her eyes. His hands stilled.

"We'll talk to Justin tomorrow," she said. "We'll check out of here and go to Robin Hood Yard, and I'll keep on investigating while you find somewhere to lie low. No, don't argue. If you get caught as Templeton Lane, it's all for nothing. We'll see to that tomorrow." Her thumb brushed his skin. "For now…come to bed."

CHAPTER TWELVE

James packed in the morning while Susan took a last opportunity for a bath. She might as well get her money's worth given the likely size of the bill. James had said Crozier would bring funds as well as clothing, and that he'd pay her back for the hotel. It was a small relief: there was only so far she wanted to push Justin in the way of expenses.

They left around ten-thirty for their 'Paris honeymoon' with good wishes from the staff, and took a hackney to Charing Cross from where the fictional Ranelaghs were supposed to catch the boat train down to the coast. James and Susan took the other exit instead, and a different hackney to Farringdon Station, from where they walked to Robin Hood Yard. Susan didn't think they'd be followed, and she didn't think James did either, but they would be fools not to take precautions.

Susan hadn't enjoyed the previous evening with her family. They'd all spent seventeen years believing James Vane was a shit, which could be disputed, and five knowing he was a criminal, which couldn't. It had not been easy to persuade them to help, or at least get out of the way, especially since she had had no intention of admitting to her…whatever it was. Affair. Relationship. Thing.

She'd have to at some point, if she and James carried on with the thing, but that was hedged about with so many ifs that she felt justified in not thinking about it quite yet. If she pinned the murder on its true culprit. If James actually reclaimed his name and left his old life behind him, once he had a free choice. If he continued to want a scrawny, scrappy, ill-tempered, and not even young woman who was unsuitable for polite society.

Enough, she told herself. They were almost at Robin Hood Yard, heading through the back way. She shot a glance up at him. "Nervous?"

"I rely on your protection."

"Ha."

Susan let them in the back door. There was no sign of Emma. James left the suitcase in the kitchen, and they made their way through to the front of the building.

"In here," Justin called from his study. James squared his shoulders visibly, and they went in.

Justin stood by his desk, arms folded, grey eyes glittering. Susan gave him an evil look, which he returned before switching his gaze to James. "Vane."

"Mr. Lazarus. Thank you for seeing me."

"So, I'm told you aren't quite as much of a prick as I had thought. By a small margin."

"Justin!" Susan snapped.

"No, I'll take it," James said. "I've done a lot of things a gentleman wouldn't be proud of. But I did not abandon Susan by choice, or attempt to cast blame on her when there was nothing to blame her for, and if you were told otherwise, that was a lie."

"You're calling your father a liar."

"Yes." James held Justin's gaze with impressive steadiness, given her guvnor was doing his famous impersonation of a venomous snake.

"And those other things a gentleman wouldn't be proud of?"

"You cannot possibly be coming the moral high ground on other people's criminal past," Susan said. "It'd make a cat laugh."

"On the contrary," Justin told her. "My experience gives me an informed perspective."

"I shan't apologise," James said, ignoring the show. "I'm not ashamed of my career, whatever a gentleman ought to think about it, but I did not kill the old man or his valet. And I do intend to change how I live."

"So you're abandoning jewel theft for…what, bank robbery? Embezzlement?"

"Lord, no, far too much work," James said cheerfully. Justin's expression didn't change exactly, but Susan saw the tiny twitch. "I thought I'd reclaim my name, and work it out from there. In a legal, above-board, and gentlemanly fashion."

"Really." Justin's eyes flicked to Susan and back. "And who's paying for this?"

"The assembled ranks of the British aristocracy have been very generous." James sounded as though he was enjoying this conversation now. "I have substantial savings."

"You intend to live this new above-board life on the proceeds of crime. I *see*. One might think a moral man would return stolen money to its owners, or at least give it to an orphanage."

"A moral man might," James agreed. "Did you?"

Justin's face cracked into his wicked, sharp grin. "Do I look stupid? All right, sit down, you've wasted enough of my time. I've put Nathaniel on to finding the real Harrison Stroud. He has a lawyer friend in Calcutta who he's telegraphed to set an enquiry in motion. If we can find the real man, dead or alive, that will throw the cat among the pigeons. Meanwhile, on this side of the ocean…" He pointed at James. "You did the Cyrus-Price job, yes?"

James nodded. Susan remembered it well: a wholesale jewel dealer's new and supposedly impenetrable safe opened and emptied.

"There was around twenty thousand quid's worth of diamonds in the safe. About half of them were a private client's property," Justin said. "We didn't spend any time on that because they were uninsured, and anyway the culprits were clearly this bastard and his mate. Remember, Sukes?"

"Yes."

"Remember the private client's name?"

"I can't say I do," Susan said slowly. "I have a vague idea it was a lawyer."

"Any particular lawyer?"

"Are you going to tell me it was Cecil Brayton?"

"Give the lady a cigar. I went back through the files. Montmorency's lawyer lost ten grand's worth of diamonds to your light fingers, Vane."

James's mouth had dropped open. Susan said, "How would a not-very-important lawyer have a fortune in diamonds? Why would he hold them with Cyrus-Price instead of Montmorency?"

"Montmorency was a very reputable dealer," James said. "He wouldn't have taken stones without provenance from his own mother. If Brayton wasn't dealing with Montmorency, it's probably because he didn't want to be examined on where he got them, or who they actually belonged to. Because—"

"—he was holding them for someone else," Susan said over him. "He had a halo of respectability by association. If you wanted a significantly better return on dirty stones, Montmorency's lawyer would surely be a good name to bring into it."

"But a reputable lawyer wouldn't hold unspecified jewels under his own name for any old client," Justin pointed out. "So who was the owner?"

"If I can get a word in?" James said. "When we did the Cyrus-Price job, we stole from Kammy Grizzard."

Susan and Justin both sat up straight. "Come again?"

"After the job, Kammy informed us we'd trodden on his toes. He said he'd been putting a large quantity of stones through the wash—providing a new provenance for them—and we'd lifted his property. He wanted it back, he said. We weren't inclined to take his word for it. He wasn't pleased."

"Suppose Grizzard was using Brayton to launder stolen jewels," Susan said slowly. "Would Grizzard have swallowed the loss himself, or held Brayton responsible?"

"The latter," James said. "Fairness wouldn't come into it."

"So Grizzard has Brayton on the hook for thousands, just when Montmorency is searching for his lost nephew. He comes up with the scheme of a fake heir, which entirely depends on Brayton's cooperation. Daring, but worth it if he can get access to Montmorency's entire fortune."

"He wouldn't tell Brayton the intent was murder, of course," Justin said. "Why, it's just fraud. Barely that, really. The old man won't come to any harm, and he hasn't got long to live. We'll give him a nice young nephew to keep him company in his declining days, no harm done. It's practically an act of charity."

"*Was* the intent murder, do we think?" James asked.

Justin didn't comment on the 'we', for which Susan found herself grateful. "Mph. The sooner Montmorency drops off his perch, the quicker everyone gets paid, and the lower the chances of discovery. But, equally, murder brought the police into it which a discreet death would have avoided."

"Maybe the Samsonoff changed things," Susan said. "Maybe Kammy thought it was worth the risk to settle his score with the Lilywhite Boys, and specifically James, since I should mention he threw Kammy's nephew out of a second-floor window."

"*Dropped*. Not threw."

"I'm glad you cleared that up, I'd have worried otherwise," Justin said. "Yes, that would work. It's also possible Messrs Grizzard or Brayton might have an urgent need for money. You said our villains have started disposing of Montmorency's jewels without waiting for probate, yes?"

"Stan Kamarzyn, my colleague, is looking into that," James said. "And Jerry is trying to find out who Peevy really was, and link him to Kammy. If you can get that photograph, Susan, it would help."

"I see you're trying to be useful," Justin said. "However—"

The doorbell clanged. He glanced at the clock. "Expecting anyone, Sukes?"

"No."

"Nor am I, and Mark's out." Their eyes met. "Keep quiet in here, will you?"

He went out. James stood, without the slightest scrape of the chair, and gave her a questioning look. Justin's voice rang out in the hall, pitched for clarity.

"Come in here, Inspector Wilby. We can talk in comfort."

That was the police inspector on James's case. As Justin ushered the man in to the front room, where most agency business was conducted. Susan tiptoed to the wall, and opened the discreet hatch Justin had installed so that one could overhear proceedings between rooms. A sampler hung over it on the other side.

"What can I do for you?" Justin was asking.

"Actually, I'd like to speak to Miss Lazarus." Wilby's voice.

"I'm not sure if she's in." Justin went out into the hall again and called, "Susan?"

She ghost-walked to the door, catching James's eye on the way. He gave her a casual grin; she puffed out her cheeks to signal, *No rest for the wicked.* Apparently neither of them intended to show they were worried.

She stuck her head into the hall. "What is it, Jus?"

"Inspector Wilby."

"Oh, good. I wanted to see him." She headed into the other room, past him.

"Do you need me?" Justin asked from the hallway. He could have been asking Susan or Wilby. She looked at the policeman, who said, "No," and waited till Justin had shut the door.

The inspector looked significantly less cheerful than at their last meeting. Susan decided not to notice that. "Hello, Inspector. I was going to come and see you today."

"Were you, Miss Lazarus? What about?"

"The valet, Francis Peevy. Was the body photographed?"

"It was, yes."

"Can I have one?"

"Why?"

She put her hands on her hips. "He'd been in service to Montmorency just a few months, unlike all the other servants. Someone drew the bolts on the side door to let Lane in. Come on, Inspector."

"He's dead. Does it make a difference if he was Lane's accomplice or not?"

"Well, if he wasn't, someone else in the house is an accessory to murder," Susan pointed out. "Do you know what happened to his predecessor?"

"I'm looking into it," Wilby said, with a twitch of irritation Susan ascribed to his dislike of not having answers. He was one of the brighter policemen she'd met, a serious man whose dark complexion suggested ancestry from the further-flung parts of Empire. "That's not what I came about. How was your trip to Mortlake?"

"Inconclusive. Mr. Stroud let my expert look through the saferoom, where he did *not* see the particular sapphire bracelet that's supposedly been offered for sale, but Mr. Stroud wouldn't give him an inventory to check. I didn't ask specifically about it to avoid alerting anyone. To be honest, I wasn't convinced by Mr. Stroud or Mr. Brayton."

Wilby's eyes were hard on hers, as if he was trying to convey a message, or receive one. "Were you not. Reasons?"

Susan ran quickly through the options for what she could reveal. "Mr. Stroud looked highly uncomfortable. Perhaps that's just because he's selling jewels before probate, but if he is, I'd like to know why, given he's about to inherit a fortune. And I was confused by his accent. Why does he speak like an Australian if he's only ever lived in India?"

"Does he? I've never met an Australian."

"He does, but he specifically said he'd never been there. Something's odd about him. I'd like to dig into it a bit more."

"But this isn't your case, Miss Lazarus, or your business," Wilby said. "Mr. Stroud isn't currently a suspect in his uncle's murder, and I've received strong representations about the impropriety of your visit. He was extremely distressed, and Mr Brayton has made a complaint."

"About what?"

"He says Mr. Stroud considered your questioning aggressive and accusatory."

"A lot of men say that," Susan remarked. "I don't know if it's being asked to account for themselves to a woman, or just my manner."

"I couldn't speculate," Wilby said, sounding very much as if he'd like to, "but the fact is, you have no official standing to ask questions of any kind."

"Indeed not. Hence I stopped and left when they asked me to stop and leave. Is that a problem?"

"Mr. Brayton felt you used the letter I wrote you to claim an authority you didn't have."

"I showed it to Mr. Stroud. I can't help it if he can't read. Tell me, Inspector, on the subject of authority, why did Mr. Brayton come to you about this instead of, say, Mark Braglewicz, or Justin, or me? Because if his problem is that I don't work for you, why would he talk to you about my work?" She caught the tiny twitch. "Or was it not to you?"

Wilby's face tightened. "Mr. Brayton lodged a complaint to a superior officer who passed it on to me."

"I didn't realise he was so well connected."

"It's not a matter of connections, Miss Lazarus, it's about police business and not overstepping the lines. The Metropolitan Police has been happy to co-operate with your agency in the past where justice might be served, but that cooperation can be withdrawn at any time. It's my duty to inform you that we'll have to consider the relationship extremely seriously if there is any further unwarranted interference."

"Is that so," Susan said, equally levelly. "I'm sorry to hear it. Did you say it was Mr. Brayton who lodged the complaint?"

"That's right."

"Who with?"

"Superintendent Tennick."

"Really."

They looked at one another. Wilby didn't blink.

"Well," Susan said after a moment. "I shan't return to Mortlake, so you can assure Mr. Brayton of my cooperation. Can I have that photograph of Peevy? Purely for my own investigation, of course."

"I warned you about overstepping, Miss Lazarus."

"Yes, you did, just now. I was here."

Wilby gave her a look. "Who was the man who came to Mortlake with you?"

"A jewel expert we use occasionally. Why?"

"Apparently he was a very big man."

"Yes. He plays…oh, I don't care, prop forward or full back or whatever it is. But as far as I know he keeps his violent tendencies on the rugby pitch, so I hope nobody's accusing him of misconduct. The worst you can say of him is he's keen. Why?"

"Any mention of a big man in relation to this case interests me."

Wilby was watching her closely. He was welcome to; Susan had been lying for a living since she was eight. She gave him a half-second of blank look, then a snort of amusement. "Right, yes, the killer returning to the scene of the crime disguised as a detective. That's a little bit desperate, Inspector. Is the Yard embarrassed that you can't lay your hands on Templeton Lane?"

Wilby tipped his head. Susan added, "Stroud seemed fairly sure he drowned in the Thames. I don't know what he's based that on, unless one of his bullets found its target."

"Perhaps. What's his name?"

"Who?"

"Your man."

Susan couldn't remember the alias for an alarming half-second, which she filled with a pitying look, then recalled the tribute to James's aunt. "Rawling, Harry Rawling."

"Could you produce him?"

"Whenever you like. Except Saturdays, of course, when he plays rugby. Anything else?"

"I don't think so, Miss Lazarus. Just remember what I said, won't you?"

"Oh, I will," Susan assured him. "Give my regards to Inspector Tennick."

She ushered him out, glared at the door once it was shut behind him, and returned to find James and Justin both in the other room, waiting for her.

"I suppose you heard all that, gentlemen. Looks like we've been warned off."

"Tennick takes bribes," James said. "His hands are always open. Word is he's in Kammy's pocket."

"It seems your jaunt south of the river had an effect," Justin said. "Brayton panics and runs to Kammy for help, Kammy leans on his pet policeman to shut us up. That would link Brayton and Kammy nicely, if one could get Tennick to admit it. Decidedly unsubtle of Mr. Grizzard, though. You have him worried, Sukes."

"The question is whether he'll cut his losses or dig his heels in," Susan said. "On the one hand, double murder. On the other, he's made a big investment in this job, and there's a lot of profit to come if his people can hold their nerve."

"So what now?" James asked. "If the police won't cooperate with us—"

"Now is that you clear off," Justin interrupted. "That was what I was saying before we were interrupted: we have to get rid of Gogmagog here, sharpish. Preferably ship him out of the country."

James appeared unmoved, except that his eyelids drooped to the point he looked half asleep. "Sadly, the ports are watched," he drawled. "So inconvenient. And I must admit, I should prefer to play some small role in my own salvation, since I don't think I'm entirely useless."

"I admire your optimism."

"Shut up, Justin. But he's right," Susan added to James, with more reluctance than she wanted to feel. "We talked about this. And you did say you need to get out of the country at some point, so you can come back. It might as well be now."

His face tightened. "If that's my marching orders—"

"We need somewhere safe for you to go while we sort your passage out," she said over him, because she didn't want to hear whatever it was. "Justin, can you come up with something? I need a private word with James."

Justin gave her an irritatingly perceptive look, but said only, "Of course, my dear. I'll go and work miracles for you, shall I?"

"Yeah, do that."

James looked after him as he shut the door. "He's mellowed with age, then."

"Gentle as a lamb. James, you must see you need to get out of sight, and the sooner the better. We've kicked over a hornet's nest in Mortlake—"

"And you want me to leave you to face the consequences alone," he finished. "I did that last time."

"I want you to listen to me, which you *didn't* do last time." She held his gaze until he gave a reluctant nod of acknowledgement. "The police don't have a thing on me as it stands. But if they catch you before we have rock solid proof of Stroud and Brayton's guilt, they'll identify you as my companion in Mortlake, which will make me look like an accessory to murder after the fact. We need you out of sight, and me squeaky clean. And that means you out of the way. No more hotels."

James took a step closer, looking down at her. "No more hotels?" His voice was very deep. He slid a finger lightly over her cheek. "I would regret that greatly. I liked that hotel."

"Hotels won't get you out of this mess, and that's the important thing."

"No, it isn't," James said. "It hasn't been the important thing for some time, except as a means to an end. I don't want to leave you, Sukey."

She didn't want him to go. That was ridiculous. She'd done very well without him for seventeen years, and she'd spent less than three days with him now. It was hardly as if he was going to vanish for another decade, anyway. He'd just drop out of sight, slip out of the country as soon as it became possible, go off to America, and do whatever he needed to do to re-establish his name.

It would take months. They loomed like years.

Susan was quite used to being solitary, but she had a horrible feeling that now she'd be alone again, the sort of alone she'd felt when he'd gone the first time, or after Cara died. Alone in England, wondering what James was up to in America that was more fun than returning to a life and a name he'd never wanted in the first place.

"What I said," she told him, or at least his shirt front. "About your name, before. You don't have to do anything, you know that. If you don't want to, that's up to you. I don't care." She made herself say it: "But if you aren't coming back, you might let me know."

James's big hand closed round hers. "Do you promise not to burn my letters unopened this time? Because that really would help."

She sighed. "All right."

"Whereas I won't promise anything, not even to come back." She looked up, startled. He gave her a wry smile. "What I'd like to promise you isn't in my power to fulfil yet, and even if it was, I'm not sure I ought to. You might not want what I have to offer, and then where would we be?" He pulled up her hand and stooped to kiss the fingers, a bizarrely courtly gesture done with grace that took her breath. "So I want a second promise from you instead."

"Oh, really?" Susan said, trying for snide but not quite making it. "What would that be?"

"Don't decide against me in my absence. Don't tell yourself your instincts were wrong, or convince yourself I'll do something terrible. I'm enough of a villain without adding sins to my list. Give me a chance to come back to you before you decide I won't."

"Are you suggesting I'm judgemental?" Susan asked. Her throat felt thick.

"Yes. I'm quite sure you'll dwell on all the damn fool things I've done, from which it would be very reasonable to draw conclusions about all the damn fool things I might yet do." His hand cupped her cheek. "Please don't."

Her chest hurt. She hated that, and also wasn't a great enthusiast of having her flaws pointed out, no matter how lovingly. "If I'd believed you before—" she managed.

"If I'd listened to you before," James said. "How fortunate we're now both rational adults who can do better."

Susan gave that the snort it deserved. James kissed her lightly on the lips, his hand still covering hers. "I don't want to sit around taking care of myself while you work yourself ragged. I'd prefer to be useful. But I know perfectly well which one of us will do a better job of saving my skin, so if my role is that of a parcel of contraband goods to be shipped, I'll be an obedient parcel."

"You need to get out of the country, and sort yourself out a story that explains the last seventeen years," Susan said. "That's enough to keep you busy."

"While you take on Kammy Grizzard."

"At a remove. We'll get Stroud and Brayton, but my guess is that Kammy will manage to keep himself out of it, and find an inducement to keep them quiet, one way or another."

"Yes, well, that's what worries me too," James said. "Did you know Long Ikey Latham? He was set to testify against Kammy but mysteriously died in prison awaiting trial."

"I saw a woman who had vitriol thrown in her face. Same thing."

James grimaced. "He's a ruthless bastard. Something of a coward, too, which is probably why he's so ruthless. Anything to avoid personal harm."

That was too true, and another reason they couldn't risk James's arrest: he'd be a sitting duck in a gaol cell. Kammy's reach was long, and he had a great deal to lose.

"He's not the only ruthless one," she said. "If he tangles with me and Justin, we'll dissect him."

"He holds grudges," James said. "Be careful."

"I always am."

A smile spread across his face, touching his eyes. "Extraordinarily careful while doing extraordinarily reckless things."

"Isn't that what the Lilywhite Boys were all about? Not getting caught? It would be a shame to break a winning streak."

"So it would." James exhaled, warm breath ruffling her hair. "Hell and the devil. All right, I said I'll be sensible and I will, if it means I can come back. If you want me to."

"That's the plan."

James kissed her again. His big hand tightened on hers, almost clinging to her, and Susan kissed him back as hard as she could, as if that would make any difference at all.

She went straight out, rather than linger on goodbyes which were merely a waste of time for a busy woman. When she got back to Robin Hood Yard that evening, he'd gone.

"You already found somewhere to put him?" she demanded of Justin. "Where?"

"I didn't," Justin said. "We decided the important thing was to keep you entirely separate from him."

"Who are you, Lord Dickie Vane?"

"To avoid making you an accessory after the fact," Justin said patiently. "We can't hide him with anyone connected to you, or by extension us."

"So where is he?"

"I don't know."

"What?"

"He's gone off somewhere safe, he says. I don't know where, so I can't say. When I'm ready to ship him out, I'll get in contact via Alec Pyne."

Susan made a face. "I'm not sure I want Alec involved in this."

"He's already up to his neck. When you fall in love with a criminal, you get problems." Justin gave her an expectant look. Susan gave him back a malevolent one.

"Watch out, the wind might change," he recommended. "I don't want to interfere in your affairs—"

"Good."

Justin rubbed a hand on his hair. It had faded to grey over the last twenty years, and his crows' feet were multiplying. Before too long, she'd have to stop thinking he was getting older, and accept he was getting old.

"I actually don't, this time," he said. "I handled your business with Vane extremely badly back then, and I've kicked myself for it since."

"It wasn't your fault."

"I could have done a lot better. I didn't try, because I didn't believe he was any good to you. I think I'm sorry about that."

"Think?"

He shrugged. "I might have been quite right about him. I still could be, come to that. Ugh. I wanted you to have a safe harbour,

Sukes. Someone you could rely on, someone decent who'd never let you down and help steer you right—"

"Someone like Nathaniel."

Justin glowered at her. "Yes, if you must. I dug myself a bloody great hole and I don't know if I'd have got out of it without him. I wanted someone who'd do that for you, whereas Vane—"

"But I don't want that," Susan said. "I don't want to be looked after, or taken responsibility for, or helped. I want someone who listens to what I say, respects it, and trusts me to look after myself."

"I tried the 'I stand alone' business for years. It really doesn't work."

She sighed heavily. "I wouldn't know, because I haven't stood alone since I was eight years old. I don't need someone else who'd never let me down, Jus. I've always had you."

Justin's lips parted. "Susan— Oh, ratface, if I thought I'd managed that, I'd be a proud man. Come here."

Susan walked over for a hug. He was only a couple of inches taller than her; she dropped her head on to his shoulder anyway, briefly missing the days when she'd had absolute faith in his omnipotence. That would have been nice now.

"Do you know what you're doing?" Justin asked, voice buzzing in her ear.

"Did Nathaniel know what he was doing when he started up with you?"

"Didn't have a clue, which hasn't stopped him being intolerably smug about my reformed character for the best part of twenty years. I may kill him yet."

Susan detached herself and returned to her seat. She'd wanted to talk to someone about what was bothering her; it was possible the answer had been under her nose. "I remember when he came along. You disappeared for ages, and then you came back with him and you even looked different, and I realised everything was about to change."

"It had to. We couldn't have gone on in the life. It was rotting me from the inside out, and look at you. You'd have been one hell of a medium, but you make a better enquiry agent."

"Even so. I was terrified, Jus. It had been just us for ages, and then suddenly there was Nathaniel and it was all different. It turned my life upside down, and I don't think I ever thought how much worse it would have been for you."

"It wasn't worse," Justin said. "*Worse* would have been keeping on as I had been. Nathaniel's the second best thing that ever happened to me, after picking up a snot-nosed brat from the gutter."

"It can't have been easy though," she pressed. "You say standing alone doesn't work, but you can't get hurt that way."

"Oh, you can," Justin said. "Just differently."

She took a deep breath. "Were you scared? When you decided to trust Nathaniel?"

"Scared? What, to hand over my heart and pray he was the man I hoped he was, because the world would be unbearable if I was wrong?"

"Well. Yes."

"Nah, piece of cake," Justin assured her, and they were both cackling when the door-knocker sounded.

Justin nodded in the direction of the hall. "Talking of, that's probably him. He's missed you while you've been avoiding us, ratface."

"Sorry."

Susan hoped it was Nathaniel. She wanted to see him—to have her whole family around her, in fact, with noise and laughter. She didn't want to go back to her empty rooms, with nothing but James's absence and a picture of Cara on the wall.

It didn't sound like Nathaniel, though, she realised a moment after the door had opened. His voice was deep and penetrating; this speaker had been ushered into the next room but she could only hear a mumble. A few seconds later, Emma stuck her head round the door.

"Um, Sukey? Someone to see you." Her eyes were wide. "It's Kammy Grizzard."

Kammy was seated in the main parlour opposite Mark, the original owner of the enquiry agency. Mark's expression was not pleasant. Kammy looked sadly let down by this wicked world

Susan strode in with Justin at her heels. "Mr. Grizzard. What a treat."

"Miss Lazarus. Mr. Lazarus." He nodded at Justin. "My apologies for calling so late in the day."

"Our door is always open," Justin said. "What can we do for you?"

"I believe you can put me in touch with someone I'd very much like to meet." Kammy pressed his fingertips together. "Very much indeed."

"It's an enquiry agency," Mark said, with unconcealed hostility. "Not matrimonial services."

"I know what you do, Mr. Braglewicz, and who you do it with. I heard all about Miss Lazarus's trip to Castle Speight earlier this year, and your encounter with the Lilywhite Boys."

"It received a lot of publicity. And?" Justin asked.

Kammy's eyes looked like those of a mournful puppy until you gazed into them and realised they showed all the warmth and depth of a funereal slab. "I want to know who you've been working with, Miss Lazarus. Your 'assistant'. The big man you took on a recent visit. I want Templeton Lane."

Mark raised a brow. "Cards on the table, I see."

"Admirably frank," Justin said. "And close to an admission of involvement in the events in Mortlake."

"Not at all," Kammy said. "In fact, the opposite. Templeton Lane murdered poor Mr. Montmorency and his unfortunate valet. He deserves to hang for his crimes."

"And what's it to do with you?" Susan asked. "A high-minded devotion to public service?"

"I don't want to see a murderer escape," Kammy retorted. "I'll admit I've a score or two to settle with Lane; why shouldn't I? And I have a certain interest—nothing to do with the murders—in certain persons that makes your interference unwelcome. I think you've already been told to keep your noses out of the business."

"Indeed we have," Justin said. "This very morning, by Inspector Wilby."

"And yet Miss Lazarus spent the afternoon doing what? Nosing around," Kammy said. "Sticking her neb into my business, in a way that will only cause trouble for yours." He evidently caught the flicker of a glance that passed between Mark and Justin. "Or did you not know what she was up to? I think it's time for you to put her on a shorter leash, Mr. Lazarus. You've been told the police will brook no further attempts to obstruct a murder case; well, I won't have any more interference either. I don't want it to come to a falling-out, gentlemen. I don't see any reason we shouldn't all go about our own affairs like reasonable men. But I'm afraid Miss Lazarus here has exposed your agency very badly. Working with professional thieves is one thing, and quite bad enough. Spending your day in efforts to save a murderer's neck is another altogether." He paused before landing the blow. "Particularly if you're spending the nights with him in the honeymoon suite of Thurgood's Hotel on Frederick Street."

"You have a nasty mind," Susan observed levelly.

"No, Miss Lazarus, I have witnesses. Witnesses who will be quite ready to testify, if your baseless attempts to blame someone else for Templeton Lane's crimes should ever reach court."

Justin stood. "I think you've made your point. If you make any more points, I might have to conclude they're threats."

"Not at all, Mr. Lazarus." Kammy stood as well. "I hope I've clarified my position, and that you can persuade Miss Lazarus to consider hers. So good to meet you, gentlemen."

Susan drew in breath to speak. Justin held up his hand to stop her, a commanding, almost angry gesture. "Enough. We understand each other, Mr. Grizzard. Let me show you out."

CHAPTER THIRTEEN

By the third day of life in hiding, James was starting to climb the walls, albeit only metaphorically. That was a pity, because activity would have helped. So would drinking himself unconscious, which he couldn't do either.

Jerry had housed him in a little place up by Victoria Park. It had a way out the back and one over the rooftops, and was near the railway line and Homerton station, as well placed as a bolthole could reasonably be. A cautious man, Jerry Crozier. James lived in the back room with the shutters closed, to avoid anyone seeing him. He hoped Lazarus would come up with some scheme for him to get out of the country soon, and not simply leave him to rot.

At least he had possessions again. Jerry had visited James's own lodgings in the small hours to pick up shoes, clothes, papers and a small box of valued items, most of them opals. If he'd kept anything to read in the place other than old copies of the *Turf Gazette*, he might have been the perfect friend.

They were sitting downstairs, the curtains safely drawn, around eight o'clock that evening, talking through the situation for about the fifteenth time.

"No word yet?"

"Not a dicky bird," Jerry said. "Don't get twitchy. I'm sure Lazarus senior is as keen to see the back of you as everyone else, but they have plenty on their plate."

"Nothing more from Alec?"

"Are you under the impression I'd have forgotten to mention it?"

"Sorry."

Alec had brought the news of Kammy Grizzard's visit to Robin Hood Yard, and also produced a sketch of the valet Peevy that looked a lot more like him than the photograph of his corpse did. Stan, the little genius, had tracked down the sapphire bracelet, which had been sold by an elderly man who matched Cecil Brayton's description. The Lazarus firm were 'in communication' with India. Things were undeniably in motion, just without James.

"It's too quiet," he said. "We kicked over a hornet's nest: there should be hornets. What's Kammy up to?"

Jerry grimaced. They'd been over this several times, since there wasn't much else to talk about. "If he can't find you and the fraud is exposed, he'll need to stop Brayton and Stroud implicating him. If he gets rid of them, bang go his chances of getting his hands on Montmorency's money, so he won't want to move too early. But if he leaves it too late, with the case against them building, one of them might crack and inform. All of which leads us to one conclusion: Kammy's somewhere between foiled and fucked whatever happens, unless he can get hold of you. If he can deliver you to the police as the murderer, a jury might well be persuaded that allegations of a conspiracy are an elaborate tissue of lies created by your mistress to protect you. And that would probably be easier if he hands you over dead."

"I have to stay uncaught, I know. But aside from trying to get hold of me, what's he going to do? Wait and see, or silence his accomplices before they crack?"

"I'd cut my losses," Jerry said. "Eliminate Brayton and Stroud, clear out Montmorency's jewel store to cover my expenses, and go to ground for a while."

"You're a ruthless bastard, aren't you?"

"A logical bastard, please. Do you disagree?"

"No, probably not. I wonder if Brayton and Stroud have reached the same conclusion. If I were them, I'd be looking for a way out. Brayton at least could turn Queen's Evidence, couldn't he?"

"He'd need protection from the Met, and I mean that in both senses given Kammy has police in his pocket. The other possibility, of course—"

There was a sharp knock at the door. They exchanged looks. Jerry went to answer, while James slipped into the back room, where a bag was ready for him to grab and run.

"Oh, hello," Jerry said from the hall. "Come in." The door closed again. James heard him start to say something else, but Alec Pyne's voice cut across him, sharp with nerves. "Is Templeton here? James, I mean?"

James let go the bag handle and came back through. "I am, but if you two want privacy— What is it?"

"Alec?" Jerry demanded.

Alec was pale, breathing fast. "It's Susan. I think Kammy Grizzard's kidnapped her."

There was a brief silence, then Jerry said, "Well, that was the other possibility."

"What do you know?" James demanded. "What happened?"

Alec recoiled at his tone, but answered steadily enough. "I went round to Susan's lodgings but she wasn't there, so I dropped by Robin Hood Yard on my way home. Emma was there, on her own, in an awful state. She said Susan hadn't come back, and a boy had turned up and said he'd seen a man push her into a cab, struggling, and Mr. Braglewicz had gone to get Mr. Lazarus. So I came here, I didn't know what else to do. It must be Grizzard. He's kidnapped her, and you told me what he tried to do to Stan, he *kills* people—"

"Calm down," Jerry said, the words an order.

"I *can't*," Alec said through his teeth. "He's got Susan, and God knows what he's doing to her! Don't you care?"

"We care calmly, and we act calmly. Don't we, Temp?"

"I'll rip his fucking head off calmly," James said. "Where will he be?"

"Thirza Street, I expect. We should start there. However—"

"Fuck however."

"He'll be expecting you."

"Fuck his expectations."

Jerry sighed. "Like that, is it? Ah, well, needs must. Alec, get your arse over to Miss Chris's place. Let her know what's going on, tell her to contact Stan, then keep your head down till I'm back."

"Oughtn't you…" Alec evidently wasn't sure what they ought to do. "Tell someone? Get reinforcements? Join up with Mr. Lazarus?"

"What supplies do you have here?" James asked Jerry, ignoring that.

"I'm good for knives, brass knuckles, and coshes. Why are you still here, Alec?"

Alec made a strangled noise. "But you can't just go off without talking to Mr. Lazarus, or the police, or anyone!"

Jerry gave him an affectionate look. "You didn't come here to watch us sit on our hands, my dukelet, so let's not pretend you did. Scarper."

Alec's mouth tightened for a moment, then he sighed. "As long as you're careful."

"Oh, come now." Jerry's dark eyes were positively glowing at the prospect of trouble. "You *know* I don't promise that."

***

"You realise this is a trap," Jerry said as they walked along the Commercial Road towards Kammy's headquarters. They'd taken the train to Stepney rather than a hackney whose driver might prove inconveniently good at faces. The carriage had been half empty and cold; the night air was freezing.

"Of course it is."

"And you're going to walk in?"

James nodded. Jerry shot him a glance. "I always thought you were a romantic soul at heart."

"Takes one to know one."

"I've been forced into it. Blame Alec."

"Rubbish. If you had a cape you'd be throwing it in puddles for him. You'd need a wardrobe of the bloody things in this country, mind you."

Jerry grinned. "Perhaps. You know, there's a perspective-changing quality to this business that I hadn't previously understood. I find myself concerned to come out of this alive and free, which is far more for Alec's sake than my own convenience. He'd be so upset."

"Can't have that. You realise you don't have to do this. As you say, it's an obvious trap."

"Nonsense," Jerry said. "Look how badly you fucked up last time I let you go off alone."

Kammy's place of business was on Thirza Street, where Whitechapel edged into Shadwell, between the old Ratcliffe Gasworks and the Rope Walk. They approached through darkest Whitechapel, passing no more than a stone's throw from Dorset Street, perhaps the worst street in London. A madman had killed and mutilated five women around here just a few years ago and it didn't look like anything had improved. The sooner it was all knocked down the better, in James's view: the air round here stank of ordure, human waste, rotting vegetables, rotting houses, rotting bodies. It was enough to make a man believe in the old miasma theories of disease, even without the tendrils of November fog that caught in his throat.

"Ah, Love Lane," Jerry said, pointing down towards the river as they crossed a road. "Did you know it comes to a junction with Cock Hill? I'd buy someone a pint for that."

James laughed raucously, because he could see what Jerry had spotted: two policemen on patrol. Unusual for them to travel in pairs, but they were near enough Dorset Street to explain that. He paused at the next alley-mouth, from which shrieks, whoops and a strong odour of gin drifted out, as well as the savage snarls that announced a dog-fighting court.

"Gawd, what a pit," he remarked. "Think it's a fair game? Worth a stop?"

"Doubt it." Like his own, Jerry's accent had slid steeply down the social scale. "Bessarabians run the whole thing round here."

"Bloody Greeks," James agreed, as the policemen passed behind them. "Oh well. Come on."

They strolled off again, turning right up Devonport Street, which led on to Thirza Street. There was no gas lighting here, and very few people out on this miserably cold night. James wore thick gloves to keep his hands warm and supple; he stripped them off now, and pulled on a thin pair of black leather. The cold bit at his fingertips.

The houses at this end of Thirza Street were a low, shoddy terrace. He and Jerry strolled down it together. There didn't seem to be any dog-fighting or anything else going on; the place was very quiet. A handful of idlers lurked in doorways, tall shadowy figures bundled against the cold.

As they approached the far end, there was a little nameless entrance to a court before the buildings took a jump to three stories. Kammy's was the first of those taller buildings. No sound came from the court, but a few men were gathered on the other side of the street, muffled in huge ragged coats. Neither Jerry nor James broke stride as they passed the court, and turned left, out of Thirza Street.

"Well. Balls to that," Jerry said, when they were a few moments away. "If I were you—"

"Slate road," James agreed. "I'll go up, you lurk. No, I insist. If I get you in trouble, Alec will have my hide."

"I can see you quaking. All right. See you later."

James picked a house on the corner of Brook Street, which ran parallel to Thirza Street, had a quick look round, and shinned his way up the wall and onto the slate road: the connected rooftops of the terraced houses. He kept to the spine of the roof where he could, since you should never trust a gutter, and threaded his way through the chimneys with care. A knocked slate would be bad news.

The terrace ended at the court, but the roofs and walls offered a continuous run to the back of Kammy's building. He could see a couple of men in the open space below, presumably guarding the door, hunched against the cold and wet. They didn't even look up.

He made his way up the fog-wet brickwork, the gloves giving him grip despite the chilly slime. This wasn't the easiest wall he'd scaled but it was far from the hardest either, with a reasonable distribution of window ledges and metal hooks used for hoists. He sent a fond thought to the architects of commercial buildings.

James's disadvantage in climbing was his weight; his advantage was his reach. He had long arms even for his height, and extremely powerful shoulders, and he used them both, pulling himself up with steady control. He didn't think about what he would do when he got in, or about Susan: he considered only the next grip. A wrought iron nub, sweating cold, a jutting brick. One leg went out to the metal collar that fastened a drainpipe to the wall—you couldn't trust those to climb up but they did for a foothold, especially sideways—and he had a very comfortable perch on a second-floor window ledge.

He took a moment to let the strain in his shoulders subside to a dull ache and, while he recovered, to think.

He hadn't made a plan. It was so very obviously a trap that his actions probably didn't matter. The only important issue was that Kammy was inviting him to turn up, and if he didn't, there was an unacceptable risk the bastard would take it out on Susan.

Hurting her wouldn't be Kammy's primary aim. He was vicious, but he damaged people for reasons, not for fun. His best option was undeniably to make James the scapegoat for the murders, using Susan as his pawn, and that gave him no pressing reason to set his men on her while he waited. James had been telling himself that for some time in an effort to keep calm.

There was no sound from the inside of the room, and no light. The window-catch was easily slipped and he let himself in.

No sound on the second floor. No screaming from anywhere below, either, which suggested that the evening's main business hadn't started yet.

He squinted down the stairs. On the floor below, a man was leaning against a door—a scrawny sort with a greasy cap pulled down low, smoking a noxious cigarillo. He'd be there to raise the alarm. James found a stub of pencil in one pocket which he stuck in his mouth, came down the steps soundlessly, and patted his pockets as the man finally noticed him. "Ah, bollocks," he remarked, not breaking stride. "Oi, mate, got a light?"

Nobody ever called for help when you asked for a match. James reached the lookout in three deceptively casual long strides while extending a hand in request, slammed his palm over the man's mouth, and thumped him in the stomach. The man went forward with an airless gasp, and James caught his jaw coming down with a fist swinging up, then grabbed his coat as he fell. He lowered the body to the ground, opened the two exterior bolts, and wiggled the door handle. It was unlocked, so he went in, dragging the unconscious man with him.

The room he entered was bare-walled, with shuttered windows and no furniture except for two chairs. Susan sat on one of them. She had a dark red mark on her cheek and a swollen look to one eye that would doubtless turn into a shiner. She did not look like a woman overjoyed to see her rescuer.

Kammy Grizzard sat on the other chair, legs crossed at the knee in a relaxed pose. His mouth was twisted into an up and down curve, the closest he got to a smile. The three big bruisers who stood behind him looked fairly pleased with themselves too.

"Ah," Kammy said. "Templeton Lane. I wondered when you'd get here."

"Sorry I'm late. Dreadful traffic." James dropped the limp body and locked the door behind him, since the key was there. "Good evening, Susan."

"You arsehole," she said. "What are you doing here?"

"Well, you couldn't expect me to sit around waiting."

"Couldn't I?"

"You don't pay my debts. You wanted me, Kammy, I'm here. Let Susan go now, and we can discuss our business like gentlemen."

Kammy gave that the look of contemptuous pity it deserved. Susan sighed. "Is that it? Really? Was it *really* worth inserting yourself into this situation for that?"

"Well, we'd all be better off," James said. "Kammy and I could have a nice chat, you could go home and put your family's minds at rest, and the—I think ten?—policemen about to raid this house could get on with their job that much quicker."

Susan's eyes met his. James smiled into them. "Looks like Inspector Wilby has a very high opinion of you. It's buzzing with bluebottles out there."

Kammy sneered. "Am I supposed to believe you went to the police and laid accusations against me? You'd be sitting in a cell right now."

"Me? Good Lord, I haven't done anything," James said. "I'm the monkey; Susan's the organ grinder. In every sense." Her mouth twitched at that. "She's been in charge all along, and that includes the last few hours. You might not have noticed."

"If that's what you think, what are you doing here?" Susan enquired.

"Belt and braces, beloved. I know you don't need me, but I thought you might want me. Kammy's a very bad loser."

Kammy's nostrils flared. "Balls. You're bluffing."

"Tell me that when they kick the doors in. Come off it, Kammy. You thought you could pick Susan Lazarus off the street? That it would be easy?"

"I'll show you what's easy," Kammy said through his teeth. "If the police come in here, what they'll find is you, you sodding murderer." Something nasty dawned in his eyes. "Maybe you killed her. Maybe—that's right—maybe the pair of you came here as part of your plot to cast doubt on my good name and you argued with your tart. Killed her and cut your own throat after, and that's how they'll find you. Did you bring a knife, or will we have to get you one?"

James made his lungs fill with air. "Don't take the trouble. I'm going to use my hands on you."

"Actually, that's not a bad idea," Susan told Kammy, a schoolmistress being kind to a rather slow child. "It would be a very good idea, in fact, if silencing me would make your problems go away. But it won't, because we heard from India. Harrison Stroud—the real one, not your Australian lackey—died of cholera aged seventeen, and there's a certified copy of the death certificate on its way now. Cecil Brayton is currently in a gaol cell. They arrested him for selling stolen jewellery, but I expect the conversation's gone on to other topics. And we found a name for the valet you planted in Montmorency's house: Alfred Priestly, who did two years for robbing his employer a decade ago and has worked for you on at least three occasions since." She gave him a smile that could have frozen the Thames. "Oh, and while we're discussing your many mistakes, Mr. Lane didn't need to contact anyone about my whereabouts, because I had shadows on me who let Wilby know as soon as you made this very obvious move. All of which is to say, you're cat's meat, you vitriol-throwing fucker, and I hope hanging hurts."

Kammy's mouth was moving soundlessly. He started to speak, and that was when the house shook with the application of what sounded to James's experienced ear like a police battering-ram to the front door. Kammy leapt up, barking an order. One of his men grabbed Susan's shoulder, and the other two both came straight at James.

He couldn't have been more grateful. Three endless days in Jerry's bolthole, the best part of two weeks as a hunted murderer, months of exile yet to come, seventeen bloody years of wasted past: he really did need an outlet. He put a brass-knuckled fist into one man's stomach with a surge of almost sexual satisfaction, caught the other's blow on his forearm, and settled in for a joyous couple of moments' mayhem before Kammy's shout got through to him.

"Templeton Lane!"

Susan stood, arms tight to her body and clenched fists pressed to the sides of her head, a picture of frozen fear. Kammy's remaining henchman had his arm round her waist and a knife in his other hand, its tip digging into her torso. Kammy stood on her other side, his eyes wild and darting. There was a lot of noise downstairs. It sounded like a brawl.

One of his assailants was straightening up from an airless crouch. James punched him in the back of the neck, sending him down for good.

"I'll kill her," Kammy said savagely. "You do as I tell you or she's dead."

"Let her go and I'll help you get out of here," James said. "I don't give a damn about Montmorency. Don't hurt her and I'll make sure you get away clean."

Kammy sneered at that, though his raised lip was more like a snarl. "Get on your knees. Now. Hands up and kneel, or watch her die!"

James held up both hands and went down to one knee, then the other. He could see the thrumming tension in Susan's body, and in the man who held her. The tip of the knife pressed deep into her dress at the base of her ribcage. It would slide in very easily indeed if her captor got over-excited.

"It won't do you any good," he said.

"If I'm going to swing for murder anyway, what's one more?" Kammy demanded.

"Yes, but he's not." James nodded at the man who held Susan. "I'd let your boss do his own dirty work, if I was you, mate."

The man's eyes flicked to Kammy, then widened. There were feet coming up the stairs, deep voices. "Kammy—"

"Shut up," Kammy told him, or James, or everyone. Panic squirrelled in his eyes, the look of a man who couldn't see a way out. He'd overstepped, gone too far to retreat, and there was nothing he could do now to make it better.

Unfortunately, that also meant nothing would make his situation worse. "You shit, Lane," he snarled. "You'll hang with me. Kill her, Slater. Do it!"

"I'll confess," James said sharply. "All right? I'll confess to Montmorency's murder, if you let her go. You can prove I did it. I've got the Samsonoff with me."

Kammy's lips parted. James forced calm into his voice. "I'll show you. In my inside coat pocket. It's proof I did it. Look." He kept his left hand up and wide, pushed his jacket open with his right hand splayed, and fished the opal necklace out with a finger and thumb.

Thousands of pounds worth of gold and dark fire glistened in the gaslight. The henchman Slater inhaled sharply. Heavy fists banged on the door, and James flicked his wrist and sent the priceless opal necklace flying right at Kammy Grizzard's face. Kammy and Slater both jerked back instinctively, and Susan's hands shot down from her hair in a vicious stabbing motion, like a two-fisted Lady Macbeth.

Slater screamed. That wasn't surprising, because Susan's eight-inch steel hairpin had gone right into his elbow joint. Susan twisted out of his loosened grip, extracted another hairpin, and planted it in his shoulder where it met the neck. James had already launched himself up and at the man, dropped him with a brutal blow to the gut as if Susan didn't already have it under control, and turned vengefully on Kammy.

The fence was bent double and keening, a terrible high-pitched noise that ought not come from a man's throat. James grabbed him by the shoulder, pulled him up straight for a punch that was intended to shatter his jaw, and saw the hairpin that jutted no more than three inches out of his groin.

He recoiled with pure horror. "Christ alive, Susan!"

"Get out," Susan said sharply. "Now."

The door shook and splintered under a heavy kick. "Miss Lazarus!" someone bellowed.

"In here!" she shouted back, and jabbed a commanding finger at the window.

James grabbed her hand. "Marry me."

"What? No! Go *away*."

They were out of time for discussion. He shoved up the sash window, told her, "I love you," and got the bloody hell out of there as the police kicked down the door.

The only possible way was up now, metaphorically but also literally, because there would be police in the court below, and he didn't want to face the consequences either of arrest or of ruining Susan's plans. He gave the wall a quick scan, and started moving sideways as the window gently slid shut behind him. An old iron hook gave him a foothold to reach the window ledge of the next room, which had a sill over it. He muscled his way up, reached the smaller window on the second floor, and plastered himself to it and the wall. This one did not have a jutting sill, and the roof edge was a good seven feet above the ledge on which the balls of his feet were planted. That meant he couldn't quite reach.

He didn't greatly want to leap for it with so little purchase, but he couldn't delay much longer. Sooner or later someone would look up, and when Kammy regained the power of speech, he would unquestionably point the police to where James had gone. Jump or nothing. He took a breath.

A dark shape appeared over the roof ledge—a head and shoulders, plus the softest whistle he'd ever heard. James let the air out in a wave of deep gratitude, and reached up to grasp the rope Jerry was extending down to him.

They waited in silence until the noise from below had long stopped, worked their way over the rooftops towards Hardinge Street, made a rapid descent, and set off at a brisk pace down Labour in Vain Street to the river.

"That sounded like fun," Jerry said once they had melted into the Ratcliffe docks. "What was the screaming about?"

"Susan put a steel hairpin into Kammy's trouser front. Several inches deep."

Jerry cringed visibly. "Ah, the gentle sex."

"Ministering angel. She wasn't frightened, you know. She put her safety in the balance to get Kammy, and she wasn't afraid at all. You should have seen the look in her eyes when he suggested having her killed. She was spitting."

"He was probably lucky just to get the hairpin."

"He really wasn't," James said with certainty. "And he'll be getting a lot more than that anyway. They've nailed the bastard, her and Wilby. I wonder if they're aiming to nab Kammy's pet police superintendent too."

"It must be tiresome for decent policemen when their colleagues take bribes," Jerry remarked. "Not that I've ever met one, but I suppose they must exist. If that hand comes near my pocket I'll break it off, you little turd."

The lurking pickpocket fell back. Jerry made an annoyed noise. "That's the problem with this city, the criminal element. What now?"

"I get out of the country. They'll doubtless call off the search for Templeton Lane within the next day or so. I'll head up north, take the boat from Harwich."

"Lose yourself in the Continent, get over to the States. Stan and I can transfer funds out to you. And when you come back, assuming you do?"

"Start from the beginning, I suppose. Make myself acceptable."

"You seem all right to me, you know," Jerry said. "An apelike mockery of the human form, of course, and a pig-headed idiot to boot, but all right. You don't need to grovel."

"She isn't asking me to. But she doesn't trust lightly and she doesn't trust words, and that's fair enough. It's why I had to come tonight, just in case she was relying on me to turn up."

"Was she?"

"Not at all, no. She seemed quite annoyed to see me."

Jerry sighed theatrically. "Given a choice of the love that dare not speak its name, and the love that can't spell it without two tries—"

"Sod off, Alec plays you like a fiddle. Anyway, I'll do my best and wait for her to decide." He shrugged at Jerry's look. "It's how she works. I've nothing better to do. And she's worth it."

"Look at what 'it' means, though. The inconvenience, obstacles, arguments, narrow evasions of the law, and unexpected need to change one's extremely comfortable life, all in the desperate hope of what? Winning the love of another thoroughly flawed person?"

"Yes," James said. "And, as I said, she's worth it."

The laugh in Jerry's voice was all amusement, no mockery. "Bloody nuisance, isn't it?"

CHAPTER FOURTEEN

April 1896

The sky was blue. Birds sang, insects buzzed. There were trees in blossom, and flowers sprung in bright profusion amid the fresh green of Regent's Park. Susan's feet scrunched on the gravel, step by step.

"You're walking like you want to kick something," said Greta, Countess of Moreton.

"I do."

Greta indicated one of her twin sons, who was executing a graceful handstand on the beautifully manicured lawn, just behind the sign that said *Do Not Walk On The Grass*. "Make it him, will you? William Taillefer, get back on your feet and the path right now!"

They were on a family excursion, strolling at a respectable but not intrusive distance behind Penny, Greta's daughter, since she was walking on the arm of some bloody man. Susan had no idea how women could bear to have daughters and then watch them grow up to be courted by bloody men.

"Nothing?" Greta asked.

"No."

"How long has he been back?"

Susan growled in her throat. "Eight days."

Eight days since James Vane had landed, in his own identity, with notices to that effect in the newspaper, and she hadn't had a single word from him. She hadn't been at the port waiting for his ship to dock: that would have been stupid. He'd written via Alec to say he would be back soon, that he wanted to make sure there would be no reception committee, that he did not intend to visit her immediately. *I will take my time*, he'd said.

For eight days, after five months, after seventeen bloody years. That was taking your time with a vengeance.

"Tired of waiting for him?"

"Yes," Susan said, with feeling. "And who says I've been waiting?"

"Spare me, Susan. And for heaven's sake, give him a chance. He's worth waiting for, isn't he?"

"How would you know? You've never met him."

"But I've met you, and you're waiting for him. Therefore he must be worth it," Greta said. "Because otherwise you wouldn't be waiting, would you? Logic."

"Women are wrong about men all the time."

"And also right," Greta countered. "I fell in love with Tim in about twenty-four hours and I've hardly ever regretted it."

"Hardly ever?"

"You can't be married for two decades without regretting it occasionally. When I was giving birth to the twins, I felt very strongly I should have become a nun instead."

"I can understand that." Susan kicked a stone. "Does it annoy you, being married? Not to Tim, but in principle."

Greta didn't need that explained: she was a suffragist too. "Not personally, because it hasn't brought me anything but good. It's revolting to consider how much Tim *could* abuse and exploit me with the law on his side, of course, but the root of that problem is the man."

"You have to pick the right man, yes, yes. What if you get it wrong? What if he changes? What if you change your own mind?"

Greta's entire life had been shaped by her father changing his mind about his marriage. She made a face. "It's a leap in the dark, and many people land on rocks. The entire apparatus that punishes women for immorality and children for illegitimacy is there to force us into wedlock by making the alternative even worse. Don't tell Tim I said that."

"Don't tell Dad what?" William asked, appearing as if by magic.

"Go away, you vile eavesdropper." Greta flapped a hand at her son. "Marriage is fraught with pitfalls in principle, and the best thing I ever did in practice. Square that circle if you can."

"You're a lot of help."

"Thank you, I practice on the children. Talking of marriage, unless I'm changing the subject entirely, are you aware that James dined with the Cirencesters the other day? Tommy told me all about the prodigal's return. She said he was charming and she'd hardly have taken him for a colonial."

'Tommy' was Thomasina, Marchioness of Cirencester. Naturally James would go to see the noble heads of his noble family before he contacted Susan. "How nice. I'm glad he's having fun."

Greta sighed. "Oh, be fair. If you were involved in machinations, and you usually are, you'd expect him to trust you to play your game out, wouldn't you?"

That hurt in a way Greta couldn't have known. Susan would indeed expect James to trust her to play out a game: that was why she wanted him back. "I don't know what machinations he's up to."

"If you did, you wouldn't have to trust him," Greta pointed out. "It sounds to me like he's establishing himself before he risks involving you. You said yourself, you couldn't be sure the police wouldn't connect him with his past self, or that he mightn't have trouble with friends of that dreadful man."

"There won't be friends," Susan said. "Kammy Grizzard didn't have those, only lackeys."

He'd swung last month. Cecil Brayton had turned Queen's Evidence and sung like a linnet, confirming that he'd been in debt to

Kammy and had followed his directions in endorsing the false heir. The subsequent trial had been brutal. Kammy had instructed his lawyer to come down hard on Susan's moral character in an effort to discredit her. That included telling the world she'd spent a couple of nights in a hotel with a man she wasn't married to, and claiming it was Templeton Lane, notorious jewel thief. At least the police hadn't pressed charges for kidnap, so Kammy hadn't been able to bring up the events of that final night without incriminating himself further. That meant that he couldn't substantiate his claim that Templeton Lane was alive, well, and involved. Even so, the shocking affair of a woman detective's unlawful goings-on had lasted hours in court and made the newspapers for days. Susan had had to remind herself quite frequently that she didn't care what people thought. It felt very like she did.

Kammy's malice hadn't saved him. The Crown's barrister had dismissed it all as an irrelevant distraction, part of the conspirators' effort to cast the blame for the murders on a burglar who was probably dead, and the judge and jury had agreed. The chain of evidence against Kammy was irrefutable, and Templeton Lane a mere footnote in the judge's summing up. Kammy and the false Stroud had hanged; Brayton was serving a six-year sentence.

Too bad for them, still not wonderful for Susan. She'd had to accept that she wouldn't be able to set up her own detective agency as soon as she'd wanted, since her professional reputation would take a while to recover from this: Mark had already thrown out three prospective clients who'd come seeking a different kind of service. It would have been one more nail in the coffin of her suitability for the scion of a noble house, if she'd ever had ideas of that in the first place.

James had put months of effort into making himself look like a respectable man while Susan had become a notorious woman. Not that it mattered, since she'd never asked or wanted to dine at the Cirencesters' table. Merely, she'd have preferred it to be her own choice, not the result of public humiliation.

"Good heavens, you look thunderous," Greta said. "Let's talk about something else. How is Alec's chap doing at the music hall, do you know? Pen seemed very pleased with him when we last spoke. He says he strikes just the right note for a front of house man, perfectly balanced between hail-fellow-well-met and a reign of terror."

"Sounds about right," Susan said. "Alec's happy. I don't know if Crozier or whatever he calls himself these days intends to stay there long, but it's honest work, and it keeps him busy while he learns to behave like a normal person."

"Well, he won't learn *that* in the music hall," said the Countess of Moreton, ex-trapeze artist, and they walked on.

Susan had tea with Greta and the twins, and returned to Robin Hood Yard some time past five that evening. She was living there now, since she'd been asked to leave her lodgings during the trial: Mrs. Hewson, stiff with outrage, had informed her this was a respectable house and women of her stamp weren't welcome. Susan hadn't argued. It hadn't seemed worth the effort.

And the truth was, she was happy to be home, or at least happier than she'd have been anywhere else. She had the guvnors, and Emma, who had gone round and given Mrs. Hewson an extensive and colourful piece of her mind, and frequent visits from Alec and the Moretons. She could neither lurk nor brood with her family around. Perhaps decent clients still preferred not to see Miss Lazarus, but that would pass and meanwhile she could get the filing done.

She pushed open the back door and came in, hoping for a bit of peace. A day with the exuberant Taillefer twins did that to you. Instead Emma poked her head into the hall and shrieked, "She's here!"

Oh God. Susan went into the sitting room, and found Emma, Justin, and Nathaniel, all poised for her entrance. "What?" she enquired.

"Letter." Justin indicated the table.

She told herself it wouldn't be a note from James, and indeed it wasn't. The letter on the table was in a thick, expensive, vellum envelope with a crest, addressed to her name only in an unfamiliar, spidery scrawl.

"Hand delivered?"

"This afternoon, by a footman," Justin said. "That's the Vane arms."

"I know."

It looked like trouble. She picked it up, ripped it open, and glanced at the subscription before embarking on the task of reading it. "It's from his father. James's, I mean. It's from Lord Dickie."

Nathaniel's dark grey brows drew together. "If it contains a threat, I suggest we do what we should have done last time."

"If by that you mean go in so hard that the old bastard won't ever walk straight again, yes," Justin said. "I suppose we'll find out if that's necessary once Sukey reads it. Take your time."

She made a face at him, and lifted the letter again. She might as well read it. It would only be words; they couldn't hurt.

Dear Miss Lazarus
It appears that I owe you an apology.

She read it three times as the others waited in commendable silence. Nathaniel cracked first. "Well? What *is* it?"

She folded it up, stuck it back in the envelope, and handed it to him. "Lord Dickie Vane has learned he was labouring under a misapprehension, before. He offers me his deepest regrets for the insult and offence he caused me in the past, and hopes I will forgive his behaviour."

"Well," Justin said. "Well. Bugger me."

"That's a point to young Vane, I think," Nathaniel said, examining the envelope. "We can assume this is his work. I further deduce—"

"Is that your job?"

"Do be quiet, Justin. I further deduce that we are likely to see him here in person." He held the envelope to his head like a spiritualist might. "Tonight, around six o'clock, I'd say, so Susan might want to hurry up and get ready. Or bolt the doors, if that's your preferred tack."

"What are you talking about?" Susan demanded.

Nathaniel tossed the envelope back at her. "There's a note in there as well, you young fool. Call yourself a detective?"

She scrabbled for it. Emma's eyes widened. "Six o'clock? You've been waiting for months, he'll be here in *half an hour*, and you look like a rag-bag!"

"I have not been—"

"Yes, you have!"

"No fighting, girls," Justin said. "Well, this is exciting. We'll leave you to it, but ratface?" He waited for Susan to look at him. "I trust your judgement, and you should too. Don't be scared."

"That isn't the problem," Emma said forcefully. "Her *hair* is the bloody problem, now get upstairs!"

Susan put on a new blue dress that she'd thought made her look less drab than usual, and let Emma dress her hair. She insisted on her own pins, though, not pretty ones. There were limits. She wouldn't want to give the wrong impression.

She made it downstairs in good time and sat around for a full three minutes, leafing through the newspaper without seeing it, until the knock came. It was one minute to six.

"At least you're punctual," came Justin's voice in the hall. "Susan's in the back parlour." He added something in a lower tone that Susan couldn't hear, except for the last syllable, which might have been *luck*, or possibly something that rhymed. It was hard to guess, with Justin.

And then James came in.

The sight took her breath. He seemed larger than she remembered, possibly because he was standing taller, shoulders back, taking up more space. His suit was cut to accentuate his size as well, and he'd parted his hair on the other side.

"That's good," she said. "Makes you look different. Clever."

"Precaution." His eyes were locked on hers. "Hello, Susan. I've missed you."

"You took your time turning up." The words gave her a sudden, horrible urge to cry. She pressed her lips together.

"I'm sorry about that. I wanted to be sure I wasn't liable to be arrested, for a start, and I had a few other things to put in place. You got my father's letter?"

"Yes. Did he mean a word of it?"

"I doubt it. I told him that I had come back solely to discover if you would forgive me, and if he didn't write it he'd never set eyes on me again. Hence he did."

Susan blinked. "You mean, he *wants* to set eyes on you again?"

"He is a picture of senile remorse," James said, with no discernible sympathy. "My brother is impatient for him to shuffle off this mortal coil so he can get his hands on the family money, such as remains. Father is deeply distressed. He became quite tearful as he complained about Neville's greed and ingratitude, apparently impervious to the irony. I think he wanted my sympathy."

"Your family really is something."

"It is indeed, and Neville's a chip off the old block. The first thing he said to me was, 'I suppose you're back for the inheritance.'"

"Rude," Susan said. "Particularly since you're actually back to establish an alias."

James grinned. "Yes, how dare he think so poorly of me? Anyway, my continued existence gives Father a weapon against Neville, so he's acknowledged me and so has Cousin Roddy, the marquess. James Vane is back."

"Good."

"The story is I knocked about the world a bit—Australia, South Africa, the States but never the big cities. Assorted business dealings, a decent but not particularly eye-catching fortune made, a respectable return to the bosom of my family accomplished without drama. Nothing to see."

"Right."

"So here I am. And here you are."

"Mmm."

James exhaled. He clearly found this conversation as hard going as she did. "I saw the papers. The trial reports. I'm extremely sorry, Susan."

"It's not—"

"Don't say it's not my fault, because it is. You came into the business because I begged for your help. Kammy hurt you because you prevented him from hurting me. You were made an object of scorn because of our nights together, you took all the punishment so I could get away scot free, and I am desperately sorry. I've done you so much harm, and it makes no difference that I never wished it."

"I chose to take your case on," Susan said. "I took that hotel room, and I decided to sleep with you. You said that I don't pay your debts: well, you don't take my consequences."

"They oughtn't be your consequences."

"But they are, and that isn't your fault. Anyway, if you'd been around to take your share of the blame, you'd have been arrested and for all I know Kammy would have managed to pin the murders on you after all. Don't worry about it. Life's not fair."

"That doesn't change the fact that I owe you too much. I owe you everything, Sukey, starting with my neck." He stepped forward, closer, but not reaching out to touch. "I've thought a great deal over the last five months about myself, and you, and us, and I reached an important conclusion."

"Which is?" Susan asked warily.

"Right. Well. This is the tricky part. By which I mean, *please* let me finish talking before you interrupt. I did listen to what you said about marriage. I know you've always wanted to be Susan Lazarus, yourself, nobody's appendage. However, your reputation has been stained by my actions, not for the first time, and failing to offer you the protection of my name would be the act of a shit. Unfortunately, offering it is somewhere between a ridiculous piece of patronage and a bad joke. I also loathe the idea of marriage as some sort of moral obligation on either of us, because I adore you and I'd be on my knees begging if I thought you would do anything except tell me not to wear out my trouser-legs. In fact, I have no idea how I should proceed now, which leads me to the obvious conclusion. So." He took a box from his pocket and opened it. "The stone has the merit of being honestly earned, by the way."

Susan stared at the ring within. Its stone was nothing like she'd ever seen: an opal of a bizarre, jagged triangular shape. "What *is* it?"

"What it is, is a possum tooth turned to opal," James said. "From the skull I found in the mines. I worked for this as hard as I have worked in my life, and I missed you every day while I did it. What it represents is up to you. If you want to wear it on the fourth finger of your left hand, I will marry you and count myself the luckiest bastard unhung. If you'd rather wear it on a different finger, as long as you choose to wear it now and again, I'll take that and still call myself lucky as hell. It's your decision, Susan. I'm not going to ask you to be mine, but I very much want you to know that I'm yours." He took her hand, and closed her fingers gently around the box. "If you would care for my name, it's at your disposal. If not, I would be proud to live in sin with you, and I'm rather good at sin. And if you don't want me at all…to be honest I've tried not to dwell on that, but let me know. You can interrupt now. Or take the ring. I do wish you'd say something, though, you're making me nervous. Susan?"

Susan couldn't take her eyes from the box. "This ring is made of a *tooth*."

"Well, it's beautiful and unique and it bites, so it seemed to suit you. Don't you like it? Shit. If you'd prefer a diamond, I can—"

"Shut up, James." She took it from the box, her hand hardly shaking at all. It was a stunning thing, delicately wrought curling gold tendrils holding the jagged jewel at the centre. It looked unmistakably like a tooth, now she knew what it was, and it shone with rainbows. "Did you have this made?"

"Yes."

"For me?"

"Nobody else could wear it. Will you?"

Susan held the gold band, turning it to see the colour flicker. "You don't mind what finger I wear it on?"

"I mind very much," James said. "I absolutely insist that it goes on the finger that makes you happiest. Marry me, don't marry me, marry me in secret and remain Miss Lazarus to the world, or call yourself Mrs. Vane without benefit of clergy. I think that's all the options? Whichever you choose."

"What would your family say about us marrying?"

"Who cares? I came back for you. And to see Jerry engaged in honest toil, of course, that should be funny."

"You've spent the last five months making yourself respectable—"

"For you," James said. "You told me I should do it for myself, but I regret to report I failed. I don't give a fuck about rediscovering the noble Vane heart under the jewel thief. I want to be with you, because you are and always have been the best thing in my life. If that means respectability, I'll do it; if you want to chuck the detective business and go back into mediumship, or take up thievery, count me in. I'm yours however you want me, if you want me, and I'd very much like to know that at some point because it's been a bloody long five months."

"Yes, it has." Susan looked down at the ring, up at him. "Justin told me not to be scared, and I don't think I am. I trust you, James."

"You can. I swear it."

"I know. You turned up."

He made a face. "I really wasn't sure you'd be pleased about that."

She hadn't been, until he'd made it clear he'd come as support, not rescue. Support was, perhaps, a thing she did want. If it was the right kind, of course, the kind that didn't have to be asked for, and respected her judgement, and placed her higher than opals.

"I'm not going to do anything just to prove I'm not scared to do it, and getting married would be stupid while people might link you to Templeton Lane because of me. So I won't marry you—not now. Maybe not ever. I'll think about it." She drew a steadying breath. "But my guvnors don't have a marriage licence either, and what does for them will do for me. So if you want to be the man I'm not married to—"

"Oh God. Yes. Please."

She held out her right hand. James brought it to his lips as if she were a queen, then took the ring and slipped it on.

"It fits," she said, looking at the play of light.

"Of course it does, give me some credit. Christ, you look good in opals. I have a lot of them for you."

"Stolen ones?"

"Let's not split hairs."

Susan reached up to pull him towards her, and their mouths collided, hungry and perfect. His arms wrapped around her, drawing her onto her toes, and she kissed him with all the force of five months of fear and loneliness and waiting.

"I love you too," she mumbled into his mouth.

James pulled away. "What was that?"

"Shut up."

"I heard you."

"Yes, and I heard you ask me to marry you right in front of Kammy Grizzard, you idiot!"

"He wasn't paying attention," James said, with certainty. "That was the most painful experience of my life and it didn't even happen to me. I notice you're wearing your lethal weapons now."

"You never know when they'll be necessary."

"Your trust is very beautiful. Talking of grievous bodily harm, will you want me to explain myself to your guvnors?"

"It'll be fine," Susan said. "You can come with me. Not yet, though." She snaked her arm round his neck again. "I'm busy."

James picked her off her feet for a kiss in a movement that made her squeak. "You do realise that if we don't have the benefit of clergy, we don't get the benefit of a sanctioned double bed? We'll just have to work our way through London's more gullible hotels."

"I hope you've got a lot of stolen loot to pay for that."

"Right," James said. "Er."

Susan pulled back to look at him. "What's 'er'?" She knew that expression. "James Vane, what did you do?"

"Nothing! It's what my family did. It—now, *please* don't overreact—it appears my father had a point about me currying favour with my great-uncle, because the old man left me a certain amount of money in his will, held in trust to be given to me when I turned twenty-one. Father didn't tell me about it at the time, I expect because he was trying to find a way to spend it, but Great-Uncle was a far-sighted man. It's been sitting there for more than two decades."

"Your father's an arsehole."

"Yes, dear, but the thing is, if you keep a certain amount of money well-invested and untouched for two decades, it turns into a significant amount of money. One might even say largish."

Susan stiffened. "How large is that? Do you mean you're rich? James—"

"I'm saying, what with my ill-gotten gains and Great-Uncle's generosity, *we* are in a position to make choices. Travelling, working our way through accommodating hotels, establishing your own enquiry agency with extra staff. Making you a home, if you want one. I'll decorate."

"With your money."

"I did wonder if I should have told you," he muttered. "It's just money, Sukey, tokens one exchanges for convenience. It doesn't mean anything. If it helps, imagine we stole it from my father. I'm fairly sure it's how he felt."

Susan let her hackles subside. She had an instinctive distrust of wealth—those who had it, what it did, how people with it behaved to those without—but scrabbling for pennies did nobody any good either. More to the point, she had a fair idea that the gift did mean something. "Your great-uncle thought about you, and he loved you. I won't complain about that. Especially not if it pisses your father off."

James's smile was enough to make a lesser woman's knees weak. "Thank you, Sukey."

"What, for taking your money?"

"You cared for me when I didn't care for myself. You listened to me when nobody else did. You fight. And you are without a doubt the bravest soul I've ever met, particularly when you're facing up to the terror of having someone love you." He cupped her face. "I hope to get you used to that."

"That's the easy part. What's hard is the loving someone else. People change, they die, they let you down—"

"I'm sorry for that. I will always be sorry."

"And other people run away," Susan ploughed on. "Or even if they don't go anywhere they still push people away because they don't want to get hurt again. That's not good either."

"If you had a crest it would be a hedgehog couchant," James agreed. "I know that relying on others is not easy for you and I haven't made it easier in the past." His hand tightened on hers. "I promise I won't make you regret this in the future. At least, not more than I can help."

"Standards still low, I see. Anyway, if I'd run away this time, Cara would probably have started haunting me like the bloke out of *A Christmas Carol*. She couldn't bear people who give up without a fight. She'd have been quite ashamed of me for a while." She shot him a look. "And I know what she'd have said about you."

"What?" James asked, with some foreboding.

"Nice thighs."

James gave a shout of laughter, pulling her close. Susan leaned in to him, smiling herself, and let her shoulders relax as she rested against him.

Probably she'd regret this now and again. Certainly he would, because she had few illusions about herself. But she didn't think they would regret it more than she could reasonably expect, and definitely a great deal less than anyone who crossed the pair of them when they stood together.

And that, Susan thought, would do very nicely indeed.

Acknowledgements

Massive thanks to May Peterson, whose book doctoring skills hauled me out of the mire, to Veronica Vega for editing, Vic Grey for the stunning art, and Lennan Adams for the cover design.

The Lilywhite Boys Series

London, 1890s. A pair of care-for-nobody jewel thieves make a nice living at the expense of the aristocracy, and pride themselves on staying one step ahead of the law. But pride goes before a fall—and the Lilywhite Boys are about to fall hard.

The Rat-Catcher's Daughter (Lilywhite Boys 0.5)

Music-hall singer Miss Christiana is in serious debt, and serious trouble. She owes more than she can pay to a notorious criminal, and now he plans to make an example of her. There's no way out.

But Christiana has an admirer. Stan Kamarzyn has watched her sing for a year and he doesn't want to see her get hurt. Stan's nobody special, just a dodgy bloke from Bethnal Green, but he's got the sort of friends who can get a girl out of trouble—for a price. Christiana's not sure what it will cost her...

The two slowly reach an understanding. But Christiana is no criminal, and she can't risk getting mixed up with the law. What will happen when Stan's life as the fence for the notorious Lilywhite Boys brings trouble to his doorstep?

Any Old Diamonds (Lilywhite Boys #1)

Lord Alexander Pyne-ffoulkes, the younger son of the Duke of Ilvar, holds a bitter grudge against his wealthy father. The Duke intends to give his Duchess a priceless diamond parure on their wedding anniversary—so Alec hires a pair of jewel thieves to steal it.

The Duke's remote castle is a difficult target, and Alec needs a way to get the thieves in. Soldier-turned-criminal Jerry Crozier, one half of the notorious Lilywhite Boys, has the answer: he'll pose as a Society gentleman and become Alec's new best friend.

But Jerry is a dangerous man: controlling, remote, and devastating. He effortlessly teases out the lonely young nobleman's most secret desires, and soon he's got Alec in his bed—and the palm of his hand.

Or maybe not. Because as the plot thickens, betrayals, secrets, new loves, and old evils come to light. Now the jewel thief and the aristocrat must keep up the pretence, find their way through a maze of privilege and deceit, and confront the truth of what's between them...all without getting caught.

"The sparkly heist qualities of this book hide some sharp, painful edges, and Charles' brutally gorgeous prose offers up gem after gem after gem to make the reader laugh and gasp and weep and swoon."—Seattle Review of Books

"Super fun, yummy romance, twisty plot, more-ish characters, excellent revenge, lots of banging. Get it now for all of your comfort read needs."—Malka Older

"This book is gorgeous from cover to cover. I inhaled it in a single sitting."—Red Hot Books

More Victorian shenanigans from KJ Charles...

The Sins of the Cities series

London 1873. As one of the worst fogs of the nineteenth century closes in on the city, long-buried crimes are crawling into the light. Clem Talleyfer is an unassuming lodging-house keeper; Nathaniel Roy is a lawyer turned journalist who likes nothing more than a crusade; Mark Braglewicz is a private enquiry agent. And all three friends are about to find themselves dragged into an aristocratic family secret that turns deadly.

An Unseen Attraction (Sins of the Cities #1)

Lodging-house keeper Clem Talleyfer prefers a quiet life. He's happy with his hobbies, his work—and especially with his lodger, taxidermist Rowley Green, who becomes a friend over long fireside evenings together. If only neat, precise, irresistible Mr. Green were interested in more than friendship.

Rowley just wants to be left alone—at least until he meets Clem, with his odd, charming ways and his glorious eyes. Two quiet men, lodging in the same house, coming to an understanding—it could be perfect. Then the brutally murdered corpse of another lodger is dumped on their doorstep and their peaceful life is shattered.

Now Clem and Rowley find themselves caught up in a mystery, threatened on all sides by violent men, with a deadly London fog closing in on them. If they're to see their way through, the pair must learn to share their secrets—and their hearts.

"both an intriguing and engrossing story and a tender romance between two well-drawn protagonists whose unique personality traits inform their emotional and sexual relationships."—All About Romance

"A plot that's unabashed pulp, made poignant by its effects on the two bruised souls at its center."—Publishers Weekly starred review

"I never thought taxidermy could be this sexy."—Aliette de Bodard

An Unnatural Vice (Sins of the Cities #2)

Crusading journalist Nathaniel Roy is determined to expose spiritualists who exploit the grief of bereaved and vulnerable people. First on his list is the so-called Seer of London, Justin Lazarus. Nathaniel expects him to be a cheap, heartless fraud. He doesn't expect to meet a man with a sinful smile and the eyes of a fallen angel—or that a shameless swindler will spark his desires for the first time in years.

Justin feels no remorse for the lies he spins during his séances. His gullible clients bore him, but hostile, disbelieving, utterly irresistible Nathaniel is a fascinating challenge. And as their battle of wills and wits heats up, Justin can't stop thinking about the man who's determined to ruin him.

But Justin and Nathaniel are linked by more than their fast-growing obsession with one another. They are both caught up in an aristocratic family's secrets, and Justin holds information that could be lethal. As killers, fanatics, and fog close in, Nathaniel is the only man Justin can trust—and, perhaps, the only man he could love.

"A great story that's excellently written and researched; characters who are well-drawn and appealing; a book that stimulates intellectually as well as emotionally… An Unnatural Vice has it all and is easily one of the best books I've read so far this year."—Romantic Historical Reviews

"fierce and frantic enemies-to-lovers romance … a powerful and fascinating conflict."—Romantic Times, Top Pick

"Hot hate-sex that gradually develops into cross-class understanding and respect—now that's a romance writing achievement that you don't see every day." —Romance Novels for Feminists

An Unsuitable Heir (Sins of the Cities #3)

On the trail of an aristocrat's secret son, enquiry agent Mark Braglewicz finds his quarry in a music hall, performing as a trapeze artist with his twin sister. Graceful, beautiful, elusive, and strong, Pen Starling is like nobody Mark's ever met—and everything he's ever wanted. But the long-haired acrobat has an earldom and a fortune to claim.

Pen doesn't want to live as any sort of man, least of all a nobleman. The thought of being wealthy, titled, and always in the public eye is horrifying. He likes his life now—his days on the trapeze, his nights with Mark. And he won't be pushed into taking a title that would destroy his soul.

But there's a killer stalking London's foggy streets, and more lives than just Pen's are at risk. Mark decides he must force the reluctant heir from music hall to manor house, to save Pen's neck. Betrayed by the one man he thought he could trust, Pen never wants to see his lover again. But when the killer comes after him, Pen must find a way to forgive—or he might not live long enough for Mark to make amends.

"I love the way KJ Charles has incorporated the elements of Victorian popular fiction into her plotlines; the writing is sublime"—All About Romance

"With a lively cast and a tangled, entertainingly pulpy plot, Charles delivers a sensitive, powerful romance full of humor, humanity, and suspense."—Publishers Weekly starred review

About the Author

KJ Charles is a RITA®-nominated writer and freelance editor. She lives in London with her husband, two kids, an out-of-control garden, and a cat with murder management issues.

KJ writes mostly historical romance, mostly queer, sometimes with fantasy or horror in there. She is represented by Courtney Miller-Callihan at Handspun Literary.

For all the KJC news and occasional freebies, get my (infrequent) newsletter at kjcharleswriter.com/newsletter.

Find me on Twitter @kj_charles

Pick up free reads on my website at kjcharleswriter.com

Join my Facebook group, KJ Charles Chat, for book conversation, sneak peeks, and exclusive treats.

Printed by Amazon Italia Logistica S.r.l.
Torrazza Piemonte (TO), Italy